King Triton's Lair

Northern Caribbean Islands

St Beatrice Island, Ruby Island,
Antigua and Barbuda, and Guadeloupe

THE
EXPEDITIONERS

THE EXPEDI

McSWEENEY'S McMULLENS

www.mcsweeneys.net

McSweeney's McMullens and colophon are copyright © 2014, McSweeney's & McMullens
Manufactured by Thomson-Shore in Michigan
ISBN: 978-1-940450-20-9
Manufactured by Thomson-Shore, Dexter, MI (USA); RMA596CG310, July, 2014

IONERS

WITHDRAWN

and the Secret of
King Triton's Lair

by S. S. Taylor

illustrated by Katherine Roy

BOOK I

I, James Rickwell, aged 16 years, of the city of Southampton, in the country of England, on this 3rd day of May, 1823, do hereby put down this record of the voyage of the Adelaide, captained by the mapmaker and explorer Gianni Girafalco, in the hopes that our expedition will prove of historic value ~~_____~~. It is my hope that if our expedition is successful, this journal may prove of interest to future generations of

One

The forest was thick around us, the huge Derudan Bast Trees crowding in on all sides, filtering the late-day sun.

"Where's the entrance to the cave, Kit?" whispered my brother, Zander. "We've been out here too long. The other team must be close and we're leaving our scent everywhere. Who knows what's—" He snapped his head around at the sound of something moving in the thick undergrowth and held his machete out in front of him. "We've got to get back on the river."

"Hold on. Hold on. It should be right here." I scanned the map again, cursing the hack cartographer who'd drawn it. It looked like it had been through a volcanic eruption, burn marks everywhere and patches where the paper had worn down. There were no contour lines and no scale, just a crude rendering of the river we'd come up and some trees and bushes drawn in as landmarks. Down in the right-hand corner of the map, southeast of the largest trees, was a little drawing, a line and an open triangle, like the forked tongue of a snake, that I knew to be the universal mapmaker's symbol for a cave entrance. The compass and navigation instruments in my Explorer's vest were of no use whatsoever, so I did what Dad had always said Explorers should do first: I raised my eyes from the map and focused on the surrounding landscape.

We were searching for the lost caves of Upper Deruda, where, if all went according to plan, we'd be able to recover documents from the body of an Explorer of the Realm who'd disappeared ten years ago. All of the information that the Bureau of Newly Discovered Lands had given us indicated that his remains and the documents, which would include important information about routes around a deadly mile-long stretch of quicksand, were in one of the caves. But I couldn't find the entrance.

"Just a second." I focused on the map again and turned it slightly, noticing a big Bast Tree, skeletal against the horizon. Something was bothering me. According to the map, the tree was only a few feet from another, smaller Bast Tree. It wasn't there and I'd assumed it had fallen down in the years since the map was made.

We all looked up quickly at the faint sound of voices, coming from the direction of the river.

"It's them," Zander said. "They've landed. Where's that cave?"

"We don't have much time," my sister, M.K., whispered, brushing a muddy piece of her blond hair out of her eyes, leaving a long, dark smudge above her eyebrows. "Kit? You're the map master."

I scanned the landscape again.

"What's that over there?" I took my spyglass out of my vest and focused on something just barely sticking up behind a far-off tree. "What does that look like to you? Is that a Bast tree?"

M.K. narrowed her eyes, searching the horizon. "I don't know," she whispered. "Maybe. Looks like the top got knocked off." We heard the voices again, nearer this time. It was only a matter of time before they reached us.

Rotating my spyglass, I zoomed in on the jagged line of the broken trunk. "That's it. That's the tree! I was working off the wrong landmark." I looked down at the map again and pulled my compass out of my Explorer's vest. "So, if that's the landmark, then the entrance to the caves should be south-southeast of the . . ." I spun around, facing a wall of rock covered with thick, trailing vines. "This is it! Zander?"

He gave one last, wary look at the dense undergrowth all around us and turned to the vines, hacking at them with the machete. The sound of his blade against the vegetation seemed horribly loud.

"I can see something," he called after a few minutes. "Come on!" M.K. and I followed him, shoving the vines aside. I pushed a button on my Explorer's vest and a strong light illuminated a disappearing cavern ahead of us. It was large, high enough to stand in, with lots of entrances to other, smaller caverns in all directions. It was cold and damp inside, rivulets of water trickling down the walls. "Start looking," I told them. They put on their vestlights too and we took off in separate directions.

I explored a couple of small offshoots of the main cavern, walking slowly, aiming my light directly down at the ground, but I didn't see anything except for some bones—too small to be human.

"Nothing," M.K. said once we were all back at the entrance.

"Me, either." I was frustrated. We'd come all this way. Maybe it was some kind of trick. "Zander?"

He was just standing there, lost in thought.

"Zander? Wake up, Zander."

He blinked. "Oh. I was just thinking. Deruda has these things called Derudan Ground Adders. They're really poisonous and they're tiny, so you don't know they're there until it's too late. I remember Dad telling me about them."

"What does that have to do with anything?"

"Well, they can't climb. If I were trying to sleep in these caves, I know where I'd want to be."

We all looked up.

"There he is!" M.K. exclaimed. The lights from our vests bouncing on the wall, we ran over to a makeshift hammock hanging between two rock formations at the far end of the primary cavern, about eight feet off the ground. Zander boosted M.K. up on his shoulders, and she used a small scissor utility from his vest to cut the ragged ropes on one side, holding on to it so it wouldn't fall, and then handing it to me so she could cut the other side. We let it down as carefully as we could.

Somehow, I hadn't really grappled with the fact that we were looking for a *dead body*, and when I saw the white of the skeleton,

clad in a tattered red jacket and breeches, I jumped back. *Dad disappeared too,* I thought. *Is this what happened to Dad?*

"It's just a bunch of old bones," M.K. said matter-of-factly. "Keep it together, Kit. What are we looking for again?"

"A piece of parchment, twelve inches by fourteen inches, with words in Derudan and numbers on it," I said. Zander had already started looking through the pockets of the jacket. It was made of a rubbery material and covered with zippers and little ports for lights and gadgets. The guy had been a Neo, one of the breed of Explorers who embraced new technologies and dressed in colorful, synthetic clothing, sporting strange, spiky hairstyles and jewelry with flashing lights that pierced their ears and faces.

"Get the documents and let's go," M.K. said. "The other team must be almost here."

Zander kept searching and finally pulled out a stack of maps and notes. "This looks like it," he said, handing it to me. "Let's get out of here."

"You're sure?" I asked him. "I don't think any of these are the right size."

"That's all there is."

"Okay." I tucked the stack of paper into the hidden pocket of my Explorer's vest and we took off, running out of the cave and into the light. We stopped to replace as many of the vines over the entrance to the cave as we could and then we ran northwest by my compass, through the thick vegetation towards the river, Zander hacking away as we went. Just when I was starting to get worried we'd gone the wrong way, we came out onto the muddy shore of the river.

"There's the boat," M.K. called.

She splashed into the dark water and fiddled with the outboard. It was a new SteamBoard engine, made for small river craft, but it hadn't sounded very healthy on the way down.

"Ready, M.K.?" Zander had his machete up and he was looking suspiciously at the trees banking the river. "I thought I heard something."

"It's not starting," she called back. "It sounded a little raggedy when we pulled up on the bank. Hang on."

"Hurry. Come on, Kit. Get in."

But I was looking back in the direction of the caves. "He was a Neo," I said, thinking out loud. "They didn't tell us that in the briefing."

"Why does it matter?" Zander was still focused on the trees. "Come on. Get in the boat."

"It's just . . . Zander, I have to go back. We didn't get the parchment."

"I got everything out of his pockets." He sounded annoyed.

"No, you didn't. I'll be right back. You get the boat started and wait here." I started running back the way we'd come. It was much faster this time because Zander had cleared the path, and I was back at the caves in five minutes. Unsure of where the other team was, I pointed my spyglass in the direction of the path and turned on its voice amplification utility. I heard a familiar voice say, "That map is a piece of garbage! There aren't any caves here," and dropped down to the ground to keep myself hidden from their view.

A female voice answered, "But it says they should be right here. Lazlo, are you sure you didn't mess up the navigation?"

For an answer, Lazlo Nackley just gave an indignant snort. I stayed as still as I could and a few minutes later I heard another male voice say, "Joyce is right, Lazlo. Not an uncommon occurrence, I might add. We'll have to go back to the place where the landmark tree was and try again from there."

Lazlo Nackley cursed. "Stop trying to impress Joyce, Jack."

The female voice muttered, "Don't worry, it's not working. Let's get out of here," and I listened to the *chunk, chunk* of a machete retreating in the other direction. When they'd gone, I dashed back into the caves, careful to replace the vines over the entrance again in case they came back. My vestlight illuminated the Neo Explorer's jacket, and I ran a finger slowly over the edge of the right sleeve. Sure enough, there was a hidden pocket there, disguised in the seam, and I slid my fingers into it and pulled out a folded piece of old paper covered with unfamiliar words and a series of numbers. It didn't make any sense to me, but this had to be it. I tucked it into my vest and left the cave, crawling along the ground until I was sure Lazlo and his team couldn't see me above the thick vegetation. Then I broke into a run and was back at the river in another five minutes. Zander and M.K. were still hunched over the boat, fiddling with the engine.

"Got it!" I called to them, holding up the paper and making my way down to the boat.

Zander was sweating and he ran the back of his hand across his eyes, wiping away the perspiration. "How did you know?"

"His sleeve," I said. "A lot of Neo Explorers used these secret sleeve pockets . . . Sukey told me about them. What's wrong with the boat?"

"Still won't start," M.K. said. "I think it's a fuse." She was fiddling around with the wrench, which was attached by a thin piece of wire to her Explorer's vest. "I'm going to try to construct a new one out of this wire on my vest, if I can get it out of here . . . Yes! There it is. Now I'll —"

Suddenly, we heard a loud crashing in the undergrowth. We looked up to find a Carnivorous Derudan Hippo. It was standing between me and Zander and M.K., blocking my path to the water and the boat.

The hippo was smaller than the African hippos I'd seen in paintings, with a streamlined shape and a wide mouth full of small, razor-sharp teeth. I remembered hearing about an Explorer who'd come home without his arms thanks to a Derudan hippo. It stopped right in front of me and stared, as though it was figuring out what to do.

"Stand still," Zander whispered. "Don't move." I could feel the hippo waiting to see what I was going to do, calculating its next move. Every cell in my body told me to run, but I forced myself to stay put. Zander whispered something to M.K. and she quietly turned back to her work on the boat engine. The little outboard motor coughed and then went silent again.

"Come on, M.K.," Zander whispered. "Come on."

The hippo charged.

I dove to the ground, rolling away from it, but it kept coming, so close to my face that I could smell rotting vegetation and spoiled meat. I cowered on the ground and closed my eyes, waiting for the attack.

"Arrrrrrhhhhhhhhhh!" I opened my eyes again to see Zander leaping out of the water, swinging his machete at the hippo. He struck its rump with the handle end and it turned away from me to see what was attacking it from behind. And then Zander did something really strange. He grabbed the hippo around its neck as though he was going to hug it and screamed right into its ear. The hippo sank down on its front legs, docile as a house cat, twisting its head this way and that as though trying to escape the sound.

I rolled away, toward the river, just as we heard the outboard motor spring to life.

"Get in!" M.K. called. I got into the boat and Zander stopped screaming and leapt through the air over the hippo, joining us just as Lazlo Nackley and his team came running through the underbrush. They halted and stared at the scene unfolding in front of them.

M.K. pulled away from the shore as the hippo, on its feet again, charged the boat. It splashed into the water behind us snorting and grunting, but the boat was faster, and a moment later we were racing down the river, my heart still pounding, my fear only now catching up and washing over me. A shockingly loud horn sounded, and M.K. pulled the boat up to the riverbank again.

"Okay. Simulation over! Let me see the document," called Parker

Turnbull, the Simulated Expedition instructor. He strode out of the woods around the man-made river and jungle, surrounded by his assistants who helped him create the Simulated Expedition tasks for students of the Academy for the Exploratory Sciences.

"Hand it over," Mr. Turnbull shouted. "Let's see if you passed the challenge."

Two

We jumped out of the boat. My heart was still pounding and my hands shook a little as I reached into my vest. I handed over the papers and a small smile started at the corners of Mr. Turnbull's mouth. He was very tall, six-and-a-half feet in his field boots, with a shiny bald head and a stern face. He always wore his khaki trousers and jacket embedded with gadgets and devices, and he was always armed with a variety of weapons, pistols, stun guns and knives. Apparently, he was one of the best big-game hunters in the world. He examined the parchment. "So this is why you went back to the cave."

"That's right," I said, "I remembered that—"

But before I could tell him what I'd remembered about the Neos' jacket pockets, he put a hand on Zander's shoulder and said, "That was a stroke of bravery in the face of that hippo, son! I don't think

I've ever seen such courage! You remembered that Derudan hippos hate high-pitched noises and you saved your brother's life, sure as I'm standing here."

"And an impressive bit of on-the-fly engineering on the part of this young lady," said Frannie Quincy, the Engineering instructor, waving her toolbox in the air. "Fashioning a fuse from a wire on your vest . . . Brilliant, just brilliant." She was a tiny, plump woman, with a lot of very curly hair streaked with gray, which she always wore pinned up with some kind of metal clip, and a pair of brass welding goggles perched atop her head. Her mechanic's jumpsuit was covered with pockets filled with tools of all sizes.

"Thanks, Quincy." M.K. let Quincy give her a big hug.

Turnbull took a step toward Zander, clapping him on the shoulder again, and stepped square on my foot. It felt as if someone had dropped a piano on it.

"I've never seen anything like it," Quincy was saying to M.K.

I was still holding my throbbing foot when Turnbull said, "Well, congratulations. You three are the winners of the Document Recovery Challenge." Lazlo and his friend Jack Foster stood there scowling, but Joyce Kimani, the third member of their team, gave us a big grin and mouthed, *Well done*, as Lazlo's father, the famous Explorer of the Realm Leo Nackley, stomped over in his high leather boots, his glossy black mustache twitching with irritation. He was a tall man, his shoulders stretching his black cowhide Explorer's jacket at the seams, and he stood nearly eye to eye with Turnbull. "I demand to see the briefing materials and map," he shouted. "I don't believe that this was a legitimate result." Next to him, Lazlo straightened his shoulders and stuck out his chest, glaring at Turnbull.

"Mr. Nackley, I assure you. These students won fair and square, As you could see from the spectator's area, there was a hidden—"

"I said I want to see the briefing materials, Mr. Turnbull. There was no indication that the Explorer was a Neo. Therefore, the challenge is invalid."

"Mr. Nackley. I am happy to—"

"I will expect the documents in my room within the hour." Leo Nackley met my eyes and I could feel how much he hated me. I wasn't exactly sure why, but I knew it had something to do with his relationship with my dad, Alexander West, who had also been a famous Explorer before his disappearance. I looked away before Leo Nackley did. He took his son by the arm and they marched off toward campus. Jack, who seemed to care about girls a lot more than he cared about winning expedition challenges, cast a smarmy grin at Sukey and M.K. and wiggled his fingers at them in farewell before he trotted off behind the Nackleys.

"Don't worry," Turnbull muttered. "He'll get over it. He never did enjoy losing."

"Well, *she* looks happy enough," M.K. said, pointing back at the hippo in the river. One of Turnbull's assistants was tossing huge pieces of bloody meat to the hippo. Our friend Sukey Neville, who'd already been at the Academy for a year, had told us that the hippo's name was Petunia, and that when she wasn't playing her part in the simulations, she liked to chase Mr. Turnbull's dogs. We watched as Turnbull's assistants led Petunia back to her climate-controlled enclosure in a complex of barns at one end of the training grounds. The complex was well disguised behind a man-made rock face, and when you were in the middle of a simulation you almost forgot it wasn't real.

"You must have been scared, son," Turnbull was saying to Zander, who grinned proudly.

"When she charged the second time, I did think I was a goner, but then I remembered that—" A black form came racing through the sky and landed on Zander's shoulder. It was his Fazian Black Knight Parrot, Amerigo Vespucci, whom we called Pucci, and following him was Sukey, her bright blue flight suit and tall plastic Neo boots shining against the dark green transplanted foliage of the simulated Derudan jungle.

Hippo! Pucci squawked. *Big hippo!*

"I had the worst time keeping him from flying to you when the hippo charged," said Sukey, grinning. "You did it! Well done, you three. And you left Lazlo in the dust. He couldn't even figure out the map!"

Turnbull waited until she'd finished hugging us to ask, "How's your mother, Miss Neville? She coming up for the kick-off dinner tomorrow night?"

"Not this year," Sukey told him. "She's in Deloia again. But she'll be up for the Announcement Banquet. She always likes to be here for the announcement of the expedition teams." Sukey's mother was the famous pilot and Explorer Delilah Neville. Even Turnbull seemed a little starstruck by her.

Sukey had told me she understood why Delilah was always off on her expeditions, but I remembered how lonely the house had seemed when Dad was away. "Well, Raleigh can't wait to see you," I said. "You can sit with us."

"If you promise not to lord your new status as one of the chosen elites over us," Zander said with a wink as we headed back toward campus. Sukey had been training for some sort of top-secret Academy flying squad and Zander loved to give her a hard time about it.

"Where are you four going?" As we turned off the main path we ran right into Security Agent DeRosa. We had met DeRosa over the summer when he was working as a special agent for the director of the Bureau of Newly Discovered Lands, or BNDL. He didn't like us very much, on account of the fact that M.K. had knocked him and his partner out with a wrench so we could escape from them. He'd been reassigned to BNDL's Academy for the Exploratory Sciences right around the time we'd become students, which I was pretty sure wasn't a coincidence.

DeRosa pushed his dark hair out of his eyes and smoothed his flowing mustache. He was a dangerous-looking man and he was very proud of his mustache. A friend of Sukey's claimed she'd seen him grooming it with a little comb behind a tree at the far end of campus. His dog, a Deloian Shepherd trained for guard duty, growled a low growl as we passed.

"To dinner," Sukey said, in an annoyed voice. "Don't worry, Agent DeRosa, we're not trying to escape." I looked down at the ground, hoping he wouldn't notice me, but M.K. gave him a sappy-sweet smile that made him scowl, and we all glanced up at the high razor-wire fence that surrounded the campus, guard posts every mile or so around the perimeter. It was supposed to keep intruders out, but the fence and the guards worked just as well to keep us in. Sukey said that the security was much tighter this year, since we'd arrived; I couldn't help but take it personally.

We'd been students at the Academy for the Exploratory Sciences for a month and a half and I still couldn't believe that we were really here, really eating in the Longhouse, where Dad had eaten all of his meals as a student, really taking classes in the forest lodge, really learning about cartography and big-game hunting and survival foraging on the Training Grounds where Dad had learned about these things too. Dad was gone, "disappeared and presumed dead," according to BNDL, on an expedition in the Fazian jungle, but we could still find traces of him here, his initials scratched into the wood of a table in the library, his name on a locker in the mountaineering hut.

Zander and M.K. had jumped right into life at the Academy, M.K. spending most of her time in the engineering buildings with Quincy, learning about new steam engines developed for exploration, practicing small-engine repair and building boats and vehicles with scavenged materials. On the second day of classes, Zander had walked right up to an enraged Grygian bear during his Fauna of the Newly Discovered Lands class and scratched it on the back. He'd also grown another three inches since the summer and was now almost six feet tall. Despite the fact that I'd turned fourteen in September, I still only came up to his shoulder. Last week, a girl had asked me if I was really only a year younger than Zander. "Your brother's so brave," she'd said with a dreamy look on her face. "Everyone thinks so."

It was taking me a little longer to get used to life at the Academy. The agents were everywhere, watching us while we ate and trained, and Sukey had warned us that you had to be careful about criticizing President Hildreth and BNDL. There were students who would inform on you if you did. "Lazlo's an informant, of course," she'd said. "But there are rumors about others, too—people you wouldn't expect."

Now she stopped on the path, letting Zander and M.K. get a little bit ahead of us. Her dark red hair, the color of shiny copper, was full of the late daylight. It was October and the maple trees were turning red and gold, the mountains around campus covered in a wash of autumn color. "You okay?" she asked.

"Yeah, I'm fine," I said quickly, but I could tell she didn't believe me.

She looked around carefully before leaning in and whispering in my ear, "Have you figured out anything about the map?"

The map. Last fall, six months after our father had disappeared on an expedition to Fazia, we had followed a trail of clues—and risked our lives in the process—to a remote canyon in Arizona. It had been waiting for us there, a mysterious bathymetric map showing the contoured floor of some unknown lake or ocean, a gouge in the center labeled "Girafalco's Trench." For the past four months I'd cursed Dad for disappearing in Fazia and leaving me to try to figure out what his mysterious maps meant. There had been a note for us too, a maddeningly brief message that raised more questions than it answered. *Well done, Expeditioners,* it had read. *Here's the next piece of the puzzle. All my love, Dad.*

But what was the puzzle we were trying to solve?

I could smell Sukey's hair, clean and faintly spicy, as she leaned in, and felt her warm breath on my cheek. "Nothing," I whispered back, feeling the frustration of the past month rush through me. I'd searched every atlas I could find for mention of Girafalco's Trench and compared Dad's secret map to them with no luck whatsoever. "Officially, Girafalco's Trench doesn't exist."

Which was exactly the point, of course. Like the map that had led us to Arizona in the first place, it was highly likely this map's secrets were somehow hidden, coded and waiting for me to discover them.

If I could.

A stray curl had escaped from behind her ear, and it brushed my cheek. I wanted her to stay just like that, so I went on, a little desperately, "I keep thinking that maybe it's like the other map, that maybe there's another half somewhere. But *where?*"

"You don't think someone's supposed to *give* it to you, do you? The way that Explorer gave you the book?"

"Maybe, but how would they get it to us? This place is locked up tight and protected like a military base."

"Some people say it *is* a military base," Sukey muttered.

"What do you mean?"

"Nothing." She thought for a minute. "So you've looked through all the maps in the library?"

"Yeah, everything I could find."

"Who's Girafalco anyway?"

It was a good question. "I don't know. I've never heard of him."

"Or her," she said grinning. "Maybe Girafalco's a she. Why didn't you think of that?"

"Maybe she is."

Sukey stared thoughtfully into the darkening sky, the sun hovering over the peaks to the west. "Well, whoever this Girafalco is, your Dad must have trusted you to figure it out the same way you figured out the map of Drowned Man's Canyon."

"I guess. I just wish he'd *explained* what he wants us to do."

Her amber eyes twinkled with mischief. "That would be too easy."

We caught up to the others and walked the half-mile back to the Longhouse along the razor wire fence. "Aren't you coming to dinner?" Sukey asked me when I hesitated outside. Zander had been telling her a funny story about Pucci stealing a pair of eyeglasses from Mr. Wooley, our History of Exploration instructor. Lately, Pucci seemed to think he was a magpie. He was always stealing people's pens and compasses. The students thought it was funny, the teachers not so much. Pucci's presence at the Academy was barely tolerated as it was. Like other unfortunate animals and birds, he'd been modified by the government for use during protests and crowd situations, his legs replaced by metal ones. He'd escaped somehow; Zander had found him on the verge of death and nursed him back to health. His presence on campus must have been a reminder of the government's cruelty and we were worried they might take him away from us. But so far, they'd left him alone.

"I'll be there in a bit," I told them. "I want to go to the library first." I eyed the three agents stationed in front of the Longhouse, watching every student who went inside. Suddenly, I couldn't stand the thought of them watching me while I ate. Besides, the food was terrible here. The shortages were getting worse and there wasn't much coming in from the territories and colonies now.

"Okay," M.K. said cheerfully. "We'll make sure to save you some disgusting, unidentifiable slop."

Three

The Academy for the Exploratory Sciences had been built into a wide valley of the White Mountains, most of the dark-timbered academy buildings nestled together at the foot of Mt. Arnoz, with the Simulation and Training Grounds stretching out in all directions, and the Mountaineering Hut high up in the foothills of the mountain.

The centerpiece of the campus was the huge Longhouse, constructed of gargantuan pine logs, the bark smoothed or worn away in places, pine sap still glimmering here and there on the walls.

The boys' and girls' cabins were a half mile north of the Longhouse, and there were many other log buildings around, some of which I'd never been inside. Sukey had told us that she'd heard rumors there were secret caves and tunnels through the mountains, but she'd never seen any evidence of them and no one knew what they were supposed to be for, so the stories may have just been . . . stories.

I turned up the collar of my Explorer's vest against the chilly breeze coming down off the mountains and trudged along the path to the library, thinking about Sukey. Lately she had seemed preoccupied, her amber-brown eyes always darting around worriedly, her forehead scrunched in thought.

She'd told us that she'd been asked to be on a top-secret flying squadron of Academy students. They'd been taking extra classes and practicing at night and she was tired. I wondered if that was what was on her mind, or if it was something else. Before I knew it, I was standing in front of the Cruthers Memorial Library, looking up at the statue of the famous Explorer George Cruthers seated on the horse he'd used to explore Deloia and other Newly Discovered Lands.

The library was three stories high and, like the Longhouse, it smelled of the pine logs from which it was constructed. The walls of the big main room were lined with books and document boxes and, on one side, a winding staircase leading to three floors of tables and study nooks and shelves around the outside walls that were filled with books and maps.

Most of the books were new, printed since the Muller Machines had failed, taking their huge libraries of computerized books and maps with them. But one of my favorite things about being at the Academy was that there were also some really old books from before the Muller Machines. I loved to pore over them, smelling the smooth leather and musty paper. The maps and nautical charts were stored in special wooden and glass boxes that allowed you to slide them out on trays. You could examine the winding lines showing places that we'd known about for a long time, as well as the places discovered by Dad and his fellow Explorers. I'd been through them a thousand times, looking for Girafalco's Trench. I'd had no luck, but something Sukey said had gotten me thinking.

I couldn't find a record of Girafalco's Trench, but maybe I could find out something about Girafalco himself—or herself.

The Academy librarian, Mrs. Pasquale, sat behind the big desk in the main room, stamping books and keeping an eye on the students working at tables on the first floor. Next to her was a pair of IronGrabbers, steam-powered gloves that got longer and longer and reached high up into the shelves with their chrome fingers to pull down the books you wanted. Mrs. Pasquale was an elderly Neo, her acid-yellow hair in a bun and her glittering spectacles suspended from her neck by a chain of flashing lights. She always thought people were trying to deface the books and maps and she kept a close watch on the students, making notes in a little notebook next to her desk about what you were reading or checking out.

I spent a half hour in the clockwork card catalog, looking for books about famous explorers, and gave her a list of the first five texts I wanted. She slipped her hands into the IronGrabbers. They clicked and whirred as the wrists telescoped, getting longer and longer until she could reach the shelf where my books were. Then, with more clicking and whirring, they shrunk down again and she handed me the books.

"Thank you, Mrs. Pasquale." She just scowled, so I took them back up to my favorite leather armchair by the big windows on the third floor and started checking each index, skimming for mention of a Girafalco. When I finished the first pile, Mrs. Pasquale and her IronGrabbers got me another, and I went through those, feeling more and more frustrated as I failed to turn up any reference to a Girafalco, male or female, living or dead, human or animal. Ready for a break, I got up and went over to the big bureau where the Academy kept its collection of maps and nautical charts.

I'd been through them over and over, looking for a reference to Girafalco's Trench, and now I tried yet again, straining my eyes to see the fine lines of the old documents, the strangely shaped continents and coastlines, the big, wide-open spaces of the oceans, where cartographers had drawn in sea serpents and mythical beasts. But no matter how many times I squinted at the maps, the words I was looking for weren't going to magically appear. Dad had taught me how to memorize maps, and I was good at it, scanning the loops and whorls and lines and making a picture of them in my mind. I had most of these committed to memory now, I'd looked at them so much. By the time dinner was over and students started streaming into the library, the IronGrabbers had had a good workout, and I had made my way through all of the general histories of exploration and all of the biographies of Explorers and had started on the shelves of textbooks that were kept on reserve by the front desk.

Every time I came down with a stack of books and she had to get the IronGrabbers out again, Mrs. Pasquale would make a little notation in her notebook and look up at me with growing admiration. She must have thought I was some kind of speed reader.

I had finished the animal biology and cartography textbooks and had moved on to geology, and then suddenly there it was, at the end of a textbook called *Understanding the Earth*:

"The Italian scientist, mapmaker, and explorer Gianni Girafalco developed an early theory about the permeability of the earth's surface, but it was overshadowed by Tyler's more mainstream hypothesis during the New Modern Age explorations of . . ." That was it. Nothing more about Girafalco. *The Italian scientist, mapmaker, and explorer Gianni Girafalco.* I put the book aside and started on the rest of the geology texts. I found a few more references to Gianni Girafalco, most of them noting that he had explored the Caribbean in the 1800s and was an early believer in something called "trench theory," or the belief that the planet was covered with trenches that represented entry points to the inside of the earth. Girafalco seemed to have believed that if you could enter these trenches, you could actually travel deep inside the earth. He hypothesized that many of these entry points were under the sea and that if you could explore the ocean floor, you could access the center of the earth. I found another reference in an old book about nineteenth-century exploration that contained crew lists from his voyages.

So what did Dad's map mean? Had Gianni Girafalco found one of these undersea trenches? Had Dad gone there? And how was that possible? The New Modern Age inventors had made suits that would let you stay under water for a few hours at a time, but would that have been enough? And how was I supposed to find it, anyway? I couldn't just search the floor of the entire Caribbean Sea.

I got more geology books and kept reading. In a huge textbook called *Men of Earth and Fire*, I finally found another clue in a chapter on geologic exploration before the New Modern Age. "In 1823," I read, "Gianni Girafalco made the third in a series of trips to the northern Caribbean Sea in the Atlantic Ocean, to a region known for its strange weather phenomena, and where many ships had foundered and been lost. Girafalco believed that the rough seas and unusual weather patterns were a direct result of an ocean trench and that the points of access to the trench might reveal a mysterious source of fuel. In a stroke of bad fortune for scientific knowledge, Gianni Girafalco's ship, the *Adelaide*, sunk in May of 1823. The sole survivor, a boy native to Southampton, UK, described rough and turbulent seas just before the ship had foundered. The boy was found floating on a piece of wood by a fisherman."

The library was full of students now, and as I read, I could hear the low murmur of whispered conversation around me, the scratch of pencils on paper, the sound of books being opened and closed.

I turned the page.

There was nothing more about Gianni Girafalco. But remembering that Dad had pointed us to the map of Arizona by leaving coded messages in a book, I flipped through again, checking carefully for notations in the margins, even gently shaking it to make sure nothing was tucked inside.

I slipped the paper cover off and checked out the binding and the endpapers, but everything seemed in order. It was as I was flipping through the title pages and copyright information that I noticed the name of one of the book's authors: R. Delorme Mountmorris.

Was it a sign? Dad had left a code for us in another book by Mr. Mountmorris. But Mr. Mountmorris was a historian. He'd written lots of books. Still . . .

I checked to make sure no one was watching me, then examined the endpapers once more.

Nothing. I turned the book over again.

The spine was stamped in gold, and I checked it with the paper cover off. Closed, the spine lay flat against the bound pages, but when I opened the book all the way so that the front and back covers touched, there was a gap between the stiff board and the glued edges of the paper. I peered down into it, but I couldn't see anything out of the ordinary.

So I poked a pencil down into the space. The first time I didn't notice anything. The second time I poked the pencil through, I felt some resistance, as though the pencil was hitting something. I checked to make sure no one was watching and used the pencil to pry whatever it was away from the inside of the cover.

Suddenly I felt it give way, but before I could catch it, it fell out on to the wooden floor with a metallic *clang*.

Trying not to attract attention, I looked down.

A shiny silver key lay on a square of glossy wood near my foot.

Four

I sat very still, not even daring to lean over to pick it up. Instead, I inched my foot forward over the key.

Joyce Kimani was sitting at the table directly to my right, her Kenyan Snake Falcon, Njamba, dozing on her shoulder. Joyce was fifteen (like Zander), the daughter of a sea captain from Mombasa, Kenya, and one of the best Explorers in Training at the Academy. I knew she hadn't asked to be placed on Lazlo's challenge team, and I was pretty sure she disliked him as much as we did. At the table next to her were a couple of boys M.K.'s age. They were drawing pictures of naked ladies in their notebooks and giggling. I was pretty sure they weren't watching me.

Casually, keeping my eye on Joyce, I reached down and slid the key out from under my shoe.

"Hey, Kit."

I sat up suddenly, clutching the key, and found Kemal Asker standing in front of me. Kemal was my age, a tall, quiet boy who was in most of my classes. His family was from Ottomanland—the country on the Simerian border that some people called Turkey—and they had fled the Indorustan Empire a couple of years ago. His father had been some kind of adviser to the Emperor, but he had gotten into trouble for speaking out about corruption at the Emperor's palace. Now his dad worked for our government, advising them on the Indorustans. I had the sense that the other kids at the Academy didn't quite trust Kemal.

"Oh, hi," I said quickly, conscious of my closed fist, the awkward angle of my foot. "What's up?"

"Uh, I was just wondering whether you know which chapters we're supposed to read for History of Exploration tonight." His accent was pretty strong, and he seemed self-conscious about it. He often looked down at the ground when he spoke, his eyes hidden behind his dark bangs, and he didn't seem to like being called on in class.

"Oh. Five, six, and seven," I told him, my voice too high.

His eyes narrowed. "Okay. Thanks."

When he was gone, I got up and went down to the boys' bathroom, holding my breath as I passed two agents in black uniforms, red BNDL patches on their jackets. They were always patrolling the library, on the lookout for someone stealing a book or putting one back on the wrong shelf. I waited until I was safely locked in a stall to look at the silver key.

It wasn't more than three inches long, designed simply, with a solid oval head, and decorated with little star-shaped flowers. I didn't know if it fit a door or a padlock or something else, but I felt certain that Dad had left it for me. I tucked the key into the new hidden pocket M.K. had sewn into the collar of my vest, got my things together, and went out into the night.

"A key?" Sukey repeated. "A key to what?"

"That's the question, isn't it? That's what I can't figure out. It has these little flowers carved into it, but no writing or anything."

It was late afternoon and we were walking down to the Academy gates to meet Raleigh's taxi. Most of the agents were up at the Longhouse, getting ready for the Kickoff Dinner, and it was a relief not to have to whisper for once.

"There's Dad's old locker up at the Mountaineering Hut," Zander said. "The one that he scratched his initials on. But it doesn't have a lock."

I had given the key to M.K. to look at, and she examined it carefully with the little magnifying glass utility from her vest.

"I already checked with my spyglass, and there isn't anything written on it," I told her.

"I think it must be for a door," she said, handing it back to me. "It's small, but it looks like a deadbolt key. I can't tell anything more than that. I don't know what these little flowers are supposed to mean."

I looked at it again before putting it away in the hidden collar pocket of my Explorer's vest. Dad had customized the vests for Zander, Sukey, and me, and mine had come with a hidden map pocket on the back panel. But ever since government agents had discovered the pocket, I didn't trust it anymore. M.K. had helped me construct a new one, accessed through the collar of my vest, where I was also keeping the map of Girafalco's Trench.

Sukey had been silent, but now she said, "You don't think it's a little—I don't know—*strange*, do you? That he would leave it in the book like that?"

"But the book is here. Somehow, he knew that we'd be here at the Academy, and he put the key in the book about Gianni Girafalco. A book written by Mr. Mountmorris."

"*If* it was him," Sukey reminded me. "You don't know that it was. Maybe someone just left it there. Another student."

"Maybe," I said. "But if so, it's kind of a crazy coincidence."

"And what did he leave us, exactly?" Zander asked. "I don't understand what you think you're going to find." He reached out and brushed a bit of grass off Sukey's jacket, prompting her to smile.

"Zander," I said. "Don't you get it? There's another map somewhere. The map to Girafalco's Trench was just a clue to lead us to the one that actually tells us where to go."

He was silent for a long moment. "Do you think he's trying to tell us where he is? Do you think he's trying to tell us where to find him?"

M.K.'s eyes were wide. "You still think he's alive, Zander, don't you?"

"All I know is that it's really strange that he's supposed to be dead, and yet he's leaving us maps all the time."

"Kit, what do you think?" Sukey asked, her eyes focused intently on me.

"I don't know. I wish it was—I wish I could believe he's still alive. You know I don't believe what BNDL told us about where he disappeared, but I think it's about something else. I think he's trying to lead us to another place. I just don't understand why."

"Why don't we ask Raleigh?" M.K. said. "He might know if there's somewhere Dad would have had a key to. He might even recognize it."

"I thought we said we weren't going to get him involved," I said.

"We don't have to tell him about the key," Zander said. "We can just ask if there were any places that he and Dad used to go. I'll do it really casually. You'll see."

"Look!" M.K. shouted all of a sudden, as we heard the chug-chug of a gleaming chrome-and-brass SteamTaxi making its way up the mountain road. "There's Raleigh!"

Raleigh! Pucci shrieked. *Raleigh!*

We watched Raleigh clank out of the taxi on his prosthetic IronLegs, his messy brown hair and gray beard even longer than when we'd said goodbye to him in September. I didn't realize until that moment how much I'd missed him.

"All right," he said once he'd wrapped us all up in an enormous hug, surrounding us with the familiar clovey scent of Dramleaf and wood smoke. "Let's get up to the Longhouse. I'm not going to miss a chance to have a meal on BNDL's dime."

41

We have now been at
sea for three days and
the nausea I initially experienced has
abated and I have decided to detail how
I have come to be aboard the Adelaide.

My father is himself a ship's captain
and I had gained some experience with
navigation and cartography by the
time I reached the age of eighteen. One
evening last spring, Father took me to a
dinner at the home of his
fiend Captain Sibley,
who had just returned
from the Orient. I was
examining a chart on
the table in Captain
Sibley's study when a thin man with
a foreign accent and strange, sharply
pointed beard entered the room and asked
me if I was interested in maps. I said
that I was, and he introduced himself
as Captain Gianni Girafalco. I had
heard his name before, of course. He is

an Italian explorer and cartographer who gained some fame in his exploration of the South Pacific.

He asked me why I liked maps and charts, and I explained that growing up, I would always watch the ships set sail for exotic ports and try to imagine their voyages. It was when I first saw a chart showing the route around the Cape of Good Hope, which so many of the ships took, that I was able to imagine their journeys by trailing a finger across the lines on the paper; imagine that I was going along with them.

Captain Girafalco seemed very interested, and we talked for nearly an hour before he took his leave. I didn't think I would see him again. Fate had other plans for me.

Five

"What is this stuff?" M.K. asked, letting the gray soup we'd been served as our first course dribble from her spoon back into her bowl. We all watched as she pulled a little cord on her Explorer's vest and a tiny metal canister appeared out of a hidden pocket. She shook it on her food and then tucked it back into the pocket. "Everything here needs salt," she said. Zander lifted a bone out of his bowl and examined it for a minute. "Could be human, actually. This is an articulated thumb bone, with cartilage that . . ."

"Zander," Sukey protested, spitting out the mouthful she'd just spooned in.

Zander grinned, his blue eyes lighting up exactly the way Dad's had lit up when he was joking with us. "Just kidding. I'd say it's rat, marmot, something like that. Though *this* bone is kind of human looking." Sukey laughed, slapping him on the arm.

It was warm and festive inside the Longhouse for the dinner kicking off the Final Exam Expedition season; we'd each be proposing our own expeditions, and the ten best proposals would be announced in six weeks at the Announcement Banquet. The room was full of energy and anticipation.

The long tables were filled with parents and special visitors, all of us watched by the stuffed heads of lions and Elebeests, Shadow Leopards and other exotic creatures, the huge Doolandan Elk antler chandeliers casting flickering candlelight on our conversations.

"We'd better be getting roast beef for the next course," Raleigh said. "I've been looking forward to the roast beef."

"This is gross." Sukey put her spoon down and pushed her bowl away. "Is it my imagination, or has the food been getting worse?"

"What's the matter, Neville?" We all looked up to see Lazlo Nackley standing over our table, holding his empty dinner tray. "The food isn't rich enough for you? They say real Explorers can eat anything. I once ate a cockroach when I was exploring in Deloia."

"Don't they also say, 'You are what you eat?'" I muttered. Everyone at the table laughed, and Lazlo flushed red.

"Excuse me?" He fixed his pale blue eyes on me.

"Come on," Sukey said. "Leave us alone, Lazlo. Or are you still mad you lost to them in the challenge?"

Lazlo fixed his cold eyes on her. "I *let* them win."

"Must have been hard losing in front of your dad," M.K. said.

Lazlo's eyes narrowed. "Did you hear I may win the Arnoz Prize for my find in Arizona?"

"No," Sukey said flatly, stirring her stew. "That's great. Congratulations."

"Thanks." He gave a smug little smile.

I shouldn't have done it, but I couldn't help myself. "Congratulations, Lazlo. Daddy must be really proud of his little boy."

He flushed again and swung his gaze around to me, eyeing me coldly, then turned and went back to his table.

I felt a little stab of caution. The summer before, we'd found ourselves in a race to reach a golden treasure in the Arizona desert before Lazlo and his father could. We'd ended up letting Lazlo take credit for it in order to protect a much bigger secret. So far, Lazlo had seemed willing to accept that he'd found the gold in Arizona and that there hadn't been anything more to it than that, but I didn't want him thinking about it too hard.

Sukey raised her eyebrows at me and hit herself on the side of her head with the flat of her palm before turning her attention back to her soup. She was right. I'd been dumb. When I looked up, Lazlo was whispering something to his father, and they were both watching us from across the room, underneath the gigantic head of a Munopian Mammoth Elephant, its polished and lethal-looking tusks catching the candlelight.

"What are you going to propose for your expedition?" I asked Sukey.

The expeditions were the most important thing that happened each year at the Academy. We all knew that leading a successful expedition was the only way to ensure that you would be made a full-fledged Explorer of the Realm, that BNDL would let you travel the

world, that you'd get to be a member of the Expedition Society.

It meant everything.

I knew that Sukey's dream was to head a polar flying expedition, taking her glider to a part of the New North Polar Sea that had never been accessed by aircraft and was too full of ice for ships. Now she wanted to prove that gliders could be trusted for polar exploration. M.K. had been helping her modify her glider to use solar power.

"I want to plan an expedition to southern Africa," Zander said, "to study the migration patterns of Munopian Wildebeests."

"M.K.?" I asked.

M.K. raised her eyebrows and said noncommittally, "I've got something I'm working on."

Sukey grinned. "What, you're not going to tell us?"

"Not yet. I want to get a little farther first."

Zander looked at me. I shrugged and said, "Not much point in my thinking about it, is there? At the rate I'm going, I'll be lucky to get assigned to one of your crews. Everyone here hates me."

"I'm sure that's not true, Kit," Raleigh said kindly. "When I was a student, I remember feeling like I was always playing second fiddle to your dad. He was so talented. Everyone loved Alex. But we all have our own skills and things we can offer."

Zander reached across the table for the little dish of rancid butter next to Raleigh and asked, "Did Dad have any secret places he liked to go on campus, Raleigh? We need to know."

Raleigh looked confused for a moment. Then he said, "Your dad loved hiking, Zander. Loved it. He'd spend hours and hours on the trails, up near the Mountaineering Hut. I used to kid him about having a secret girlfriend, but I think he just loved being on the mountain. Still, I always wondered if—"

"Enjoying the meal?" We looked up to find Cameron Wooley, our History of Exploration instructor, standing next to our table, wearing his gray synthetic leather longcoat and tweed hat pushed down over his spiky platinum-blonde hair. Though he couldn't have been older than forty, his face was weathered, lined and permanently tanned, lines feathering the corners of his wide brown eyes. I liked his soft Irish accent. "Hello, Raleigh. Lovely to see you. You're looking well. Hello, Neville," he said, nodding at Sukey. He was a Neo, as she was, and though they weren't supposed to play favorites, everyone knew that the Neo instructors looked out for the Neo kids at the Academy. While Mr. Wooley had completed a few moderately successful expeditions in the North Atlantic, he was best known as a scholar of New Modern Age exploration history.

"I just wanted to say congratulations to you three. I was watching the challenge. And I wanted to tell you, Kit, that that was a nice bit of thinking on the map and on the sleeve pockets." He smiled at me. "Aren't a lot of Archys who would have caught that. Well done. Well done, all three of you."

"Thank you, sir," I stammered.

"How about that?" Raleigh said after he'd returned to his table. "That was nice of him."

"See," Sukey said, grinning at me. "Not everyone here hates you."

"Yeah." Zander punched me on the shoulder. "Just most of them."

Six

The hired waiters served us small slices of fatty, overdone roast beef for our second course. As we started to eat, there was a flurry of activity up at the front of the dining room.

"Your attention, please!" We all looked up to see our headmaster, Hilde Magnusdottir, standing up at the front of the huge room, under the giant mounted head of the Munopian Mammoth Elephant. She wore her white leather jacket, britches, and high boots. Her thick, snow-white hair hung in long braids down her back and her Explorer's vest, tight over her tall, thin frame, was covered with loops and pulls that I knew turned into ice picks and climbing equipment. She had made her name scaling the frozen ice walls of the Newly Discovered Lands north of her native Iceland. Everyone, even the students, called her Maggie.

"Quiet, everyone," she called. "Welcome to all of the parents and special guests who have joined us for the traditional Final Exam Expedition Kickoff dinner. As you know, the dinner is a beloved ritual of the training year here at the Academy.

"Now, I am happy to announce that we have two *very* special guests tonight, Mr. Francis Foley, the Director of the Bureau of Newly Discovered Lands, and Mr. R. Delorme Mountmorris, a well-known historian and advisor to BNDL. Welcome, gentlemen."

They gazed out at us, Foley looking angry as usual in his black BNDL uniform, Mr. Mountmorris smiling devilishly, his shiny suit and top hat a sparkly blood red. Foley was very thin, with small eyes that shifted back and forth when he spoke, and a too-wide mouth of very white teeth.

I hated him. I'd hated Foley ever since the day he'd come to tell us that Dad had disappeared on an expedition in Fazia, ever since he'd seized Dad's maps and chased us across the country, ever since he'd killed the one person who could tell us something about why Dad had left the mysterious map for us. I hated him for that and a lot of other reasons besides.

If it was possible, I hated Mr. Mountmorris even more. We had gone to him to ask about Dad's map of Arizona and he had told us that it might show the location of a fabled treasure in gold. He had acted pleased to meet us and to show us his collections of artifacts and specimens from all over the world. He'd made us feel like we could trust him, and then he'd betrayed us, telling Foley and Leo Nackley about the map and trying to get it away from us so the government could find the gold.

Most of all, I hated him because he held our futures in his hands. We were only at the Academy because he'd said we could be, and I knew he could send us away any time he wanted to. And now he was the only person who'd be able to tell me about Gianni Girafalco. And yet there was no way I could ask him.

"Security seems a little tight, don't you think, considering we're in the mountains and about a thousand miles from civilization?" I said to the others. "Look at all those agents." There were ten of them, dressed identically in their black BNDL uniforms, the red patches on their jackets identifying them as agents of the Bureau. They were watching all of us carefully, standing close to Foley and Mountmorris.

Raleigh lowered his voice. "You heard about the bomb in New York last week, didn't you? Some people say that Foley was the target. They think it was East Simerian terrorists."

Sukey lowered her voice too. "When Delilah came back from Mooristan, she came up for a visit and told me that people think there's going to be a major uprising in Simeria. War, maybe. If I were Foley, I'd be nervous too." "Look who else is here," M.K. whispered. "Isn't that . . . ?"

"Dolly Frost," I said, finishing her thought. I met the reporter's eyes, then looked away when she recognized me. She was the exploration correspondent for the *Times,* and I knew she had questions about what had happened in Arizona, too.

"As you all know," Maggie went on from the front of the room, "you will all soon be submitting your Final Exam Expedition proposals for our consideration. The Final Exam Expeditions constitute 50 percent of your grade for the entire year and are the most important work you will do here at the Academy. Your proposals will be read and evaluated by the faculty, and ten will be chosen—the ten *best* plans. Those expeditions will be carried out during the spring term. You may make suggestions about the crew members you want for your expeditions, based upon your needs, but the final choice will be up to the faculty. Now Mr. Foley and Mr. Mountmorris would like to address you. But before they do, I have a very special announcement."

She looked out at the crowd in the Longhouse, the enormous head of the Munopian Mammoth Elephant scowling down at her from above, and hesitated before saying, "Earlier today, President Hildreth announced that he has named Mr. Francis Foley as the new Director of the Agency to Defend the Realm, and has asked Mr. R. Delorme Mountmorris to take over as the director of the Bureau of Newly Discovered Lands. We are greatly honored to have both of these talented and patriotic men with us today."

There was a low murmur in the Longhouse as everyone took in the news and then stood to applaud. I thought for a moment about staying seated but changed my mind. There were too many agents. I happened to look over at Leo Nackley during the long round of applause and was surprised to find him scowling and barely clapping his hands.

"Director of ADR," Raleigh said with a whistle. "Foley's moving up in the world, huh?"

One of the other parents at the table leaned in and said, "Leo Nackley doesn't look very happy. I heard he was up for head of BNDL too."

Once we were all seated again, Foley stood up, taking a piece of paper out of a pocket of his black jacket and shaking it out.

"It's always good to be back at the Academy, to see what all of our young Explorers in training are up to." After a moment of hesitation, he gave a false smile, as though someone had written "grin now" in his notes.

"I am especially pleased to be here today as my mind turns to the defense of our great nation and our allies. Make no mistake: The Indorustan Empire has designs on our lands and resources, and we must do everything in our power to defend ourselves. You young Explorers are an important part of this mission. Our ability to defend ourselves is wholly dependent on our ability to find new resources and riches in our newly discovered lands. This is where your Final Exam Expeditions come in.

"A winning expedition proposal is well researched, well presented, with every eventuality accounted for. In addition, a good expedition proposal focuses on a region that is not only unexplored but that may be of value to the well-being or the *security* of the United States and its allies.

"I don't have to tell you how important these expeditions may be to the future of our country," Foley said. "As you work on your plans, remember that though you may only be Explorers in Training now, your expeditions are very real and may yield discoveries that can improve the lives of your fellow citizens. I am expecting a lot of you. In these troubled times, your country is counting on you. Mr. Mountmorris?"

Mr. Mountmorris hopped over, joining Mr. Foley under the elephant head, and smiled a broad, jowly smile. His egglike eyes glittered, and thin wisps of gray hair sprang up from his shiny scalp. "Hello, students!" he boomed. "What a pleasure, what a truly great pleasure it is to see your happy faces, your happy, happy faces!" He looked around the room, seeming to take in the details of every one of the happy faces in the room. "Mr. Foley is right, you know. These expeditions of yours are of the utmost importance to our country and our allies. And to show you just how important I think they are, I have an exciting announcement to make. As the new director of BNDL, I am putting my money where my mouth is, so to speak. I am offering . . ." He paused. "I am offering $50,000 in gold to the leader of the expedition who makes a find that will most significantly contribute to the security of our country." A wave of excited murmurs went around the room. "Furthermore—"

I watched Francis Foley's face as Mr. Mountmorris spoke, and I suddenly saw fear flash across his eyes as we all heard a loud *boom* from above his head. A second later, there was another explosion, and smoke filled the air. The black-clad agents leapt forward and pushed Mr. Foley and Mr. Mountmorris out of the way just as the Mammoth Elephant head crashed to the ground where they'd been standing. Mr. Mountmorris gave a last, excited grin at the crowd before he disappeared beneath the pile of agents. There was another, smaller *boom* and then a cloud of smoke rose from the spot on the wall where the elephant head had been hanging.

"Get under the tables!" someone shouted, and we all scrambled for cover, overturning chairs up and down the hall.

"What was it?" Sukey whispered once we were all on the floor. "Did anyone see?" I looked down the row of students and parents crouched on the ground and saw Joyce Kimani protectively shielding some of the younger kids next to me.

"Hey, you'll be safe right here next to me. I promise I won't bite," I heard Jack Foster say to the unfortunate girl taking cover next to him.

"It sounded like an explosion. Foley looked scared," I told her.

"He should be scared. Those Mammoth tusks would have gone right through him," Raleigh said, grunting with pain. His IronLegs made him clumsy, and he'd fallen amid the confusion.

It was eerily silent for a few seconds and then we heard the agents shouting for everyone to stay down while they got Foley and Mountmorris out of the room and secured the Longhouse. I peeked out from beneath the table and saw them hurrying out, followed by a few agents, while the rest of the agents huddled around something on the floor in the corner. Dolly Frost was scribbling in a notebook and talking to the agents.

Finally, Maggie told everyone to stand up and walk single file out of the Longhouse. "Slowly, now," she said. "No pushing. I want you to go straight back to your cabins and go to bed. Guests, we are very sorry for this unfortunate turn of events. It seems that the presence of Mr. Foley and Mr. Mountmorris provoked unpatriotic elements in our society. Have no doubt that the perpetrator will be brought to swift justice."

We helped Raleigh up and filed out. The remaining agents, including Woolf, watched us carefully, focusing for a moment on the face of each student or visitor as he or she passed by.

"You okay?" I asked Sukey once we were outside. Torches blazed outside the Longhouse as agents directed everyone back to the cabins. In the yellow light, her mouth twisted down with worry.

"Yeah, mostly," she answered. "But I have a feeling this isn't the end of this. Things are going to get pretty bad here for a while." She watched the agents leading people away from the Longhouse. "Be careful, Kit. They can do anything they want now."

Seven

I didn't understand what she meant until the next day when word started spreading around campus that BNDL was calling students in for interviews about the Kickoff Dinner.

"Somebody wired up the Mammoth head with explosives," Sukey told us at breakfast. "That reporter Dolly Frost told Ava Eisenhofer this morning. She wanted to know if Ava'd seen anything." The Longhouse was quieter than usual, everyone eating and talking in low voices, very aware of the agents lining the walls. It seemed like the number of agents had quadrupled overnight. I wondered how they'd gotten them up here so quickly. "It wasn't very sophisticated, but the tusks on that head would have killed Foley if the agents hadn't pushed him out of the way. BNDL is determined to figure out who did it."

"Who do you think it was?" Zander asked her.

Sukey shrugged. "Must have been one of the visitors or students, right? Nobody else could get on to the campus without being discovered." But she didn't look so sure.

We walked down to the gates to say goodbye to Raleigh, who had been interviewed and told he could leave. As his SteamTaxi disappeared around the bend, we all looked up and watched as a huge airship rose into the cloudless sky and floated over the mountains towards the south, a thin, gray tail of smoke behind it.

"The *Grygia*," Zander said. "I guess they're hustling Mr. Mountmorris and Foley out of here."

We all watched until it was gone. And then, because we didn't know what else to do, we went to the library to study. It was full, everyone looking nervous and uncharacteristically studious as agents came in and took students out a few at a time to be interviewed. I couldn't focus on my homework, so I read through the newspapers laid out on a table by the big fireplace. The *Times* and most of the other papers were reporting that the Simerian government was accusing the Indorustan Empire of imprisoning East Simerians who weren't supporting the Indorustan authorities. INDORUSTANS COMMIT ATROCITIES, the *Times* headline shouted. INDORUSTAN TREATMENT OF UNITED STATES ALLIES GROWS WORSE, SAY WITNESSES.

Two agents escorted Zander and M.K. out of the library. When they returned, they were trailed by one of the regular school agents, who nodded at Sukey and me and beckoned for us to follow him.

"Are you okay?" I whispered to M.K.

"No talking. Come with me," the agent hissed.

We followed him outside and past the Longhouse to the Administration Building, a big log structure that housed the headmaster's office and the infirmary. The mountains loomed in the distance. Below, the trees were still bright, not quite at their autumn peak. There was a bunch of students waiting on the benches outside Maggie's office, and DeRosa scowled at us and told us to sit down and wait until we were called. Kemal Asker moved over to make room for us on the wooden bench.

"Did they tell you anything?" Sukey asked Kemal. He looked nervous, his face pale, his hands worrying at the strap on the Explorer's bag he held in his lap.

"No. But I heard some kids saying that they're searching the cabins while they interview us." His voice shook as he said it, and I wondered if there was something in his room he didn't want them to find.

I could feel Sukey tense up next to me, and I knew what she was thinking. The key and the map. But they were safely hidden in the collar pocket of my vest. I couldn't think of a way to let her know that I'd brought them with me without tipping off Kemal, so I just said, "You'd have to be pretty stupid to leave bomb-making equipment or something in your room."

"Yeah, well, I doubt it was a student," Kemal said. "I heard that—"

"Asker?" The door next to Maggie's office opened and Jack Foster came out, looking relieved, followed by a young female agent with short blond hair.

"Thanks so much for your time," Jack said to the agent. "I really enjoyed talking to you." She ignored him and showed Kemal into the office. The last thing we saw before the door closed was Kemal's terrified face.

"Jack would flirt with a Carnivorous Derudan Hippo if he thought he might get a kiss," Sukey muttered. "I don't know. Petunia *was* pretty cute," I said, trying to get her to smile.

But before I could find out if I'd been successful, Maggie's door opened and Agent DeRosa poked his head out and said, "Christopher West. In here."

I'd really been hoping it wouldn't be DeRosa. He narrowed his eyes at me as I brushed past him, and I felt very slightly relieved when I saw that Maggie was there too. At least he couldn't torture me, though after seeing the suspicious way Maggie studied me, I wasn't so sure. And then I saw Leo Nackley sitting against the far wall. He nodded, smirking. Rather than seeming upset about the assassination attempt, he looked as though he'd never been happier.

"Sit down, Kit," Maggie said. "As you know, we're interviewing all of the students at the Academy about last night's unfortunate attempt on Director Foley's life. I assume you know Agent DeRosa?"

"Yes, we, uh—"

"We certainly do know each other," DeRosa interrupted, rubbing his head as though it still stung from the wallop M.K. had given him with her wrench last spring.

"And have you met Mr. Leo Nackley? He will also be helping us during this difficult time."

"Yes, Mr. West and I are quite well acquainted," Nackley said.

Agent DeRosa leaned back in his chair. "Now, where were you when the incident occurred?"

"I was eating dinner with everyone else," I told him. I hadn't been in Maggie's office before, and I looked around at the paintings and artifacts hanging on the walls. There were Rubutan masks, the stuffed heads of two antlered Snow Deer, Lundlandian idols, and photographs of Academy expedition teams from over the years. It was a nice room, warm, outfitted with a big dark wood desk and white velvet chairs and couches, but I couldn't feel at ease in it.

DeRosa watched me, his moustache quivering. He nodded at Maggie. I expected him to interrogate me further, but instead he said, "Now, what about your fellow students? Did you notice anyone acting strangely just before the incident? Anyone seem nervous or out-of-sorts? Anyone out of his or her seat?"

"No," I said. "Do you think it was a—"

"I'll ask the questions, thank you. So you say you didn't notice anyone out of his or her seat. Are you sure?" I nodded. Leo Nackley and Maggie were watching me, waiting for me to slip up. DeRosa looked down at the paper he was holding. "What about Mr., uh, Asker. Kemal Asker. Did you notice anything odd about his behavior last night?"

"No, although . . ." Now that I thought about it, I didn't remember seeing Kemal at all.

"Although what?" DeRosa leaned forward.

"I don't remember seeing him before it happened, but he was

probably on the other side of the room. Anyway, I didn't see him doing anything strange."

Leo Nackley watched me while DeRosa wrote something down in his notebook. "And what about Joyce Kimani? She's from Kenya, I believe."

"I thought she grew up in New York."

"Well, her parents have returned to their native Kenya."

"What does that have to do with anything? Kenya is an Allied Nation, last time I checked."

Leo Nackley slammed his palm down on Maggie's desk. "Just answer Agent DeRosa's question, West."

"I think she was at the end of the table. She seemed to be eating dinner just like everyone else. I definitely saw her right after the elephant head fell. She was helping out some of the younger kids who were scared."

Agent DeRosa looked disappointed. He named a couple of other students, all of whom had come to the Academy from allied countries. When I failed to come up with anything incriminating to say about any of them, he leaned back in his chair and fixed his dark eyes on me, stroking his mustache. "You do realize that lying to the government is a very serious offense, do you not, Mr. West?"

"Of course I do."

"The last time we met, I asked you if you had been contacted by a known degenerate and enemy of the Realm who had had a relationship with your father. You said you hadn't. Has your answer to that question changed?"

I met his gaze and said steadily. "No. I haven't seen that man."
I was telling the truth. I hadn't seen him—not lately, anyway. I felt
a flash of anger. The Explorer with the Clockwork Hand had started
this whole thing. And then he'd disappeared, leaving me to face the
questions about him alone.

DeRosa nodded to Leo Nackley and Maggie and sat back down.
Now Maggie shuffled some papers and drew a deep breath.

"Kit," she said, fixing her ice-blue eyes on me. "I hope you've
enjoyed your time so far at the Academy."

"Uh, yes. Yes, I have."

"You know that you're very lucky to be here, don't you?"

"Yes, I know that." I couldn't figure out where she was going
with these questions.

"Well, we've noticed that you aren't as . . . *enthusiastic* about
your training here at the Academy as we might hope. Some of your
teachers say that you seem listless in class. Bored."

I gulped. "No, I . . . I really like it here."

"Good. I'm glad to hear that. You've been spending a lot of time
at the library lately, is that right?"

"I . . . I guess so," I stammered. "I've had a lot of studying to do."

"And you seem quite interested in geology." She read off the list
of textbooks I'd looked through while looking for Gianni Girafalco.
"Despite the fact that you are not taking any geology classes
this year."

"I like to read," I said lamely. "I'm interested in lots of different
things." A wave of dizziness hit me. It was warm in the office, and for

a couple of seconds, Maggie's face swam in front of my eyes, a blur of white. I took a deep breath and she came back into focus.

"And it looks like . . ." She consulted a handwritten list. "A couple of weeks ago you read a number of books about Simeria, again despite the fact that you aren't studying Simeria right now. I find this curious."

"Well, you know, it's in the news so much right now. I was just interested to know more."

There was a long silence, during which they all watched me as though they thought I would break down and admit everything if they just stayed quiet. Finally, Leo Nackley cleared his throat. "Mr. West, are you quite sure there's nothing else you want to tell us?"

"No. I'm sure," I said, meeting his eyes.

"Anything about the attempt on Mr. Foley's life? Or about any other matter? For instance, something about Arizona? Or a map?"

Maggie looked confused. My heart beat very fast. I'd been stupid to make fun of Lazlo. Obviously he'd told his father. And now Leo Nackley was suspicious.

"Nothing you don't already know, sir," I said, trying to keep my voice even. "There was a map. We followed it. Lazlo found the gold first. You were there."

"Ah, yes, that's right," Maggie said. "The treasure hunt. Well, if there's nothing else, I think you can go, Mr. West."

As I got up, I could feel Leo Nackley watching me. Outside Maggie's office, I found Dolly Frost trying to talk to the students who were still waiting for their interviews. The reporter had dressed up for her visit to the Academy, and her bright-pink dress and high-heeled boots looked out of place in the mountains. "Mr. West, can I speak with you?" she said, but I brushed past, ignoring her. The last thing I needed was to get in trouble for talking to the press.

Sukey caught up to me on my way back to the library.

"What did they ask you?" she asked as we walked along, keeping our voices down.

"Books." I told her about Maggie's list of the books I'd read. "And Leo Nackley asked about Arizona." Sukey raised her eyebrows. "I know, I know. You were right. I never should have been so sarcastic with Lazlo. But they seemed really interested in Kemal and Joyce and all of the other foreign students."

"Yeah, they asked me about Kemal, too. They wanted to know if I knew that Ottomanland borders East Simeria and asked if he'd ever talked about relatives of his who were still back there and were 'political activists.' Did they frisk you? I was worried about them finding the maps and the key."

"Nope. I was worried, too. I'll have to find a better hiding place. What do you think is going to happen now?"

"I don't know, but Kemal and Joyce had better be careful."

That night at dinner I searched the Longhouse but couldn't find Kemal or Joyce or any of the other foreign students.

The strangest thing was that no one said a word about them. It was as though we'd all agreed to pretend they'd never existed.

It was a fortnight

after the dinner at Captain Sibley's that Captain Girafalco came to call upon my father. They spoke in the study for nearly an hour before they called me in. Captain Girafalco explained that he was looking for an apprentice, a young man with an interest in cartography and adventure, to accompany him on his next voyage. The words were barely out of his mouth before I shouted gleefully that I would be honored to accept. I made so much noise that the housemaid flew into the study to make sure all was well.

Eight

Ever since I'd arrived at the Academy, I'd been dreaming about Dad. It was as though being in the place where he'd spent so much time had returned my memories of him to me, memories that had been pushed down during all these months of his absence. My dreams were strange, partly things that had actually happened, partly nightmares about Dad being taken away or disappearing under the surface of a river. It was all starting to get mixed up in my mind, the real world and the dream world, and it made it hard for me to concentrate in class or in the library.

That night, I dreamed that I was chasing Dad along a steep, winding mountain path. The light was strange, an oddly bright moon lighting the way like a huge torch in the sky. I kept yelling at him to slow down, but he didn't seem to hear me.

I was chasing him when I passed a bush covered with little blue flowers. They were familiar, and I studied them for a minute before I resumed my chase. But Dad was gone. I could just barely make out his footprints on the path, and it seemed to me that if I looked at them too long, they also disappeared.

I heard a bird call, and when I looked up to find Pucci, everything was murky, and I felt as though I was swimming through black water.

Caw! Pucci cried overhead as I awoke, my room still dark. *Caw!*

Zander and I had a small bunk room at the back of Base Cabin 6, the biggest of the boys' cabins at the Academy. The rooms were tiny, with a set of bunk beds, a few hooks on the wall for jackets and gear, and space against the wall for our trunks. I slept on the bottom bunk, and it took me a minute to get my bearings. It must have been Pucci outside the open window that woke me from the dream because now I could hear him chortling out on the sill.

I lay there, looking up at the underside of Zander's bunk, the details of the dream coming back. Something about the flowers bothered me. And then I realized what it was: I knew those flowers. They grew on the side of Mt. Arnoz, along the path to the Mountaineering Hut, where we had all of our climbing and mountaineering and alpine survival lessons. They'd been transplanted from Deloia around the time the Mountaineering Hut was built—I'd heard Sukey refer to them as Deloian Starflowers—and they had thrived in the mountains, spreading all over the face of Mt. Arnoz and along the hiking trails.

But then my mind turned to the little silver key and the flowers carved into its head. It had to be a sign from Dad. The mystery of the key had something to do with the Starflowers. What was it Raleigh had said, that Dad often disappeared up near the Mountaineering Hut?

For a few minutes, I considered waking Zander, but rejected the thought. Too risky. I dressed quickly in black training clothes, slipping out of the cabin into the darkness. There was a big, almost-full moon in the sky, and once I was out of the trees that shaded the cabins, I could see pretty well by its light. I kept to the woods next to the main path and listened for the agents who patrolled the grounds of the Academy at night.

Right at the beginning of the school year, there had been a boy named Frederick Carley who had been expelled for being out of his cabin at night. Sukey said that she'd heard he'd been going to visit his girlfriend. Apparently the agents didn't have any sympathy for young love.

I knew I was taking a huge risk, but I told myself that Frederick Carley hadn't had what I had: Pucci.

I whistled very softly and heard him whistle back. He'd stay high overhead, looking for danger, and alert me if anyone was near.

I made my way slowly past the Longhouse and the main campus buildings, watching through the trees and listening for agents, before starting up the winding web of trails that covered Mt. Arnoz. I was still learning the trails, but I'd already spent a lot of time at the Mountaineering Hut, so I knew the way, even in the near-darkness. The night air was chilly, and I was glad I'd worn a sweater under my vest and put on my flannel-lined trousers.

I hiked for twenty minutes or so before I saw the peaked roof of the Mountaineering Hut ahead on the trail. It was actually a fairly large, hexagonal structure, used for classes and equipment storage, and it even had a bunk room in case someone got stranded up there in the snow. Everyone just called it the Hut. The big classroom on the second floor had 360-degree views of the mountains. The lockers—including the one that had been Dad's—were on the first floor. I waited until I was past its looming shadow before I turned on my vestlight, shining it on the starflower bushes that grew along the slope. The path was well used and easy to follow, but I assumed that any hidden doors or secret compartments weren't going to be right on the path, so I made my way up the steep grade through the bushes, inspecting the ground carefully. I got the key out of my vest pocket, ready to open whatever door I was going to find.

I stopped and listened. I couldn't hear anything but the wind moving through the trees and a bird calling somewhere up the slope.

I tried not to be nervous. Pucci was watching. Surely the agents didn't come all the way up here. But then something moved in the trees. A squirrel. It had to be a squirrel. It moved again. A deer, maybe. I stopped and listened, my heart pounding, then started walking again. The wind had come up, and it whistled through the trees with an eerie hushing sound. I still had Dad's key ready in my hand, and I held it out in front of me, as though I could use it as a weapon if I needed one.

I'd gone about a hundred yards when I thought I heard footfalls on the path behind me. My heart pounding, I turned to scan the path

with my vestlight, but no one was there. The wind moved through the trees and against the side of the mountain again. I shivered and started to run. I couldn't see Pucci above me, couldn't hear him.

And then there was a rush of air behind me, and I felt cold metal go over my mouth, and a familiar voice whispered in my ear, "Don't scream." Strong arms dragged me into the woods on the side of the path and then dropped me onto the ground.

"Sorry about that," the voice whispered. "It was the only way."

It was the Explorer with the Clockwork Hand.

Nine

"Turn off your light," the Explorer whispered. "I don't want to attract attention."

He pulled me up off the ground, and before I switched off the light, I saw the familiar face, barely visible under the brim of his hat.

"What are *you* doing here?" I asked him. "Francis Foley and Mr. Mountmorris were here. Someone tried to kill Foley. The place is swarming with agents. If they find you—"

"I know," he said. "Don't worry about me. The question is, how are you? It's been a long time." He smelled the way I remembered him, like Dramleaf and unwashed clothes. His voice was hoarser, but I recognized the accent—Eastern European, I'd guessed the first time I heard it, just a little twist on his *w*'s.

"I'm . . . I don't know, how do you think I am? You gave us

the book, but you didn't tell me anything about what was going to happen. We were almost killed. Tex—well, John Beaureguard—he *was* killed."

"I know. I was very sorry to hear it."

"Why didn't you tell us about the map? About what was in the canyon?"

"Because I didn't know about the map. Or the canyon."

"But you gave me the book!"

"Because your dad asked me to. I didn't know where it was going to lead."

"What do you mean?"

"Exactly what I said."

I could feel myself getting angry at him. "Are you a member of the Mapmakers' Guild? Was Dad?"

He laughed. "You're a smart one. I can't tell you that yet, but—"

He snapped his head up, listening. "What was that?"

"I don't know. Our parrot came with me. Maybe it's him."

"No. I have to go." He stood up and tipped his hat back. Now I could hear it, too, voices coming closer. Agents. "Go up there in those rocks," he whispered. "There's a little cave that may prove useful. Try not to make any noise."

"But what's going on?"

"Shhh. Be careful. And if they catch you, don't tell them anything."

He was gone, disappeared into the trees.

I stood there, frozen, not sure what to do. And then, before I could make a decision, I heard a dog bark once, and they were on the path just below me. "There's no one up here." It was DeRosa. I recognized his voice.

"But where else would he have gone?" Leo Nackley. I knew his voice now too, and hearing it sent a chill down my spine.

"Who are we looking for, anyway?" DeRosa asked.

"A troublemaker. He may be trying to contact one of Alexander West's children. We still think West may have left behind messages for them and may be using this criminal to deliver them."

"Are you sure you saw—"

"Of course I'm sure," Nackley said. "Why would I have woken you up and brought you and your mutt all the way up here if I wasn't sure? What does the dog say, anyway?"

In answer, the shepherd gave a huge, deep bark. "He smells something," DeRosa said. "Up that way."

They were right below me, and if I stayed where I was, they were going to stumble over me in less than a minute. I didn't know what else to do, so I ran, still clutching the key in my right hand.

"What was that?" Leo Nackley shouted. "Chase him!" I heard their footsteps behind me, but I just kept on running, trying not to slip on the loose rocks on the path. They had bright lights, and I tried to stay low so their beams wouldn't find me.

Suddenly, I ran up against a wall of rock covered in the twining starflowers. I felt my way along and found what the Explorer had been talking about: a shallow crevice worn into the face, covered by a veil of vines, big enough to tuck myself into, though the dog would still be able to smell me. The moon was on the other side of the mountain now, and it was dark here. I allowed myself one deep breath and squeezed inside just as their voices came up the path below me.

They were so close. The dog was yelping, telling them I was there. I pressed myself into the rock, trying to make myself as small as possible, but I knew it was over. They'd found me.

"The trail goes up this way," DeRosa announced. My fingers sought out the little crevices in the rock. Maybe I could climb up high enough that I'd lose them. I was realizing what a stupid idea it was when I felt something under the index finger of my right hand. A metal plate, with a keyhole in the center. It was so small, I never would have found it if I hadn't been pressed up against the rock. Could it be? Slowly, trying not to make a sound, I inserted the key into the hole. I had to use both hands since I couldn't see, but I got it in and turned it.

Click.

The wall moved, swinging silently away from me, and I stepped through the opening just as the voices reached my hiding spot.

It was a terrifying feeling, stepping into darkness with no idea of what was on the other side. I carefully shut the door behind me and leaned against it, sucking at the stale air of wherever it was I was hiding. I couldn't see a thing. For all I knew I'd just stepped into a bear's den.

"There's someone in here!" I heard DeRosa shout from the other side of the door. "It's a cave! Quick, move the vines aside!" The shepherd barked.

I could see light from their flashlights through the keyhole, and I knew they were just on the other side of the door. I held my breath, the key clutched in my hand.

"There's no one here, you idiot!" Nackley shouted. "It's a cave, but it's empty."

"The dog picked up the scent," DeRosa said apologetically. "He must have headed up the mountain."

"Well, don't waste time. Let's go!"

"Come on, boy, this way," DeRosa panted. His dog barked again, as if in protest, but I heard the voices moving away from the door.

"I just don't see how he could have entered the campus without us knowing," DeRosa said.

Nackley blew up. "I saw him, you idiot! You and the Academy agents weren't doing your jobs." The voices were getting fainter.

"I don't see how that's . . ."

I counted to a hundred before turning on my vestlight. The light shone into the space around me. I was alone inside a natural cave that had been turned into a small room with the addition of the door. It was a thin, concave slab of stone that had been cut to fit precisely into the arch of the cave. If I hadn't felt the keyhole, I never would have seen it.

The room was about the size of our bunk room, with a sloping ceiling and smooth walls. The only pieces of furniture were a small wooden table and chair against one wall, covered with piles of paper, and opposite, a long couch with an old woolen blanket stretched over it. Above the table were three rows of bookshelves.

On one of the lower shelves was a square box with a screen on the front, the base covered with buttons and switches, the back sprouting wires like hair.

A Muller Machine.

Dad had been here in this room. It was where he'd been leading us. I sniffed the air and the blanket, recognizing the scent of Dramleaf and sweat; the Explorer had been here, too. In fact, I was willing to bet that this is where he'd been hiding.

I shone my light carefully around the space. I was nervous about touching the Muller Machine, but curiosity got the better of me, and I pressed a red button on the front with the word POWER printed underneath. Nothing happened. I tried a few more buttons, but the machine didn't seem to be connected to an engine or battery or anything. Where had it come from? Had it been Dad's? I knew that all of the Muller Machines had been outlawed when he was a kid. So where had he gotten it? If it had been found, it would have been confiscated.

Next I shone my light on the walls. There were some maps of the White Mountains hung up here and there, the cellophane tape yellowed and cracking, with red pencil lines tracing the hiking trails on Mt. Arnoz.

What was this place? Obviously Dad had wanted us to come here. But *why*? I kept looking around, shining my vestlight on the walls, then turning to the papers on the table. Most of them were scrawled maps and nautical charts of various places around the world. I recognized Dad's handwriting in a few places, but there weren't any notes or any obvious messages from Dad to us. Of course there wouldn't be. If someone else found his or her way in here, Dad had to make sure they couldn't decipher the clue he'd left for us.

I decided to check out the books. There was a whole series of them, with volume numbers stamped in gold on the spines, and each one was filled with maps from a different region of the world. The one I was holding had dozens of maps of various African countries: a map of Johannesburg, South Africa, the countries on the continent's east coast. There was something strange about these maps, too, but it took me a minute to figure out what it was. The wedge-shaped land of Munopia wasn't jutting out from the southwestern coast of the continent. Where the newly discovered island nation of Deruda should have been, there was just the blue of the Indian Ocean. They were Muller Machine maps, from before the discovery of Grygia. From before the New Lands.

I stared at the numbers on the spines. Gianni Girafalco had gone on expeditions to the Caribbean. Where were the Caribbean maps? It took a couple of minutes, but I finally found the right volume at the far end of the shelves. It was bound in white cloth like all the others, with blocky printed letters spelling out *Islands of the Caribbean* on the title page.

I carried the book over to the table and set it down.

The maps were black-and-white renderings of each of the Caribbean islands. Remembering what I'd read in Mr. Mountmorris's book, I flipped to the maps of the northeastern islands, Antigua and Barbuda and the Dominican Republic and Puerto Rico.

And suddenly I was looking at a map that wasn't anything like the others.

This is the next piece of the puzzle, I thought.

Even before I checked the edge of the paper and saw where it had been glued into the book instead of bound with all of the other pages, I knew this was what Dad had wanted me to find.

The map—or nautical chart—had been drawn on a torn and water-stained piece of thick, cream-colored paper. I recognized the handwriting and knew at once that it was Dad's. It showed a stretch of faded turquoise-blue water, with the islands of Antigua and Barbuda and Guadalupe in the bottom left-hand corner and the newly discovered St. Beatrice and Ruby Islands interrupting the blue above. A compass rose on the right-hand side of the chart showed the cardinal directions, North, South, East, and West. The calligraphic writing proclaimed *Northern Caribbean Islands. St. Beatrice Island, Ruby Island, Antigua and Barbuda, and Guadalupe.*

An intricate border framed the beautiful map, a many-colored design of mermaids and seashells, fish and sea turtles, and the ocean was decorated here and there with mermaids and sea horses, each of the sea horses' bodies curved like a little question mark. In the middle of the stretch of blue, there was a picture of a merman holding a shell and a trident. It was labeled *King Triton's Lair.*

I stared at the map. With absolute certainty, I knew that he'd put it here for us to find. It didn't make any sense otherwise. The rest of the maps were from the Muller Machines. This one included St. Beatrice, so it was post–New Modern Age. The map of Girafalco's Trench wasn't the map we were supposed to follow. It was a clue leading us to this one, and his hiding place was a stroke of brilliance. Even if someone managed to get inside the room, nobody would look for his map among all these dusty old irrelevant ones, or recognize it as a clue even if they did.

King Triton's Lair.

I unhooked the small paper knife from my utility tool and carefully ran the blade down the margin, removing the map and sliding it out of the bound volume. I took one last look around the secret room, trying the buttons on the Muller Machine again. Nothing. I folded the map and tucked it into the collar pocket in my vest, next to the map of Girafalco's Trench. My mind raced as I tried to put it all together. This secret room had been Dad's hideout, and at some point in the last few years, he must have visited the Academy to hide the key and this map for us, the next clue in the treasure hunt he'd sent us on.

I couldn't hear anyone outside, but as I stepped out into the dark, checking to make sure the door locked when I shut it, I was seized by the fear that they were still out there, waiting for me. I hoped the Explorer with the Clockwork Hand had made it to safety.

"Pucci?" I whispered, and the parrot came flapping down out of the darkness, alighting on my shoulder and clucking reassuringly in my ear before taking off again to keep watch as I walked back to campus and crawled into bed.

We set sail
on the
21st of April.

It was a gray, inclement day,

and as I bade my mother and father farewell, I cannot say I was sorry to be leaving England for the sunny climes of the Caribbean. Much to my surprise, Miss Mary Jennings was there to see us off. She wished me Godspeed, and the sight of her white handkerchief waving from the dock was my last sight of England, though I

Ten

"So what's King Triton's Lair, anyway?" M.K. asked. "Who's King Triton?"

"In Greek mythology, King Triton was the messenger of the sea," I told her, advancing on her with my wooden Grygian Longsword and looking over my shoulder to make sure no one was listening. "I think he was supposed to be the son of the God and Goddess of the Sea, Poseidon and Amphitrite. He had a big conch shell, and he blew it to summon the waves. Basically, it was the Greeks' way of explaining storms at sea."

We were practicing our swordfighting skills for our Combat Traditions of Newly Discovered Lands class. I'd been telling the others about my night as we swung and ducked and watched the training fights. We still hadn't seen any sign of Joyce, Kemal, or the other foreign students.

The fighting rings were at the far end of the training grounds, in the shadow of Mt. Arnoz. It was one of those brilliantly sunny fall days, and after nearly an hour of the physically taxing practice, the ground was littered with Explorer's jackets and sweaters. The ornately carved Grygian Longswords were heavy, and M.K. and I both stood panting and sweating. It wasn't much of a match. We could barely lift them. We had heard about the Grygian tree dwellers' ritual swordfights from Dad, and M.K. had been excited to try the legendary swords for herself. Now she looked disappointed as she leaned on the sword.

"Okay, switch up," Mr. Turnbull called out. M.K. and I stepped out of the fighting ring and joined Sukey and Zander over on the edge of the grounds. Two other students took our places.

"I still can't believe Dad had a secret hideout they never found," Zander whispered to me, an edge of frustration in his voice. "And I can't believe you didn't wake me up."

"I almost got caught! If there had been two of us, I bet we'd be packing our trunks for home right now, or worse."

"Shhh," Sukey warned me, gesturing to Turnbull and the other students.

Zander's blue eyes narrowed and I remembered how Dad's eyes had always narrowed like that when he was angry. "You really think he wants us to go to this place, King Triton's Lair?"

"Zander, he knew I would try to figure out who Girafalco was. He knew I would keep looking until I found the book. He knew I would find the key and look for the map." I felt so sure, but even as I said it I knew it sounded crazy. "There isn't any message, but I think there may be some sort of code. Maybe with the drawings in the border, or the pictures of sea horses and mermaids. You know, like hieroglyphics. But I don't know." I was thinking out loud now. I'd spent all morning trying to think of a possible code. I'd thought about replacing all the mermaids with *a*'s and all the shells with *b*'s and so forth, but there just wasn't enough to go on. I'd even held a lit match under the map in case Dad had used invisible ink to leave us a message.

"I still don't understand," M.K. whispered, barely moving her mouth. "What is King Triton's Lair?"

Sukey, who was watching the sword fighting, leaned in to hear my answer.

"I did some more reading this morning," I told them. I was nervous about being overheard, but we were pretty far away from the rest of the class and Mr. Turnbull and everyone else were focused on the kids sparring in the rings. "St. Beatrice Island was discovered early in the New Modern Age by the explorer Jefferson Robbins. Apparently, he decided to try to navigate a notoriously rough stretch of ocean northeast of Antigua to see what was there. For a long time, sailors had told each other to stay away from the area, and the old maps warned of sea serpents and enormous waves that could sink a ship."

I went on, summarizing what I'd read. Even before the advent of the Muller Machines and the discovery of St. Beatrice Island, ships crossing the Atlantic reported strange weather phenomena as they neared that part of the ocean. Many ships were lost, and legends and folktales on the islands told of spirits or mermaids or sea serpents drawing ships and their crews down below the waves.

"People have always told stories about mermaids and sea serpents," Sukey said when I'd finished. "But no one's ever actually seen them."

"Pirates would wait nearby because so many ships got into trouble and they thought they could get the treasure they carried. But most of the pirates went down too," I said.

I picked up a stick and drew a little map in the dirt. I drew a circle around the small, crescent-shaped island north and a little bit east of Antigua that was like a little moon above the ridge of the Lesser Antilles. "That's St. Beatrice Island," I said. Southeast of St. Beatrice, I drew Ruby Island, another newly discovered island that, from what I could tell, was mostly used as a seal-hunting station.

"Right here," I went on, making a mark in the dirt next to Sukey's foot, "is an area of the ocean known locally as King Triton's Lair. Over the years, lots and lots of ships have sunk there. Including"—I lowered my voice—"Gianni Girafalco's." I rubbed out the map with the toe of my boot.

"Mr. West," Turnbull called, beckoning to Zander to enter one of the rings. "Your turn." Zander ran over and picked up the Longsword as though it weighed nothing. He swung it back and forth in the air over his head a few times and then got into fighting stance. His knees slightly bent, his body leaned forward, the sword held high over his head. "And—Mr. Nackley, I think."

Lazlo Nackley ran forward from the other side of the field and picked up the other Longsword. He looked excited, swinging it around the way Zander had and then getting into fighting stance opposite him.

"He'd better be careful," Sukey whispered to me. "Lazlo isn't very happy with you Wests right now."

"And. . . *fight!*" Mr. Turnbull shouted, bringing his arm down and stepping out of the ring. Now everyone's attention was on Lazlo and Zander.

Zander waited for his opponent to make the first move, stepping easily around Lazlo's overhead swing and getting in one of his own that almost made Lazlo drop his sword. Lazlo seemed angry and came back with a powerful downward chop that made Zander hop back.

Zander's sword made a wide arc in the air over his head, and then he quickly stepped back and to the side to avoid Lazlo's next attempt.

"Wow," Sukey whispered next to me. "He's good. When did he get so good?"

I looked up to see Agent DeRosa coming toward us, leading his German shepherd around the training grounds on a long black leash. DeRosa and the dog passed us, but then they both turned back to study us. The dog sniffed the air, and I had a terrifying thought: Could it remember my scent from the night before?

They walked slowly past the crowd of spectators. DeRosa, seeing that everyone was intently watching the fencing match between Zander and Lazlo, stopped to watch.

Lazlo had forced Zander into a corner of the ring, and he appeared to sense that winning was within his power. He suddenly seemed to gain new strength, slashing the heavy sword from side to side, clashing it against Zander's with a dull *clang* that rang out against the mountain and echoed across campus. Mr. Turnbull was so excited he couldn't keep still, dancing around and bobbing his head along with the action.

The swords slammed against each other, Zander sidestepping along the perimeter and retreating farther and farther into the corners of the ring.

"Come on, Zander," Sukey said. "Come on."

"Get him," M.K. whispered.

And then Lazlo raised his sword and brought it down heavily. Zander raised his own sword to protect himself, and Lazlo caught Zander's sword on the hilt, hard, and then Zander was falling, dropping his sword, kneeling down in defeat in the corner of the ring.

Lazlo hoisted his sword in the air, and everyone burst into applause.

"That, ladies and gentlemen—*that* is how it's done," Mr. Turnbull said. "Well done, you two. Very well done!"

Zander got up, picked up his sword, shook Lazlo's hand, and came over to stand with us and applaud as Lazlo accepted congratulations from students and Mr. Turnbull.

He was breathing hard, a film of sweat on his brow, the armpits of his khaki field shirt stained dark. In the slanting light, I could see golden stubble along his jaw. When had he started shaving? How had I not noticed that my brother could grow a beard? We all applauded halfheartedly, but Zander made a big show of pointing to Lazlo and clapping his hands above his head.

Sukey watched him for a moment. "You let him win, didn't you?"

Zander winked at her. "Maybe I did, but don't tell Lazlo. I figure keeping him happy for a few days might give us a chance to do some sleuthing." He grinned and reached up to rub a scratch along his jawline. "It's tougher than it looks, losing on purpose. I can't tell you how much I wanted to bring that sword down on his head."

"But you didn't," Sukey said, smiling. I felt a sudden surge of jealousy. She had never smiled at me like that.

"But I didn't." He turned to me and smiled a smile that I knew to be an attempt to make peace. "Now let's figure out what Dad wanted us to do."

Eleven

We were halfway through The History of Exploration that afternoon when Kemal and Maria Montoya came in and sat down in the back. A few minutes later, Joyce followed them, her Kenyan Snake Falcon on her shoulder. Mr. Wooley nodded and Lazlo turned in his chair to give Kemal a nasty look. We had been studying Harrison Arnoz's discovery of Grygia, and Mr. Wooley went over the conditions that existed at the time Arnoz stumbled upon the unexplored mountain valley.

"It's probably hard for you to imagine the world that the enterprising biologist and explorer Harrison Arnoz left behind when, after nearly a year of living in the mountains, he ventured into that remote valley on the cusp of the Indorustan Empire only a year after the failure of all of the computer networks. His mother was Czech, and he had taken advantage of the confusion in the aftermath of the failures to make his way to Eastern Europe to study the bears of the Carpathian Mountains. Remember that there was very little fuel and very little opportunity to travel. Only a few ships made their way around the world, and Arnoz had to hitch rides on those ships and then walk across Europe to reach the Carpathian forest, where he was living when he made his great discovery. It's an incredible story of bravery and exploration. Now, Kemal, do you remember why Arnoz ventured into the Grygian Valley in the first place?" He gave Kemal an encouraging smile.

I think Mr. Wooley was trying to be kind, welcoming Kemal back and telling him that everything was okay. But I knew that Kemal was nervous speaking in public, and as he stood up and cleared his throat, I wondered if he would rather have been left alone. "Uh, well, he had been studying bear populations, and he wondered whether they had established . . ." He hesitated. "Range, I think it was. He wondered whether they had established a wider area or something that they hunted in, and when he checked the maps, he discovered that they didn't, well . . . they didn't work. The measurements were off." He looked shaken, rumpled, and worn out, as though he hadn't slept.

"Can someone elaborate?" Mr. Wooley asked.

I raised my hand, but he had already called on Joyce. Unlike Kemal, she didn't seem nervous at all. You'd never know she'd spent the night being interrogated. As far as I could tell, there wasn't anything Joyce wasn't good at. She'd beaten almost everyone at the simulations. A week ago, in Mountaineering and Ice Climbing Clinic,

I'd watched her free-climb a rock wall that no one else in the class could scale. Zander had come close, but he'd fallen ten feet short of the summit. Luckily, unlike Joyce, he'd been wearing a harness. I'd heard stories about how she'd managed to lasso a charging rhino on her Final Exam Expedition the year before.

As if that wasn't enough, Joyce seemed to know everything in every class she was in. Her brown eyes always seemed curious. Her hair was cropped close to her head, showing off her high cheekbones and heart-shaped face. Joyce wore a dark-brown alligator-hide jacket embedded with all the gadgets she used for sailing and exploring, and Njamba was always perched on her shoulder or flying overhead. I'd never heard anybody say a bad word about her—that she was arrogant, or that she tried to use her status with the teachers to get special treatment.

It was kind of annoying, how perfect she was. But today, I found myself filled with admiration for her.

"Joyce, what were the irregularities to which Kemal is referring?" Mr. Wooley asked.

She stood up and shrugged Njamba off her shoulder. The big golden-and-black bird hopped on her desk and cocked her head as Joyce said easily, "Well, the Muller Machines made digital maps based on the data that cartographers entered into them. That's what Arnoz had. Old Muller Machine maps that he'd printed before the machines crashed because he was interested in the bear populations. People really weren't allowed to explore very much. We didn't have the technology that we have nowadays, no SteamCycles or IronSteeds or anything. Kemal's right. Arnoz got there, and he noticed tracks leading out of the area that the bears were supposed to be living and breeding in. It took him a month of walking to follow the tracks all the way through the mountain range. He thought he'd discovered a new habitat for the bears. There had been a major drought the year before, and people say now that it must have been the drought that made the bears go beyond their range."

"Here, I'll show you." Joyce got up and came up to the front of the classroom. She picked up a piece of chalk and started drawing a map of Eastern Europe and Grygia on the board, scrawling in coordinates and various locations. "Here's the route he took to follow the bears." She drew a dotted line. "He came up against an incredibly tall mountain range that seemed impassable, that he assumed was the southern edge of the Carpathians. But the mileage was off. He figured he'd traveled more than a thousand miles, but the Muller Machine map placed the Carpathians here." She pointed to a spot on the map. "Most people would have given up. But Arnoz was curious. And he kept going. And during that long, cold winter, one of the worst in recent history, he pressed on over the mountain range, hunting and foraging for food. In the spring, he came down into the wide Grygian Valley and realized that he had discovered a new land."

"How did he know?" Mr. Wooley asked the class.

"The bears," Zander answered. "They were different after he went over those mountains. They were bigger and a different color, and their heads were a different shape."

"Like this." Joyce scrawled a surprisingly good likeness of the

Great Grygian Bear on the chalkboard. I looked over at Zander, who was nodding his head in appreciation.

"Thank you, Joyce," Mr. Wooley said. "That was an excellent explanation." Joyce sat down again. "Now, does anyone remember how Arnoz came across the first Grygian Tree Dwellers?"

"Didn't he get shot at?" Kemal said.

"That's right. But instead of shooting back, he took the time to discover where the arrow had come from and to establish peaceful contact with the Tree Dwellers. If it hadn't been for his . . . prudence, he would have been killed, and we would never have learned about them, and we would never have learned about Grygia itself. Okay, good work. Now we're going to move on to Admiral Piel's discovery of the New North Polar Sea. Can anyone tell me about Admiral Piel?"

"Wait," I said. "I have a question."

"Yes, Kit?" Mr. Wooley smiled at me, but his foot tapped nervously on the floor.

"The maps that Harrison Arnoz had—the Muller Machine maps. Why were they wrong?"

Lazlo Nackley jumped in. "Because the people who programmed the Muller Machines put the wrong information into them. My father says that the Muller Machine engineers were foreigners"—he glanced darkly at Joyce and Kemal—"and they wanted to undermine the security of the United States and keep all of the discoveries for themselves. So they put the wrong information into the machines."

"Wait, you mean they did it on purpose?" I looked at Mr. Wooley. I wanted to know what he had to say.

He nodded. "Well, yes. That's what we assume, anyway."

"They wanted to keep all the resources to themselves," Lazlo said. "Thank goodness they didn't get away with it. Didn't you know? Or did your father not teach you anything?" He snorted. "Of course, he had his own problems with keeping resources to himself, didn't he?" He and Jack laughed.

I ignored him. "But how did people not realize they were wrong? Why didn't they see?"

Mr. Wooley glanced at Lazlo again and took a deep breath. "You have to remember that it was very hard to get around. Petroleum was discovered in Texas in 1875, and for a while it looked like we might have a new source of fuel. We built planes and cars and furnaces and tanks and machinery that ran on the stuff—*black gold,* they called it—but then it slowed to a trickle after only seven years. The government carefully rationed what was left. There have always been rumors about fuel in Arabia, but if there is any, the Indorustans haven't found it, or they haven't told us if they have."

"Maybe Kemal can tell us," Lazlo said, snorting. "You're an Indorustan, aren't you, Kemal?"

"We escaped," Kemal said, in a tight, quiet voice. It may have been my imagination, but his accent sounded stronger than usual. "I live here now. My father works for the government. I'm American."

"Oh, you may have lived here for the last couple of years, but you're not an American," Lazlo said.

"*Lazlo,*" Mr. Wooley warned him.

"Well, it's true. Isn't it, *Mr. Wooley?*" There was something threatening in the way Lazlo said his name.

"As I was saying . . ." Mr. Wooley shot Lazlo another anxious glance. "Steam technology was inefficient then, and as the Muller Machines became more sophisticated, most agriculture and manufacturing became automated. Everything was controlled by the machines. All the coal we use for SteamCars and SteamCycles now was used to keep the Muller Machines running. There were cameras everywhere, tracking people's movements. The Muller Machines had records of everything anyone ever did. The government knew where you were at all times."

"Sounds a lot like today," I muttered.

The room went silent.

"What did you say?" Lazlo Nackley stood up and came around from behind his desk so he could look at me, his light blue eyes boring into mine. "Say that so everyone can hear."

I stared at Lazlo for a moment, then glanced over at Mr. Wooley. He looked terrified. I could feel the tension flowing from Sukey's body.

"Nothing," I said. "I didn't say anything at all."

"All right, then," Mr. Wooley said. "Let's get back to the acquisition of knowledge. Please turn to page 236."

Lazlo shot me a final look before we all bent our heads to our books, the Muller Machines and their maps set aside for the moment. A few minutes before the end of class, I looked out the window and saw a gray wall of storm clouds crowding up against the mountains.

They rolled toward us with incredible speed. When I turned my attention back to the classroom, I found Kemal gazing at me, dark circles under his eyes, which were as tense and troubled as the sky.

at night, the men on board the ship drink rum and tell stories about their voyages. Most of these stories are not to be believed, outlandish tales of sea serpents and mermaids, but last night, a sailor named John Harmon told a tale that I have not been able to force from my mind. Harmon had previously sailed the Caribbean and he was the only one of the men who had expressed trepidation about our route. He told us about a strange occurrence on his last voyage to the region.

"We had been out only a few days when the weather turned," John told the men as the ship rocked gently on the sea. "At first it was just wind, but then the rain started, then lightning. All the fury of the oceans came down on us, and I was sure we would lose the ship." He lowered his voice, as though afraid the oceans would hear him. "It was pitch black, but I was out on deck when a bolt of lightning lit up the sky and as I looked out at the water, I saw something rise up above the waves. It was like a dragon, a dragon of the sea, and it turned and looked right at me before disappearing beneath the waves."

"Oh, go on, Johnny," the other men jeered. "A sea dragon, do you say?"

John sat silently. We could hear the ship creaking and shifting on the water. Then he looked around at each of us, his eyes wide, his tone deadly serious, and said, "As God is my witness, that's what I saw. And not far from where we're going, boys."

Twelve

Zander and M.K. and I were on our way to dinner that night when we heard someone yell, "Hey! Wests! Wait for me!"

We turned around and saw Sukey running up the path behind us. Her cheeks were pink, her eyes shining, and she was breathing hard. The air was growing colder by the minute, and the wind blowing Sukey's hair across her face told us the storm had arrived.

"Sorry. I pretty much ran all the way from the library," she said. "But I need to talk to you." She pulled us off the path and into the trees and looked around carefully to make sure we wouldn't be overheard. "I had an idea, and I went and investigated at the library and, well—Stop, Pucci!" Pucci had swooped down to alight on her shoulder, and he was playing with her hair, grabbing her curls with his beak and gently tugging.

"What?" I asked impatiently.

"Your father—*Pucci!* Sorry. Your father *went* there! He went to the place on the . . ." She lowered her voice even more, just mouthing the word *map.*

I stared at her. "What? How do you know?"

"Shhh. Look." She slid a stack of papers from her jacket. "I remembered that they keep old Final Exam Expedition proposals and reports in the library. So I went and looked and, well, I had to take them when Mrs. Pasquale wasn't looking. But—read this."

We stood in a huddle in the woods, looking through the pages. During Dad's last year at the Academy, someone named Paul Mirkopoulous had proposed "An Expedition to Locate the Source of Unusual Weather Phenomena in the Northern Caribbean and to Discover Safe Passage for Ships Through the Area."

According to Mirkopoulous, a 100-square-mile region of the Northern Caribbean surrounding the newly discovered St. Beatrice Island had long been known as a dangerous passage for ships. He wrote in the proposal that newly invented diving helmets made of Gryluminum might allow him and his expedition crew to explore the floor of the ocean and discover if underwater features had anything to do with the disturbances.

"They were interested in Girafalco's trenches, too," I said.

"Look at this," Sukey said, showing us the piece of paper that had been added to the proposal, listing the Explorers in Training who had been chosen as its crew. She had to hold the papers tightly so they wouldn't blow away.

Someone named Coleman Miller had been named captain, and

Paul Mirkopoulous had been the expedition leader. Dad had been the cartographer. Raleigh hadn't been on the expedition, and neither had Leo Nackley. But I did recognize one more name: Cameron Wooley. He'd served as the expedition's historian and secretary.

"This is great, Sukey," I told her. "It's the same information I found about King Triton's Lair. The fact that Dad went there proves it. He wants us to go there, too."

"Okay," Sukey said. "But let's say he did leave it for you because he wants you to go to the Caribbean. If I remember my Greek mythology correctly, King Triton lived *under* the water."

"And how would we even get to the Caribbean?" Zander asked. "I don't think Maggie is going to give us time off from school to go look for King Triton's Lair."

"No," I said. "She's not. But look at how Dad got there."

"The Final Exam Expeditions," Sukey said, grinning. "I like the way you think."

"It won't be easy," I told them. "We're going to have to propose an expedition without making anyone suspicious, and then we'll have to get there and, somehow, look around underwater—alone. We can bring diving equipment, but none of us knows how to dive, and if the weather's as bad as they say, well, it isn't going to be easy."

M.K. had been silent, listening to us, but now she spoke up. "I can handle the underwater part," she said.

"What do you mean?" Zander asked.

"You'll see soon enough. I've been working on something ever since you found the bathymetric map. So don't worry about that part."

"You really think we can do this?" Zander asked me.

"It's the only way. We have to try, right?"

"But we can't all turn in an expedition plan for the same place," he said. "That would be sure to make them suspicious."

"Of course we're not going to turn in plans for the same place. I'll turn it in. You heard what Foley said. I need to make it seem like finding this fuel source will save the world. Or us and our allies, anyway. And we'll just have to hope we all get assigned to the expedition." I was thinking out loud now. "I'll write it so that it seems like each of you absolutely *has* to be on the expedition. "

"And if we don't all get assigned?" Zander asked me.

"Then we'll have to do as much as we can without the others." I looked up at their stricken faces and said, "I know, I know. It's awful to think of, but it's the only way. Right? I'll do some research and see if I can find anything. In the meantime, you should all be working on other plans. Do what you were going to do anyway. Just don't make them very good."

Sukey whispered. "He hasn't come back, has he? The Explorer with the—" She pointed to her hand.

I shook my head. "No, but I think we just have to go ahead."

We felt a few drops of rain, and then a few more, faster and harder. A thin line of lightning flashed over the mountains.

"This is crazy," Zander said as we heard the crack of thunder and started sprinting towards the Longhouse. "There are so many *if*s to this. A thousand things could go wrong."

We kept running. No one said anything. We knew he was right.

Thirteen

I spent the next couple of weeks looking into expeditions to St.
Beatrice Island or King Triton's Lair over the years and putting
together my proposal. Most of the Explorers who had gone there
had been looking for the gold coins and rubies and treasure that had
been on board the ships. Some were meteorologists or oceanologists
who thought that the strange conditions were caused by the weather
or by gas being released from fissures in the ocean floor or by rogue
currents. I found a few references to fishermen who had reported
"black underwater waterfalls"—from what I could tell, some of the
early Explorers of the Realm had been convinced that the substance
was an underwater oil well. A few Explorers were even convinced
that extraterrestrials were beaming ships up from the Northern
Caribbean and wanted to investigate reports of strange glowing orbs
in the water that might be alien technology.

I went over my notes again. We had to convince Maggie and the rest of the faculty that this expedition was essential to the well-being and security of the country.

A safe route for ships through the Northern Caribbean might do it. And for good measure, I'd throw in the possibility of a new fuel source and the glittering treasure aboard the shipwrecks below the water. I spent my days and nights with nautical charts and maps and lists: I would have to include an expedition budget and account for how much food and water the expedition team would need, as well as lists of the equipment we'd carry and a plan for how we'd go about securing a ship on St. Beatrice.

I was walking a fine line. I needed to include enough information from Dad's map about the exact location of King Triton's Lair that they would believe we could get there, without giving away so much that they could get there on their own.

"I think I'm just about there," I told the others at dinner on November 12, three days before the proposals were due. The temperature had dropped well below freezing the night before, and the mountains were covered with a thick layer of glittering frost. The Longhouse was warm and cozy and filled with the smell of wood smoke. Kids were clustered around the huge fire at the front of the room, warming their hands by the flames and talking excitedly about the Final Expedition Exam, speculating about whose would be chosen. Walking back from the kitchen with a plate of stringy chicken stew and withered carrots, I heard a girl say, "I bet Zander West will get chosen. He's amazing."

"I know," said the other girl. "Did you see when he walked up to get his stew? He looked so brave."

"You have a fan club back there," I told Zander when I sat down again. "Apparently the way you went up to get your stew was really brave."

"What?" He was daydreaming about something. "A fan what?"

"A fan club," I told him. "Those girls up there."

"Oh." But he wasn't paying attention. He was still staring off into the distance.

"Those girls are ridiculous," Sukey said, frowning a little.

"You can say that again." M.K. got up to get her food.

I watched Zander for minute. "What are you daydreaming about?" I asked him.

"What? Oh . . ." He turned his attention back to his plate of food. "I was just thinking about whether the indigenous rhino populations in West Africa actually experienced a genetic mutation or whether it was some sort of swift evolution. You know, how their horns have become 23 percent larger within only six generations. It's very interesting . . ."

"I've always liked rhinos," Sukey said. "Delilah and I once got to help rescue a baby rhino in Cameroon."

I leaned in and whispered: "I think I've got the proposal figured out. I just have to finish writing it." I told them about my research and about my plan to use the huge amounts of treasure under the ocean, as well as the crazy stories about black waterfalls and aliens, to ensure that they picked my proposal. "You know what Mr. Foley said about something that would contribute to the security of the nation, and all that? Well, this just might be enough to ensure that they pick us. This thing about the fuel is a good possibility."

"You're right," Sukey said. "They need gold to buy more guns for the troops in Simeria. But most of all, they need a way to get the troops over there. They're obsessed with bigger and faster engines. If we go to . . . well, if the problems over there continue, they're going to need better engines. Gliders won't cut it against the Indorustans. There are rumors that their armies have developed something with incredible power, something like an engine, but one that doesn't even need steam. It's . . ." She broke off, looking guilty.

"How do you know all that?" Zander asked her. Sukey flushed bright red.

"Never mind. What I'm saying is that it's a good idea, Kit. I think that'll get the expedition selected."

"Does this have anything to do with what you were telling us about the flying squad?" I asked.

"I can't say anything," she whispered. "But—" She cut herself off and looked down at her food. "Shhh," she whispered.

We looked up to see Lazlo and Jack Foster standing next to our table, talking in low voices. They were too close for my taste, looking in the other direction and whispering to each other, but something about the way they were standing there made me nervous. Jack glanced at us, then said something to Lazlo. He was a tall, dark-haired kid, sort of good-looking, though not as handsome as he seemed to think he was.

Whatever he and Lazlo were doing, I didn't want to risk them overhearing our plan. We waited until they were gone to continue our conversation.

"Anyway, I'm almost done," I told them. I felt excited, jittery, like the time I'd drunk Dad's coffee by mistake, thinking it was cocoa. "I just have to put the finishing touches on it. I think it's good. I think it's really good, actually. I was—What?" Sukey and Zander had glanced at each other as I was talking, and they were both looking down at the table now, as though they didn't want to meet my gaze.

"Nothing," Sukey said. "It's just, well, we were talking, and we were kind of thinking that maybe it should have Zander's name on it."

Zander didn't look up.

"With the way everything's been going, we're worried you won't get picked, and . . ." She hunched down, her head sinking into her shoulders, and chewed her bottom lip.

"But I did all the work." I could feel hot rage racing through my body. "It's my proposal!"

"I know," Sukey said. "Zander is kind of . . . well, the teachers all seem to really like him. We just think we'll have a better chance if his name is on it."

M.K. came back with her tray of thin gray potatoes and fried livers. "I think this is the grossest dinner they've ever served us. I'm giving it the prize. Don't you . . ." She saw our faces. "What's wrong?"

"We were just telling Kit that we think the proposal should have Zander's name on it," Sukey said in a quiet voice.

"Oh, is that all?" M.K. sat down and dug into her meal. "They're probably right, Kit. No one really likes you. You ask too many questions. They'll be much more likely to pick it if it has Zander's name on it. They all like Zander. They seem to think he's on their side, even if he isn't."

"Thanks, M.K."

"What?" she said through a mouthful of liver. "*I* like you. It's just that no one else does."

The terrible thing was that I knew they were right. But I couldn't let it go.

"It isn't fair. We wouldn't even know about it if it weren't for me."

"Kit, *we'll* know it was you," Sukey said. "And we'll all be there. It will be all of our expedition, even if Zander's name is on it." Her face was soft, a gentle look in her eyes. She felt sorry for me. It was worse than if she'd been mean about it. "Only if we all get on the expedition," I spat back. "And I think we all know how unlikely that is."

"Kit . . ." Sukey began, but I pushed my chair back.

"Okay," I said. Zander's eyes darted around, avoiding mine. "Fine. I'll put your name on it. Good luck."

I got up and walked out into the snow.

Three days later, on November 15, I handed Zander the stack of pages I'd worked so hard on, and he gave me his—an incomplete, badly written proposal for an expedition to study wildebeests in Munopia. Then I walked through the drifted snow to Maggie's office and turned in Zander's proposal with my name printed across the title page.

Fourteen

I finally found a chance to talk to Mr. Wooley. I had been in a dark mood, going through the motions in class, angry at Zander and Sukey, nervous about the proposals. I knew that Maggie and the rest of the faculty were spending hours every day poring over them, trying to decide which ones had a chance of success. Every once in a while, I'd start daydreaming about my proposal being chosen, hearing my name announced, before I remembered that it wouldn't be my name they called but Zander's.

One chilly night a few days before the Thanksgiving banquet where the winning proposals were to be announced, I was walking along the path leading back toward campus from the training grounds when I caught sight of Mr. Wooley walking up ahead of me, his platinum-blond head bent, his shoulders rounded. Even from far away, he seemed depressed. I knew I should leave him alone, but there wasn't anyone else on the path, and I knew this might be my only chance to speak to him with no one listening. I started running after him.

He heard me coming and turned around, a frightened look on his face. When he saw it was me, he looked relieved but also a little guilty.

"I'm sorry, Mr. Wooley," I said breathlessly. "I didn't mean to scare you, but I wanted to talk to you, and I figured this was a good place."

It was terribly cold, my breath hovering in front of my face as I spoke.

He looked around at the trees and shrugged. "About the only place one can talk, I expect. What's on your mind?" We started walking again, slowly matching pace on the path.

"I was looking at some old expedition proposals," I told him. "And I saw that you and my dad were assigned to the same expedition one of your years here. To the Caribbean?"

He looked up, his eyes wide with surprise. "That's right. The King Triton's Lair expedition. Well, that's what the locals called it."

"What happened? Did you find anything? You were trying to find out what caused all the shipwrecks, right?"

He watched me as we walked. His blue eyes were tired and bloodshot. "Did we find anything? Didn't your father ever tell you what happened?"

"No, at least I don't think he did. I'm assuming you didn't find them because I would have heard about it if you had. I'm just curious about what happened on the expedition."

Now he stopped walking and turned to me. He studied my face as though he was trying to figure out if I was telling the truth.

"You mean to tell me he never said anything about that expedition?"

"No."

He swore under his breath. "The expedition was a disaster—that's what happened," he said. "He almost died. He should have died. It was a miracle that he didn't."

"Really?" Now *I* was gobsmacked. "How?"

"We were looking for what had caused the shipwrecks, and our ship sank. Kind of ironic, if you think about it. There was a bad storm—it came in the night, out of nowhere—and we went down not far from where your father thought the shipwrecks were. The rest of us managed to get into the lifeboats, but Alex disappeared. He was knocked out and washed overboard before we could find him. We all assumed he'd drowned. We were devastated. A passing boat rescued us, and we were on our way back to school when we heard that a fisherman had found a boy floating on a raft made of driftwood and debris, confused and delirious with thirst. He said he'd been on a ship that had gone down in the ocean and had been floating for days. Alex was a day or so away from death when they found him. There were sharks . . ." Mr. Wooley stared off into the distance. "It was awful. He looked like a ghost when we finally met up with him. And he was in the hospital for weeks. He really never told you any of this?"

I shook my head.

"That expedition was a complete disaster from start to finish. Before we went, we laughed at the old tales we'd heard about King Triton's Lair. Rogue waves. Strange currents that could pull a ship under. Sea monsters. Hidden coral reefs. Weird weather. Afterward, we weren't laughing."

"Mr. Wooley, what happened to Paul Mirkopoulous?"

"Paul died on an expedition a few years back. I forget where."

"And what about the other members of the expedition?"

"I don't know. Coleman Miller was a great friend of your father's. He dropped out of the Academy afterwards, from the trauma. As for me—well, here I am."

"Thanks," I said. I was about to tell him goodbye when I realized that this might be my only chance to ask him about something else I'd been wondering about. "Mr. Wooley?"

"Yes?"

"The King Triton's Lair expedition wasn't the only thing he kept from us. We didn't know until after he disappeared that he'd been kicked out of the Expedition Society. We heard something about Munopia, but we don't know anything more than that." I lowered my voice. "BNDL says he was a criminal. Do you know why he was kicked out? I wouldn't ask, except that, well, Raleigh doesn't know, and there isn't anyone else we can ask."

Wooley's eyes got very wide. "My God, you poor children." He took off his tweed hat and ran a hand through his hair. When he looked up, his eyes were full of sadness and exhaustion. "I could get in a lot of trouble for talking about this, but you have a right to know. About a year ago, just before your father left for Fazia, I heard that he was being investigated for taking bribes in Munopia. He'd been there on an expedition to find a new river, right?"

Munopia was a Newly Discovered Land on the southwestern tip of Africa. "Yeah, a water source for the cattle farms."

"Right. Well, BNDL had lost control in Munopia. The local farmers who operated the cattle farms there weren't sending the beef to us. Instead, it was all going to Munopian markets and, it was rumored, to the Indorustans. The story I heard was that instead of turning his maps of the new water source over to BNDL, your father sold them to these farmers. But someone saw him. He was about to be arrested when he left for Fazia. After he disappeared, they said he'd lied to BNDL and they stripped him of his membership, removed all trace of him from the society. He's not the only one it's happened to."

I just stood there, taking it in. It was what Francis Foley had told us. I hadn't wanted to believe it, but it was hard to think of another explanation. "Thanks," I finally said. "And thanks for all of the information about the Caribbean."

He studied me for a moment. "Hold on. You're not thinking of going there for your expedition?"

"No, no, *I'm* not," I hurried to say. "I proposed an expedition to study wildebeests in Africa. But Zander wants to go to the Caribbean." I grinned at him. "Maybe you could be his expedition instructor and come along."

He shivered, and the look on his face made me sorry for making the joke. "You couldn't pay me to go back there," he said. "There isn't enough gold in the world."

Fifteen

I walked slowly back to campus, thinking it through. It was clearer now than ever that Dad had meant for us to look for King Triton's Lair, to succeed where he had failed.

And he must have known that somehow, we'd figure out how to get there and devise a way to explore the ocean floor.

I looked up to find the long, low workshop, tucked up against the side of the mountain, steam from who knows what sorts of machines pouring from various chimneys and pipes sticking up all over the roof.

Quincy had been the Engineering instructor ever since she graduated from the Academy. She was a gifted engineer and could take credit for many of the most impressive inventions of the new modern age: SteamOutboard motors, ultra-efficient Steam bicycles used in cities, SteamWashers, SteamPonies. . . . the list went on and on. Whenever you walked by the workshop, day or night, you could hear clanging and whooshing and all kinds of strange noises. Quincy taught all of the engineering, field repair, and gadget-design classes inside the workshop, but most of us were only allowed to work on one side of the building. The other side was for the top-secret projects that Quincy worked on with her best students, like M.K. The Bureau mostly left her alone, but that was only because they needed her inventions.

Quincy looked up and smiled when she saw me. "Mr. West!" she called out. She had been at the Academy with Dad and claimed that he'd taught her everything she knew about gadgetry and engineering. She said it with a twinkle in her eye that made me think it was the other way around, but it was clear she'd loved Dad, and by extension, she loved us. When we'd first arrived at the Academy, she'd asked if she could take a look at our vests. She'd even tuned up a few things for us. Our parachutes needed a thorough cleaning before being replaced in their hidden compartments, she'd replaced Zander's flamethrower, and she said she'd be happy to add some new gadgets once we knew where we were going for our exam expedition.

"You looking for your sister?" she asked me. I nodded, and she led me to the rear of the workshop, where I could see M.K. at a long workbench, tightening something with her wrench.

"Hey, there," she called out, grinning. "Come check this out."

I watched as she tightened the bolt on a small metal utility box. When she was done, she stepped back and held it up, then pressed a button on the side. A metal spear shot out of the box, trailed by a length of long wire.

"M.K.!" It had come within inches of piercing my upper arm.

"Sorry. In case you need to go spearfishing," she said, handing it over. "Put it in your vest. I'm making some more for the rest of us."

"Thanks," I said, tucking it into a pocket and looking around the workbench. "Whoa. Are those what I think they are?"

At the other end of the bench were four brass-and-Gryluminum diving helmets shaped like fishbowls, with glass panels in front. Tubes and wires connected them to four diving suits, each made of a blue synthetic material that shimmered in the light. The suits had small Gryluminum tanks attached to their backs—oxygen tanks, I assumed. I leaned over to inspect the gadgets decorating the front of the suits and saw a light like the one on my vest, a removable speargun, an underwater compass protected by a thick bubble of glass, and a couple of zippered pockets.

"Quincy and I based the design on the suits that Dad took on his expedition, but I completely redesigned them so they'd be lightweight and allow the diver to stay down longer," M.K. said, showing me the breathing apparatus inside the helmet.

"So this is your big surprise, huh? Pretty cool." I picked up the helmet and put it on. The room fell into complete silence as I looked out through the glass and watched M.K.'s lips move. "What did you say?" I asked her, taking off the helmet. "I said that's not the surprise. Those are just for backup."

"What do you mean, 'backup'?"

M.K. looked up at Quincy. "What do you think?"

"I think it's okay. You're almost done, right?"

"Yeah, I'm getting close now," M.K. said. "Okay. Come on."

She put down the wrench, pushing her too-long bangs out of her eyes and led me through a set of doors to a big room at the back of the workshop. In the room's center was a large swimming pool.

Floating in the middle of the pool was M.K.'s surprise.

"Here she is," M.K. said with pride. "Her name is Amphitrite." She grinned. "The Greek goddess of the sea, mother of King Triton. But I call her Amy."

Bobbing on the surface of the water was a huge brass-and-chrome octopus, its egg-shaped head made of shiny steel with a rounded plate of glass riveted to the top, forming a sort of windshield. Eight metal arms attached to the chrome body, which appeared to hold the cockpit and the machine's engine.

"She's a submersible," M.K. told me. "Specially designed for exploring"—she lowered her voice—"the floor of the ocean." Looking through the glass window, I could see four seats inside the pod, as well as a wall of controls and dials and gauges.

M.K. watched my face. I sometimes forgot she got nervous just like everyone else. "What do you think?" she said, blinking quickly. "There's an airlock, so we can dive right out of her. And I included a pressure-adjusting seal to make it safer . . ."

"I'm pretty much speechless," I said. And I was.

Quincy put an arm around M.K.'s shoulders. "She designed it herself. It holds four people, and the sealed SteamEngine keeps you under for up to six hours. She's come up with an incredibly innovative technology that addresses the problem of the steam combustion engine taking up all the oxygen in the submersible. I'm

amazed at how quickly she's pulled it together. There's a lot of fine-tuning still to do, but she's the finest engineer I've ever come across."

"That's what Dad always said."

"He was right. I haven't told anybody just how really, truly good she is. They'd start making plans for her in about two seconds, have her making bombs or something. I told her not to talk too much about this, but word gets around. Maggie came to look at it yesterday. Mountmorris will know about it soon enough. Word on the street is that they're building some kind of submersible themselves. The next frontier, and all that. Tell him about the arms, M.K."

M.K. gestured to the submersible's various arms. "Okay, well, they each have different tools: two different drills, pincers that can collect objects from the ocean floor, a hose, a light, a speargun, a jackhammer, and another supersecret one." She gave me a wicked grin. "I'll let that one be a surprise. It's all controlled from the cockpit. Here, come in and take a look."

She hauled the submersible over to the side of the pool with a rope and pressed a button on the head. The hatch door flipped up so we could step inside, then closed again, sealing us off from the water. The interior was small but cozy, with four comfortable seats in a semicircle around the perimeter. With a smile I recognized the pattern on the seats' cushions: M.K. had upholstered them with the red flowery sheets that Raleigh had bought her just before we'd left for school. She didn't like anything with flowers on it.

"Don't tell Raleigh," she said with a wink.

"What do all those levers and buttons and things do?" I pointed to the dashboard, and she launched into a monologue about adjusting pressure and conserving energy and buoyancy, then pressed one of the buttons. An engine started, and the submersible sank below the surface of the water. Using the levers, M.K. and I explored the floor of the pool. She showed me how the pincers and the other attachments worked.

"I went and looked up all those other expeditions you were talking about. The thing is, they didn't have the right equipment," she said. "A few of them had small submarines, and others had diving helmets that allowed them to go down for an hour or two. But no one had anything like Amy."

I sat back in my seat, running a hand over the smooth wood of the dashboard. "It's great, M.K."

She searched my eyes, looking older than her eleven years. "Are you still mad at Zander?"

"I don't know. Not really. I'm just . . . worried. We have to get them to send us there. It's going to take an incredible amount of luck for it to all work out."

"Well, remember what Dad always said about luck."

I did remember. Dad had always hated it when people wished him good luck on his expeditions. He would tell us, "You make your own luck. You don't wait for it to come to you. You create luck by making connections. By putting things together. It only looks like luck on the other side."

"We'll get there," M.K. said as we gazed across the floor of the pool. Midday sunlight streamed through the water, which rippled on the turquoise tiles on the pool's edge. "One way or another, we will."

Sixteen

Pretty soon it was the day before the Announcement Banquet. After lunch, I decided I needed to get up into the mountains to get my mind off the expedition proposals.

I didn't see any agents, so I left campus and started up the west slope trail that switchbacked up the far side of the mountain. It was the fastest but most challenging trail, especially with a little bit of snow on the ground, and I had to stop a few times to catch my breath.

I stopped and looked out at the vista. The sky was a cold blue, empty except for a single bird swooping and diving. For a moment, I was overcome by envy. Sukey had once told me that when she was flying, she felt like a bird, high above the silly concerns that preoccupied us on the ground. I watched as the bird hovered for a moment and then went into a steep dive. It must have seen a rodent or other prey on the ground. The bird spiraled through space until it had vanished from sight.

I kept hiking until I came out into a rocky clearing. Now it was just a mile along the ridge to the summit, and I breathed deeply, taking in the sharp scent of pine trees on the air. I buttoned my vest and then I saw the bird again, coming straight for me. I was starting to get nervous when I heard a voice from behind me call out, "Good girl, Njamba! Good girl!"

I recognized Joyce's voice, and then I recognized her Kenyan Snake Falcon.

I called hello so she'd know I was there, and I heard a great flapping as Njamba flew into the woods. A few minutes later, Joyce, wearing leather hiking boots, Explorer's leggings, and her navy-blue sailing jacket—which was covered with lengths of rope, a compass, a retractable spyglass, and various hooks and cords—came running up the path with the giant bird on her arm. Njamba was clutching a large rabbit in her talons.

"Hi, Kit!" Joyce said cheerfully, as though there was no one else she would rather have found on the path. "Look what Njamba caught!"

She took the struggling rabbit from the falcon's talons, checked it, and then set it down on the ground. The rabbit ran away, disappearing into the woods.

The bird made a funny clucking noise in her throat. "She hates it when I do that," Joyce said. "But it doesn't seem right to keep it. We're just training—she'll eat later."

"That rabbit would've probably tasted a lot better than whatever you'll get for her from the dining hall tonight."

She laughed. "You going all the way to the top?"

I nodded, and we started walking together.

"Are you looking forward to your first Announcement Banquet?"

"I guess," I said, but not very convincingly.

"It's fun. You'll like it. And it is exciting to hear who's been picked. What do you think of your chances?"

"Uh, fair to middling," I said. "How about you?"

"Oh, I won't be chosen. I'm pretty sure of it. I led an expedition last year. But this year, I want to set up a wildlife observation station and see if I can find evidence of elephant poaching. After Mountmorris's speech, I know I don't have a chance. Not much national security value in observing elephants—but it's what I'm interested in. You should see these guys. They're so intelligent. They use their trunks to communicate. They're practically human. Besides, I'm not sure I'm . . . what they're looking for this year. So how are you liking the Academy?"

"It's fine," I said. "I guess."

She slowed down and turned to look at me, forcing me to tilt my head back to meet her eyes. She was almost exactly Zander's height. Everything on the mountain was dead and finished, all white snow and dead trees, but Joyce's face was full of summer light. There was a calmness about her that made me feel calm too.

"Don't let Lazlo get to you," she said. "Everybody knows how he is."

"It's not just Lazlo. It's . . ."

"Everyone?" She smiled. "It does seem like you've gotten kind of an unfair shake. But don't worry. The nice thing about the expeditions is that it gets you off campus and lets you get to know people in a different way. You'll see. It's hard coming in, not knowing anyone. A lot of the kids knew each other from before."

"You must like it here," I said. "I mean, you're so . . ." I'd been about to say *perfect*, but then I lost my nerve, thinking it would sound as if I liked her too much.

"So . . . *what?*" Her eyes were full of mirth.

"It's just—you do so well in all your classes. Everybody likes you. The Academy must be fun for you."

Joyce smiled kindly at me, and I suddenly felt much younger than she was. "Do you know how I ended up at the Academy?"

"Not really. Your father was a ship's captain in Kenya, right?" The path had gotten steep again, and I was already out of breath. Joyce was barely winded.

"That's right. We're from Mombasa, by the sea. That's where I was born. He discovered a few shipping routes the government was interested in, and they offered him a big job at BNDL. We left Kenya when I was five. I still remember the smell of the sea and every corner of Papa's ship, but I don't remember anything from those first years in New York. It was cold and gray. Papa hated it. He realized they were never going to let him make any decisions that mattered. They wanted him for his contacts in Africa, because he could convince people to give up their rights to the fishing grounds,

133

their knowledge of the sea, to establish the shipping routes. He waited until I started here at the Academy, and then my mother and father and brother went home. I understand why they left me: I'll have more opportunities here. But sometimes I wish I'd gone back with them."

"What would you do?"

"That's the thing. As much as I love the sea, I didn't really want to work for my papa. My brother will. I always wanted to be an Explorer. But . . ."

"But what?"

"But nothing ever turns out quite the way you think it will, does it? Now I feel far away from the boats and the sea and my family, but . . . I don't know. I don't like to think about it too much."

We kept walking. Njamba led the way up into the colder, thinner air.

"Can I ask you something? Where were you for those couple of days after the attack on Francis Foley? What did they do with you?"

The muscles along Joyce's jawline tightened. "They told us not to say anything, but I trust you. It was weird. They had us in this cabin they usually use for guests. It actually wasn't too bad. The food was better than usual, and there were real beds, with good mattresses." She smiled. "They asked a few questions about the explosion, but mostly they wanted to know about our parents, about people back home. They kept asking for names, details of people's jobs, where they went to school. We left when I was five, so I didn't have a lot, but Kemal was in there with them for two days. Maria Montoya too, and that Lundlandian kid from your sister's year. It was really weird."

"I'm sorry," I said. I didn't know what else to say.

"It's okay. And you'll get used to the Academy. There are some good people here. Sukey. Kemal." She smiled. "Your brother and sister. You knew Sukey already, right?"

"Yeah." I felt myself blush and hoped Joyce didn't notice. "Lazlo, too, which is part of the problem."

She smiled again. "Lazlo's awful."

"I think his father hates me even more than he does."

"Everyone says Leo Nackley wanted to be head of BNDL. He was expecting he'd get it when Foley was promoted to head of ADR. And he's mad that he didn't. He's probably taking it out on you. You just have to ignore the Nackleys."

"That's what Zander says. But Zander doesn't seem to have any problem here. Everybody loves him."

Joyce watched me for a moment as we hiked, her brown eyes thoughtful. "It's true," she said. "The amazing thing is that he doesn't really care about what people think, does he?"

"No. He's always been like that."

I picked up the pace, and we hiked quickly up to the summit. Below us, we could see the campus spread out, the buildings like little toys. A steady stream of SteamCars and SteamTaxis were pulling up in front of the gates, and a couple of gliders and dirigibles already sat at the landing strip. The *Grygia* was there, too, casting a huge shadow.

"Looks like everyone's arriving," Joyce said. She sounded sad for a moment, and I realized that of course her parents wouldn't be coming all the way from Kenya. "By tonight, we'll know about the Final Exam Expeditions."

135

"My stomach will be glad when the waiting's over," I said. We both watched as Njamba made wide, lazy circles in the sky.

"From up here," Joyce said, "you'd never know that people are fighting and unhappy and sad and everything down there. Sometimes I wish I could just live up here with Njamba and never see another person."

I let the silence settle around us.

Joyce whistled twice and we watched as Njamba, hearing the command, fell into a sudden dive, her body dark against the smoky white clouds that had started to gather over campus. She spread her wings and sailed silently towards us, clucking as she came to rest on Joyce's shoulder.

Seventeen

Most of the parents and guests had arrived and were making their way to the Longhouse for the banquet when word started to spread around campus that something was happening in Simeria. By the time we were all seated at the long tables with our plates of roast beef in front of us, everyone knew that there had been an uprising by East Simerian factions loyal to the Indorustans. They had launched an attack on an Allied military base in Simeria, taking six surrounding towns, and were now moving troops across the Simerian Desert. The East Simerians, who were loyal to the Indorustans and had been fighting for years to bring Simeria under Indorustan control, had been stopped by our soldiers and SteamTanks, but just barely.

"Things have been tense for months," Raleigh told us. He'd taken the train up from New York and then caught a SteamTaxi from the station to the Academy. "But the East Simerians have been staging more and more protests, and finally they took over a couple of BNDL's command centers. They had weapons that had clearly come from the Indorustans. This may mean war." He leaned across the table, talking with his mouth full of meat and gravy, little droplets of grease clinging to his beard.

"Well, if it isn't Raleigh MacAdam."

Raleigh looked up and a huge grin broke out across his face. Sukey was standing there with a tall woman in a green synthetic flight suit, flight goggles pushed up on her head. Her short red hair was straight and a couple of shades brighter than Sukey's, but otherwise they looked like older and younger versions of the same person.

"Delilah! My god. It's been a long, long time." Raleigh tried to stand up, but Delilah waved him back down, and she and Sukey slid onto the bench next to him. She hugged him, laughing, and said, "I was hoping I'd get to see you, my old friend. Hi, Zander. Hi, M.K. How are you, Kit?"

We all chatted about school and her recent trip to Deloia. After she and Raleigh had caught up a bit, the conversation turned back to Simeria.

"Hildreth hasn't said a word," Delilah whispered, looking around to make sure no one was listening. "But the rumor is that it's a major uprising and we no longer have control over Simer City. The Indorustan Empire has been arming the East Simerians for years, and they aren't going to let us put down the uprising without a fight. They may see this as their chance to take us on in the Newly Discovered Lands in the east."

"Here we go," said Raleigh, his mouth full of food, as Maggie, wearing a sparkling, snowy-white arctic climbing jacket and white velvet pants approached the podium. The din in the room quieted down to a low murmur.

"Welcome, parents and special visitors," she began. "We are looking forward to showing you the amazing work that our students have done this year. And we are especially looking forward to the biggest event of the fall term here at the Academy, tonight's announcement of the Final Exam Expeditions."

After a round of applause, Maggie held up her hands. "Now, I know some of you may have heard about the rebellion in Simeria," she continued. "We had a messenger from New York this morning who brought reports that the military forces of the United States and its Allied Nations have already been quite successful in restoring peace in Simer City. We have word that many BNDL agents are serving with courage and distinction, which is something of which we can all be proud." She smiled slightly. "In any case, we can all rest assured that our government is doing all it can and that the conflict will be over soon. Now, please, everyone, enjoy the meal. When we are done eating, we will hear from BNDL director Mr. R. Delorme Mountmorris."

The dinner was bad. I had to chew the potatoes at least fifteen times before they were soft enough to swallow, and the vanilla cream pie tasted of sour milk. I didn't feel like eating anyway. Waiting for the announcement, my stomach felt as sour as the pudding in the pie.

Zander told Raleigh and Delilah about his field biology class, and M.K. was telling Sukey about her work on Amy and how she'd come up with the idea for the compressed steam engine. Sukey asked her all about the hydraulics and the rudder. Since I didn't really understand the technical details, I just sat there by myself, looking around the room. As I scanned the long table full of students and guests, I saw Kemal doing the same thing I was. He sat between a man and a woman who must have been his parents. They all looked as nervous as I felt. Kemal and I locked eyes for a moment before he looked away.

Finally Maggie returned to the front of the room. "As you know," she began, "the Final Exam Expeditions are an important part of our history here at the Academy. They provide real-world training and are meant to test you and teach you what you will need to know to become a full-fledged Explorer of the Realm.

"Now, to announce the ten chosen expeditions, please welcome Mr. R. Delorme Mountmorris, the director of the Bureau of Newly Discovered Lands."

Mr. Mountmorris, in a red suit and top hat, walked with long strides up to the front of the room.

You couldn't help noticing the twenty or so agents standing around him this time, and no mounted animal heads were anywhere in sight. Mr. Mountmorris grinned, and everyone gave a hearty round of applause. Raleigh frowned, but then he joined in the clapping, and I figured I'd better not ask for trouble, so I clapped too. Across the room, Leo Nackley leaned over to whisper to a dark-haired woman I assumed was his wife, then patted Lazlo on the back. Lazlo didn't look nervous at all.

Everyone applauded, and Mr. Mountmorris grinned and bowed. Then he took out a large envelope and opened it with a flourish.

"The first expedition will be . . ." He waited for a second, to increase the drama. "An Expedition for the Purposes of Exploring an Inlet of the New North Polar Sea." We heard a little squeal of delight from the back of the room. "To be led by Ava Eisenhofer. Congratulations, Miss Eisenhofer. Your teammates will be . . ." I held my breath. If I heard my name or Zander's or M.K.'s or Sukey's, it was all over. But she went on, "Joseph Anderson, Jonas Krowinski, Flynn Dooley, Clara Mabbo." Ava, a talented geologist in her last year at the Academy, came up and said a few words about the minerals they were hoping to find in the ice. "I only hope that our discovery will lead to a brighter future for our country," she said, to much clapping and cheering. When she was done, I let out a sigh of relief. Only nine more to go.

"The next expedition will be . . . ." He didn't wait as long for this one. "An Expedition to Map the Third New Hawaiian Island, led by Michael Fitch. The members of the expedition will be . . ." I listened to make sure that none of us were on it, and then I exhaled deeply as Mike came up to talk about his expedition. I got through the next one, and then for some reason I had the feeling that the fourth one was going to be it.

But it wasn't. It was an expedition to the Sahara.

Mr. Mountmorris grinned. "Now, this next expedition is an interesting one. There was a lot of interest in this region this year. The next expedition will be . . ." He fumbled with the paper, drawing it out unbearably. "An expedition to the St. Beatrice Region of the Caribbean to Research and Explore Possibilities for New Fuel Sources."

I looked at Zander. St. Beatrice! It was mine!

But then Mr. Mountmorris went on. "To be led by . . . Lazlo Nackley. Crew members are Alexander West., Jr., Mary Kingsley West, Joyce Kimani, Jack Foster, Christopher West . . ." Zander and M.K. and I had all been named. And just as I realized that he had one more name to say, the words came out of his mouth and my heart sank. ". . . Kemal Asker. Expedition instructor is Cameron Wooley. That rounds it out. Lazlo . . ."

Lazlo came up and started talking about how his research showed that there may be a source of oil under the ocean in the northern Caribbean. Newly invented drilling equipment would allow him to access the oil. "If we are successful, we will be providing a new fuel source to help our military secure our borders and protect our territories . . ." My head was swimming. It was too hot in the room, and I thought I was going to faint. Lazlo finished talking and grinned at the round of applause that followed him back to his seat. Leo Nackley was staring at me, watching for my reaction, and it was all I could do to keep clapping and stay on my feet.

And then Mr. Mountmorris was announcing the next expedition, something about Iceland and a new species of Snow Deer. I heard Sukey's name. Mr. Mountmorris kept talking, but I couldn't focus.

Lazlo was leading our expedition.

We were going to the Caribbean.

And Sukey wasn't.

Eighteen

Outside the Longhouse, I leaned over a trash can for a minute, hoping I wasn't going to throw up.

"He stole it," I whispered to Zander, once he had joined me. "He stole our proposal."

"How could he?" Zander looked stunned, his eyes wide, his forehead wrinkling as he tried to figure it out.

"Someone showed it to him. Maggie or someone else. It's the only possibility." I remembered Lazlo and Jack hanging around our table in the Longhouse. "Or he eavesdropped on us."

"I'll kill him," M.K. said as she joined us. I watched Raleigh and Delilah hugging old friends, everyone celebrating as though the world hadn't just ended. Ava Eisenhofer walked by with her parents and a group of friends, and we all congratulated her.

"Thanks," she said, grinning and adjusting a tool on her

geologist's belt. "From the looks on your faces, I have the feeling that congratulations aren't what you all want to hear. I'm sorry."

"It's okay," I told her. "We're happy for you."

Lazlo was accepting congratulations too, his father clapping him on the back and grinning broadly, the dark-haired woman watching him with pride.

"I'll kill him, the no-good thief." M.K. gripped the wrench on her toolbelt.

Then I saw Sukey coming out of the Longhouse, an unreadable expression on her face.

"It's okay, it's okay," she said, when she reached us. "Don't say anything. I love Iceland. I'm going to have a great time studying Snow Deer in Iceland."

But I couldn't help myself. "Maybe we could talk to Maggie. Maybe we can tell her that you have to be on the expedition, that we need your flying skills and . . ."

"Stop it, Kit," she said, then whispered. "At least you're going."

"Yeah, but it's not our expedition. Lazlo will be watching us every second. How can we find . . ."

"You'll just have to do what you can. Maybe you can go off on your own and look for King Triton's—"

"Shhh." Zander hushed us, and we saw Lazlo and his parents approaching.

"Congratulations, Lazlo," I said in a voice that I knew was dripping with sarcasm. "You must be really happy."

He gave me a funny look. "Well, it's no secret that you weren't my first choice for crew," he said, looking us over. "But I hope we can all work together and make this expedition a success." He looked nervous, his eyes darting from us to his father, who looked down at us triumphantly.

"You're a thief, Lazlo Nackley," M.K. said, still gripping her wrench. "You stole our proposal."

Lazlo frowned. "That's ridiculous. I don't know what you're talking about."

"Yes, you do," I said. "We turned in a proposal to go to the same place. It can't be a coincidence. Therefore, you stole it!"

The panicked look on his face told me I was right.

"But—" he started, as Mr. Mountmorris came up behind us.

He gave us all one of his broad, delighted grins, his froglike eyes sparkling with humor, then turned to Lazlo. "Congratulations, Mr. Nackley," he said. His red suit matched the flashing red border around his glasses. "What an exciting night. The Caribbean! Well, this is all very intriguing. And Mr. West, Mr. West, Miss West. What do you think about your assignment?"

"It will certainly be an interesting trip," I said through clenched teeth.

"Yes, I think you can say that." He caught my gaze for a moment, and as our eyes met, I knew. He and Maggie were sending us on Lazlo's expedition because he knew we had a map from Dad. Even if he hadn't been able to find it, he knew in his bones that it was there, and he thought that by sending us to the Caribbean, Lazlo would be able to follow us and steal it.

I felt a surge of anger. We couldn't let them get away with it. We had to figure out a way to get there on our own.

Once Mr. Foley and Mr. Mountmorris had left us, Leo Nackley leaned toward me and looked me right in the eyes.

"You'd better be careful, Mr. West, about accusing my son," he said. "You, of all people, should know what happens to liars."

And the two of them walked away, leaving us standing there in the cold.

Nineteen

I caught up to Mr. Wooley the next day. He looked tired and drawn, his eyes lined with worry and fatigue. "What is it, Kit?" he asked, as though he'd rather be anywhere but talking to me.

"Did you want to go on the expedition?" I asked him. "After what you said, I was amazed when they made you the expedition instructor."

"You're not the only one." I'd never heard him sound anything but kind, and the anger in his voice surprised me.

Then he gave me a little smile and said, more softly, "Look, it wasn't my first choice, but I'm a good soldier. I do what I'm told." He shrugged. "And who knows, maybe it will be therapeutic to revisit the site of the most terrifying thing that's ever happened to me."

Sukey was busy getting ready for her own expedition, and we didn't see much of her for the next few weeks while we made supply lists for Lazlo and studied sailing and nautical navigation with Joyce. Lazlo was awful, ordering us around and forcing us to do the grunt work he didn't want to do, but Joyce was a good teacher, and I was glad that she'd be captaining our ship from St. Beatrice. Even Lazlo wasn't stupid enough to do it himself.

One night, I walked by Sukey's cabin to see if she was in, but her room was dark and empty.

As I walked back toward the boys' cabins, I recognized her on the path ahead, huddled in her flight jacket, her head down. When I reached her, she looked surprised to see me. She was wearing her leather flight helmet, her goggles pushed up on her head.

"Where have you been?" I asked her.

"Oh, the flying squadron. We've been practicing more and more, but I really can't talk about it." She smiled guiltily. "How are you?"

She looked tired. We all looked tired. There was so much to do, and we'd be heading home to our house on Oceania Island the day after tomorrow to have Christmas with Raleigh. On December 26, our team was scheduled to leave on a commercial steamship for St. Beatrice Island, where we'd prepare for Lazlo's expedition.

"Fine. How about you?"

"I'm okay. I'm tired of Snow Deer already. This is going to be a long trip." She grinned, and I realized it had been a long time since I'd seen her smile. "I wish I was going with you. It doesn't seem right that I'm not." Her breath made little puffs of mist in the air.

"I wish you were too," I said. "When do you leave?"

"Tomorrow. Delilah's going to pick me up."

"When do you head north?"

"We'll head up on a SteamShip and then get the gliders and overland vehicles at an airfield somewhere near Reykjavik."

"So . . . this is it?"

"I guess so. Have you figured out anything else about the map yet?"

"Not really. I can't help feeling there's some kind of message there, but I can't crack it. I'll have eleven days on the way to St. Beatrice to think about it, though."

She gave me a hug, but it was a quick one. I felt cold and sad.

"I'll tell the others goodbye for you," I said.

"Give M.K. a hug. I already saw Zander."

"Oh." I just stared at her. Her skin was milky pale, her eyelashes dark against her cheeks.

"Good luck," she said. She started to push past me as though she had somewhere to be, but I reached out and grabbed her arm, leaned in, and whispered in her ear. "I'll show you the secret room. If you want. Come with me?"

Her eyes widened. We'd decided that it was too risky to try to go back so the others could see it, and I knew it had been driving Zander crazy that I had been there and he hadn't.

"Come on," I told her.

"I can't," she said. "I have to get back. Besides, we said it was too dangerous." A bit of light from the torches next to the doors of the boys' cabins flashed on her face, making her amber eyes swim like molten gold.

"Okay." I started to turn to go, but she pulled me in for a tight, long hug that made my heart pound. When she pulled away, I stared at her, confused and anxious.

"I hope you find whatever it was he wanted you to find. I think you will."

"I'm glad someone thinks so." My head hurt with stress and fatigue and a sudden sadness at the realization that I wasn't going to see Sukey for a long time. "I just wish I knew *why*, you know? I wish I knew why he's sending us on this hunt. What it's all for."

"I really think you're going to do it." She smiled, but it was a false, hurried smile. After she was gone, I walked for a long time, not wanting to go back to the bunk I shared with Zander.

In the morning, I stood outside the Longhouse after breakfast and watched as a glider took off and rode a warm current up and away from the mountains, getting smaller and smaller before it vanished completely.

BOOK II

and we are now somewhere east of Bermuda, having made our way across the Atlantic Ocean. We will stop in Bermuda and then make our way down the coast to the northeastern islands of the Caribbean ~~Sea~~ ~~area of the~~.

Twenty

"**F**ive," said the Lundlandian businessman. "I bet five."

"He's pretty confident . . . for a man who is about to lose!" declared the Derudan lumber merchant as he laid down seven glittering gemstone pieces. He wore a ridiculous purple cloak, and the sleeve kept falling into the glass of wine next to him on the table.

"How about the boy?" the Lundlandian asked. "You've been playing well tonight. But perhaps you're afraid to keep playing with real men." They all laughed heartily.

"No," I said, laying down ten of the playing pieces. "I think I can handle it." I met the Lundlandian businessman's eye. I had already won four hundred Allied dollars, and I wasn't about to stop now. Zander and M.K. stood behind me watching the game. Zander let out a nervous little sigh.

"Ahhhh. The little boy plays big," said the fourth player at the table, a white-haired Neo woman in a skintight green jumpsuit. The lights in her ears were all green, blinking on and off in a random pattern as she laid her pieces out.

We'd been aboard the *Deloian Princess* for three days, and I'd spent a lot of my time playing games in the lounge with an incredible variety of people from all over the world. The *Princess* was a huge, state-of-the-art SteamLiner, an oceangoing ship with ultra-efficient engines that could take her all over the Atlantic and Caribbean before she needed to stop for more coal. She could carry six hundred people and two thousand tons of cargo and she was afloat all year, shuttling BNDL officials and merchants around the Allied World.

Our expedition team, along with Mr. Wooley and Leo Nackley, had boarded in New York, and we were steaming down the East Coast toward the Caribbean, stopping in ports along the way to pick up cargo and passengers. The more ports we saw, the bigger and more interesting the world seemed.

I loved sitting on the main deck and watching the assortment of people making their way around the ship. There were BNDL and ADR and ANDLC officials on their way to the Caribbean from New York, wearing concerned expressions while exchanging hushed remarks with each other about Simeria. There were glamorous Neo couples from Paris or Milan, wearing colorful clothes made from synthetic silks and velvets and carrying small dogs, their fur dyed red or purple or green. There were rich merchants from Africa and Deloia. There were sunburned farmers from the colonies and territories in the Caribbean and South America who had been in New York making deals with wholesalers for their meat and produce.

On our first day at sea, I discovered that I could sit on the promenade deck and pretend to use my spyglass to look out at the water while actually turning it this way and that to listen to the conversations of the first-class passengers as they made their way around the deck. As I eavesdropped I would catch sight of whales and dolphins and passing ships on the horizon. A few times, we'd caught sight of the bright purple sails of the Neo pirates who cruised the Atlantic and the Caribbean, looking for smaller ships hauling produce and meat products to market. The attacks on cargo ships had been increasing as food supplies dwindled. The pirates had waved cheerfully to us but hadn't given us any trouble. They knew that the *Deloian Princess* had guns on deck and BNDL agents on board.

The agents seemed to have relaxed in the contained environment of the ship, and they let us do pretty much whatever we pleased. M.K. spent most of the voyage down in the engine room, learning about the boilers and turbines that made the huge ship run. Zander had been spending his days swimming in the pool on the recreation deck with Joyce and Kemal, sometimes fishing off the lower deck, or watching whales and dolphins and seabirds from the upper deck. Jack Foster haunted the lounges and restaurants, flirting with the waitresses, and Lazlo holed up with his father, working on the expedition plans. Poor Mr. Wooley was seasick for most of the trip, and we'd barely seen him above deck.

As for me, I'd bumped into Dolly Frost almost as soon as I'd come aboard, and I'd been trying to dodge her questions and requests for interviews ever since. When I wasn't hiding from her or eavesdropping on the conversations of the Allied world, I was in the lounge, playing chess or Deloian checkers or Simalio with whoever would give me a game.

"Okay, my friends. What have we got? I want to see those Simalios," said the Lundlandian. Despite the fact that we'd steamed into warmer waters, he was still wearing a fur jacket and pants. They made me think of Sukey. She must be wearing something similar by now.

Simalio was a Derudan game that everyone on the ship was crazy about. You played with a set of semiprecious gemstones that were dealt out to the four players in little velvet bags. You kept your thirty stones behind a little silk screen and offered up piles of them as bets, depending on what you had behind your screen and what you thought the other players had. You had to be good at remembering what the various combinations of stones were worth, and you had to be good at remembering what each player had bet, what they'd won, what they'd given up. I don't know if it was that I liked codes and numbers, but I turned out to be pretty good at Simalio. I'd won $100 the day before, and I was already $400 ahead tonight.

We each laid down our screens, revealing our collections of stones.

"You old faker. You had the Grand Simalio all along!" the Lundlandian shouted at the Neo woman.

She grinned and scooped up all of our pieces. "Come on, now! Pay up!" she said. I took most of the Allied dollars out of my pocket and handed the stack over with the others. "I got you good!" she said, cackling and coughing.

The men pretended not to care, but the Lundlandian looked a little pale as he handed over his money.

"You almost had it, didn't you?" Zander asked me when they were gone. "How much would you have won?"

"A lot," I told him. "But I didn't almost have it. I had a Simalio Brut, but the Lundlandian guy had a Simalio Gros. He would have won if she hadn't had the Grand Simalio. It's not just having one of each category of stones. You have to have the right combination of the precious ones, the rubies and sapphires."

"I don't how you remember all that," Zander grumbled.

We found a seat in the corner of the lounge and read the discarded newspapers laid out on the low table. Things were still tense in Simeria and our government had moved twenty thousand troops into position in Greece and Italy, ready for war. I read the number again. How had they gotten the troops there so quickly? Most of the steamships would take a month to make their way that far east.

Kemal came over and sat down across from us. "You playing Simalio again?"

We lowered our newspapers and M.K. grinned. "Just Kit. We're not smart enough to play Simalio."

He laughed. "My father always says there are two ways to win at Simalio. One is to make sure you never play. And the other is to steal the Simalio stones. I think he lost some money once."

"I'll remember that next time, though that Lundlandian businessman didn't look like he'd let a little thing like stealing his stones go."

Kemal picked up a paper and we all read in companionable silence, listening to the conversations as the men and women in the lounge chatted, chewing Dramleaf and drinking wine. I had gotten used to the barely perceptible motion of the big ship, the background noise of the engines. It got later and later, and a big group of Simerian businessmen wearing long white robes and red fezzes came into the lounge, discussing the uprising. "If they don't get control of this soon, it's going to be outright war," said the youngest of them, a tall man with a friendly, moon-shaped face. "I saw the papers in Miami. The Allies are telling their people it's as good as put down. It's all lies, though. They're barely hanging on. The Indorustans are sending arms to the East Simerians through the mountains."

"What about you, Musta?" said another of the men. "Whose side are you on?"

Musta laughed. "Whoever wants to pay me the most money. That's whose side I'm on. Politics don't matter to me as much as a new home in the mountains. If the Indorustans want to give it to me, what do I care?"

"You'd better be careful about saying things like that aboard this ship," said one of his companions. I looked up and met Kemal's eyes over my paper.

The Simerians left the lounge, and we read for a while longer until we heard an Antiguan landowner whom I'd seen out on deck say, "Did you hear about these kids looking for the underwater oil?" We held our papers higher, sinking down into the plush velvet chairs.

His friend laughed. "That old legend? What do you think about it? Your people are fishermen."

"My grandfather always said he'd seen it a few times, floating on top of the water. He didn't think it was a legend. But it must be said that he liked his rum."

"I heard that pirate Monty Brioux is looking for the oil too. He thinks he might be able to find it and demand the government pay him for access. He wants Hildreth to give him an island of his own. Thinks the oil is the way to get it."

The other man laughed. "Even if it is there, how would you get it? You know what they say about the water out there. It kills anyone who tries to get near King Triton's Lair. The sea doesn't want us to find it."

We waited until they were gone before we got up and headed back down to the B deck, where our cabins were. Lazlo and his father had a big suite of rooms up on the first-class A deck.

"What do you think about what those men were saying?" Kemal asked nervously when we'd reached our doors. "Do you think it's true?"

"No, it's just stories," I told him. "Get some sleep."

He nodded and ducked into his room, and Zander and I walked to our cabin. I got into bed and tried to make myself believe what I'd said to Kemal.

I didn't sleep well, and I don't think Zander did either. When we came out on deck the next morning, the sun was stronger than ever, the water a more brilliant blue.

We were almost there.

Twenty-one

As we got closer to St. Beatrice, we spotted more and more pirate ships. On our ninth day at sea we were steaming due east when a Neo woman on deck for a stroll shouted that pirates were just off our starboard side. A couple hundred yards to the east, we could see the bright-purple solar sails of the biggest boat we'd seen yet.

"It's Monty Brioux!" someone called out.

"The pirate?" Zander said. He, Joyce, Kemal, and M.K. had been swimming in the ship's pool, and they'd found me on deck, standing at the railing and looking out at the sea.

"He's the most famous pirate of all," Kemal told us as he dried his hair with one of the fancy red towels from the ship, a little DP embroidered on the hem. "Apparently, he attacked a cargo ship last week near St. John's. Got away with a couple hundred thousand dollars worth of ANDLC's goods."

"I've heard about him for years," Joyce said. "They call Monty Brioux 'the scorpion of the Atlantic.' They say he was born in the deserts of Morocco and ran away to the sea when he was only five years old."

A swift breeze blew across the deck, and the pirates passed us easily, tipping their hats as they went, their sails snapping loudly. The boat itself was huge, a big double-hulled vessel that Joyce said was called a catamaran, a popular ship in the Caribbean. It had three masts, each outfitted with purple synthetic sails covered with solar cells. M.K. pointed these out, speculating that they provided backup power to the ship's compact engine. Thanks to the cells, M.K. said with admiration, the catamaran wasn't dependent on the winds *or* fuel.

Standing on top of the deck railing at the bow was Monty Brioux, dressed in a purple cloak and plum-colored captain's hat over his long red hair. He hung on to the rigging, his alligator-skin boots shining in the sun. As they overtook us, we heard Brioux laugh loudly and shout, "We won't take you today, ladies and gentlemen, we won't take you today!" He gave a smart salute and they were ahead of us, racing through the water toward St. Beatrice.

"That's quite a boat," Joyce said, following the purple sails as they disappeared into the distant blue. "I'd say there isn't anywhere that boat can't go."

"What do you all think of this criminal Brioux?"

We turned around and saw that Leo and Lazlo Nackley were leaning against the railing next to us. They'd been watching the pirates too.

"I hope they don't follow us all the way to St. Beatrice," I said, giving them a fake smile. "This expedition's going to be hard enough without pirates to fight off."

"Is that right?" Leo Nackley said, looking down at me. He had started growing a small beard on the sea voyage, a pointy triangle at the bottom of his chin. "Don't you have faith in Lazlo and his plan, Mr. West?"

I wanted to say that in fact it was my plan, stolen by Lazlo, and that it was full of half-truths and outright lies anyway, and so, no, I didn't have much faith in him, and I certainly didn't have much faith in the plan. But I swallowed hard and just said, "Oh, yes, I'm sure Lazlo will be very, very successful." The other passengers had drifted back to whatever they'd been doing before the pirates had been sighted.

Leo Nackley grabbed my arm, squeezing it until I gasped with pain, and turned me around so I was looking up at him.

"You sarcastic little snot," he growled. "You know something that you're not telling us. I can feel it."

"I have no idea what you're talking about, Mr. Nackley." He squeezed harder. I could feel his fingers digging into my elbow.

Joyce and Zander stepped forward, but then they hesitated, waiting to see what he'd do next.

Nackley ignored them, still gazing down into my face with hatred. "You know that if you have any information you're withholding, now would be the time to give it up. On board a ship like this, things are—well, things are looser. It would be possible to overlook a breach of BNDL laws. Once we're on St. Beatrice, there will be agents everywhere."

I met his eyes. "I said I don't know what you're talking about." Lazlo stood next to his father, shifting his weight from one foot to the other and glancing over his shoulder. He looked as terrified of his father as we were.

"Your father gave you a map of the oil," Mr. Nackley said to me, his face so close to mine I could smell the garlic on his breath. "That's why *he*—" He nodded towards Zander "—wanted to go to St. Beatrice for the expedition. You know exactly where the oil is, and you're going to tell us. Where is it? Where's that map?" The veins stood out at his temples. He twisted my arm, and I felt burning pain shoot up my shoulder. He was enjoying my agony.

"Let him go," Zander said. "He doesn't have anything."

"Leo?" Mr. Wooley had come out on deck. I didn't know how long he'd been standing there. "The boy says he doesn't know anything. I think you should let it rest."

"Of all people," Leo Nackley said, sneering at Mr. Wooley. "You, of all people, are telling me how to run an expedition?"

"It's not your expedition; it's your son's," Mr. Wooley said. "And people are watching you."

We all followed Mr. Wooley's gaze up to find the Antiguan businessmen and a number of other passengers who'd gathered to watch the pirates. Their attention was now turned toward our group. At that moment, Dolly Frost, sensing the commotion, walked up the stairs and took in the scene.

Leo Nackley let go of my arm. "I'll get it from you," he hissed before stalking off with Lazlo trailing behind. "You can be sure I'll get it from you."

I leaned against the railing, trying to catch my breath, cradling my arm. "Thank you, Mr. Wooley," I gasped.

"Stay away from him," he said in a quiet voice. "You don't know what he can do. He thinks you're hiding something, and he won't let it go until he figures out what it is."

"Why are you scared of him?" I asked, still breathing hard. "Why did they make you go on the expedition?"

He laughed bitterly. "I can't tell you," he said. "But listen to me. *Stay away from Nackley.*"

I tried again and again to doze off that night but finally gave up around 1 a.m. I put on a sweater and went out, carefully shutting the door behind me so as not to wake Zander, and walked up on deck, passing a loud and very drunk group of Lundlandian businessmen and women I'd seen earlier, including my Simalio partner. They'd been very serious during daylight hours, but now they were singing cheerfully in Lundlandian. One of the men was dancing wildly, jumping up onto the railing and teetering out over the water. I passed them and walked along the deck to the starboard bow, finding a bench to sit on. The sky was full of stars, and a half moon cast a yellow light over the water. I wondered where Sukey was at this moment. On a ship like this, heading north instead of south? Flying a glider over expanses of endless white, looking for Snow Deer? Was she looking at these same stars? I had thought about her every day since we'd been at sea.

I had closed my eyes, picturing Sukey standing at the edge of a field of ice and snow, when someone sat down on the bench next to me. A man's voice said, "Stay quiet."

I opened my eyes. He was wearing the robes of the Simerian businessmen, a fez sitting uncomfortably on his thick blond hair.

"I think we can talk here," he said in a low, familiar voice. "But we have to be cautious. This disguise gets less convincing every time you see it."

Twenty-two

The Explorer with the Clockwork Hand was sunburned, shaggy, unwashed. "What are *you* doing here?" I said. "The ship is swarming with agents. If they find you . . ."

"I know," he said. "Don't worry about me. I've been on the boat for a while, and I know their routines."

"Aren't you afraid they'll find you?"

He ignored my question. "How are you, Kit? I'm sorry we didn't get to talk at the Academy. They almost caught me that night." He smiled a little, as though remembering his near capture.

"I'm . . . I don't know, how do you *think* I am?" I took a deep breath. There wasn't time to be angry. "I went to the room. I found the map that Dad left us. I saw the Muller Machine. We wrote a proposal to go to the place on Dad's map. King Triton's Lair. It's off the coast of St. Beatrice, where all those ships have gone down and where Dad almost died on his own expedition. But Lazlo stole it and turned in his own proposal. So now we're on Lazlo's expedition, and Leo Nackley knows I'm holding out on him and I don't even know what Dad wants us to find there. It may be something called Girafalco's Trench, but I can't figure out what . . ."

"Girafalco?" he asked sharply.

"Yes. Do you know who he is?"

He didn't answer. "I know the name," he said vaguely. "Now, do you have a plan?"

"Well . . . not really. M.K. built a submersible that can explore the ocean floor, and Lazlo thinks we're going to use it to find the oil." The truth was that we didn't have a plan at all.

"If you get close enough, you'll need to abandon the expedition and go off by yourself," he said. "Are you prepared to do that?"

I stared at him. "I don't know. What would happen to us?"

He grabbed my shoulders and brought his face very close to mine. "Everything may depend on whether or not you are able to do what your father wanted you to do. If you have the chance, you have to take it. Do you understand?"

I could feel anger wash over me. "How can you ask me to do that when you won't even tell me what's going on here? Where's Dad? What is this all about? What am I looking for?" I hesitated. "Is he alive? You have to tell me."

He sighed and sat back on the bench.

"You have every right to ask those questions," he said. "We don't have much time, but I'll do the best I can." He stood up and strolled casually down the deck, then came back and went the other direction, checking to see if anyone was near.

He sat down again. "For all I know, your father died in Fazia," he said. "I was given my instructions before he left on the expedition. If something happened to him, I was supposed to find you and give you the package. That was all I knew. But I can tell you that there are things that are . . . suspicious about the government's account of his disappearance. And I've heard, well . . . rumors, I suppose you'd call them. Anyway, you accused me of being a member of the Mapmakers' Guild. I can't confirm that, but you're on the right track."

"What is the Mapmakers' Guild? What do you do?"

"You've already figured out that it's a secret society of Explorers. What else do you know?"

"He's leading us to something. It's like a treasure hunt. One map leading to another, leading to another. What I want to know is what's at the end."

There was a long silence. "I don't know," he said. "I don't know exactly. But I do know that it's a matter of life or death."

Suddenly we heard voices coming our way, a woman laughing and then murmuring something to a man, who laughed in response.

We sat quietly until they had passed, arm in arm, still laughing, uninterested in what they thought was a Simerian businessman and his son sitting on the bench.

"You don't know?" I asked incredulously. "And you're asking us to risk our lives for it?"

"I'm afraid so."

"What are we supposed to do, anyway? Just jump off the boat and see if King Triton or some freaky mermaid or something swims over and says hello?"

"It worked in Arizona," he said.

"We got somebody killed in Arizona. And how do you know it 'worked'? The Nackleys found the gold. Lazlo Nackley is the hero of Drowned Man's Canyon."

"Oh, come on. Let's not play games here," he said. "I know exactly what you did in Arizona. You protected the people in the canyon. John had already pledged his life to the task. He was happy to give it up. And it was Francis Foley who shot him. You bear no responsibility at all."

There was a long silence while I decided whether I should ask him the question that had been on my mind for weeks. "I heard about Munopia. About what my father did there. Did he . . . did he really take bribes?"

He turned to look at me. "Your father wasn't perfect, but I can guarantee you that if he took a bribe, he had a good reason."

It wasn't the answer I'd been hoping for. "Look, I think there must be some mistake. Maybe we weren't supposed to start finding the maps for a couple of years. Maybe we weren't supposed to start this until we're older, until we, I don't know . . . until my brother and sister . . . They're the ones who—"

We heard voices again, two men this time, speaking English.

"I have to go," he said. "But I think you're selling yourself short. And you should know that it isn't about your brother and sister. I was directed by your father to give the book to you. Just you. Not to Zander, not to M.K. To you, Kit."

"What? But—"

"Goodbye. Good luck."

I watched him make his way all the way down to the end of the deck, where he turned left into a doorway, his white robes swirling around him, and then he was gone.

that I had been curious about the purpose of our expedition. Captain Girafalco had told us that we would map the route to Bermuda, but during my time on the ship I have become suspicious that he has another goal.

And at last, yesterday I discovered the true purpose of our voyage. Captain Girafalco called me to his cabin, where I found maps and charts spread out on every surface.

"I saw your face yesterday when I told the crew that I have completed my map of the Bermuda crossing," he said. "Perhaps you do not agree with my methods?"

"No, sir," I said, taking a deep breath. "I do not wish to be disrespectful, sir, but it is clear that the map of the Bermuda crossing is not our true purpose on this voyage. You have missed essential readings all along the way. Besides which, the crossing has already been mapped."

He laughed. "Well," he said, "you are correct. Do you have any idea what we're actually doing here?" He was laughing at me, waiting to see what I was going to say, and I told him I thought it had something to do with his theory about the trenches that

Twenty-three

"**L**and!" Pucci squawked. "*Land ho!*"

We steamed into St. Beatrice Harbor on January 7, eleven days after having left New York. It had felt much longer than that, and as I watched the island come into view, I realized how glad I'd be to be off the *Deloian Princess*. I'd gotten tired of the people, the Simalio, the smell of Dramleaf and wine in the lounge. I'd gotten tired of the endless expanse of turquoise sea.

"Lazlo, make sure you're out in front," Leo Nackley said as we all stood on deck, watching as we approached the colorful harbor ringed with palm trees. "The newspapers may be in port taking pictures. You're the expedition leader. You should be in the picture."

"Look at all the palm trees! And the flowers!" Jack exclaimed. For our arrival, he'd changed into a white suit and a bright yellow linen shirt that hurt my eyes. "Isn't it beautiful? Almost as beautiful as you look today, Joyce."

Joyce rolled her eyes.

"I don't care what kind of trees they are as long as they're growing in solid ground," I grumbled. "I'm tired of looking at water."

"Me too," Kemal said.

"You do know that our expedition includes a whole lot of *water*, don't you, West?" Lazlo Nackley said in a nasty voice.

"Really, Lazlo?" I replied without looking at him. "I thought we were sailing to the Gobi Desert."

"Okay, okay," said Mr. Wooley. "We've made it . . . this far, which is . . . good." He gulped and put a hand up to his mouth. It was only the second or third time we'd seen him since we'd left New York. Lazlo had made endless comments about the uselessness of a faculty expedition leader who wasn't seaworthy on an oceanic expedition. But even he seemed to feel sorry for Mr. Wooley at this point.

Leo Nackley raised his eyebrows at his son and smirked a little as Mr. Wooley went below deck again.

I was also looking forward to having a break from the Nackleys once we got to St. Beatrice. Zander, M.K., and I would be staying with Coleman Miller, Dad's friend from the Academy who had been on the King Triton's Lair expedition. The Nackleys, along with Joyce and Jack and Kemal, would be staying with some fancy BNDL higher-up on the island who would be helping us secure and outfit a ship.

We would have three days to stock the ship and make sure all of our equipment was ready before setting off on the trail of the oil. And Zander and M.K. and I would have three days to find out more about the exact location of King Triton's Lair and the shipwrecks.

Pucci soared into the air to check out his new surroundings as the *Deloian Princess* docked in the harbor, its horn sounding our arrival and the people onshore waving enthusiastically. We'd gotten used to the humidity at sea, but there had been a constant breeze, and it seemed much hotter now that we were on the island. We found our luggage and told the porters to hold the rest of our equipment until we could load it tomorrow. M.K. didn't want to leave Amy behind, but the porters swore they'd watch over her, and she reluctantly followed us down to the quay to meet Coleman.

The quay was lined with fishing shacks and offices, a busy jumble of people, animals, and machinery. The BNDL agents who had been on the ship took up position along the quay as we unloaded our gear. But in addition to the familiar agents, the port was full of soldiers, wearing their black-and-white uniforms and watching everyone getting off the boat. I watched as Leo Nackley went over to talk to one of them, gesturing in our direction.

Pucci nibbled on Zander's chin.

"We'll find you something to eat soon, Pucci," Zander murmured, and Pucci gave a disgusted squawk.

"He'd better be careful once we're out on the water," Lazlo said. "I heard about sharks that can leap out of the water and snag seagulls from the air."

"Are you kidding?" Joyce winked at M.K. "That parrot could whip any shark, no questions asked." Njamba flapped down and settled on her shoulder. "He's almost as brave as Njamba."

Zander grinned at her. "That's right. Any shark that messed with Pucci would be very surprised."

Surprise! Pucci chortled. *Surprise!*

"That bird is weird," Lazlo grumbled.

Finally a tall man in a tan canvas suit and pith helmet modified with lots of little gadgets came running along the quay and wrapped Zander in a gigantic hug.

"You're here!" he exclaimed. "You're finally here! I would have known you anywhere. You look just like your old Dad, you know."

"Coleman Miller," I said, and he turned to me, looking slightly confused. "I'm Kit," I said. "And that's our sister, M.K. You've already figured out that's Zander."

He wrapped me in a bear hug too, then turned to give one to M.K. "I couldn't believe it when Raleigh told me you were coming to St. Beatrice. 'They'll have to stay with me,' I told him. 'No question about it.'"

Mr. Wooley had stumbled onto the quay, looking slightly green and extremely grateful to be on solid ground again.

"Cam! My old friend!" Coleman started to hug Mr. Wooley, but Mr. Wooley put a hand over his mouth again and waved him off. "Haven't got your sea legs, have you?" Coleman said, laughing. "Don't worry, a couple nights on St. Beatrice will set you right!"

Mr. Wooley tried to smile.

"Are you going to be okay, Mr. Wooley?" M.K. said.

"We'll get him to the house," Joyce whispered. "Don't worry about him. See you back here at ten tomorrow to start on the provisions."

I was sorry to see Joyce go. I'd enjoyed her company over the past eleven days. But I was pretty happy to see Lazlo walk away, cursing as he stepped in a pile of rotting fruit on the quay, his father berating him for not being more careful.

"Welcome to St. Beatrice!" Coleman said as we shouldered our backpacks and walked through a narrow alleyway between two tall brick buildings, one painted a bright cobalt blue and the other a watermelon pink. The direct noonday sun made its way down through the alley, illuminating the hundreds of seashells set into the brickwork. They formed a giant sun.

"Wow . . ." M.K. stopped at the end of the alleyway and pointed to the scene in front of her. "It's so . . ."

"Colorful," I finished for her. "I don't think I've ever seen anything so colorful in my life."

"That's one word for the island," Coleman laughed. "Colorful. We certainly are colorful!"

Stretched out in front of us, sloping down to the turquoise-blue sea, was a patchwork of pastel-colored houses, three or four stories each, with flowering vines twining around the white filigree porch railings. Many of the houses had huge murals on their sides. The murals were so finely done that they appeared to be painted. It was only when you looked closely that you saw they were collages made of different colored shells, stones, and bits of glass.

M.K. pointed at a mural depicting fishermen unloading their catch from a boat. Another showed a group of children carrying baskets of yellow and orange fruit. Another showed a group of brilliantly colored parrots in a tree. A few of the murals, I realized with growing interest, were maps.

My first impression of the island was of a prosperous paradise. But the closer I looked, the more the picture changed. The houses looked pristine at a distance, but as we walked by them I could see peeling paint and broken windows. There seemed to be a lot of people just standing around, and almost everyone looked hungry and thin. There were soldiers and BNDL agents on every corner.

Coleman led us through the narrow streets, pointing out buildings of interest as we went, stopping every once in a while to say hello to someone or hand a few coins to a barefoot child.

"St. Beatrice was explored a few years into the New Modern Age. I don't say 'discovered' because as far as the Arawak people who were living here were concerned, they didn't need to be discovered. They'd been here for a long time. They hadn't wanted to be found. But then Jefferson Robbins showed up and reported back that they had an amazing fruit growing there, a fruit that was hardy and prolific and delicious. When the word got out about the Ribby Fruit, settlers came from all over the Caribbean. My family were farmers from Antigua, and we became farmers here. We did very well, enough that we could move to town and pay other people to tend to the crops, and I could go to the Academy for a couple of years. Fish and fruit from St. Beatrice are shipped all over the world now. When the crop is good, at least. But it hasn't been, lately, and the government forces us to sell so much of our crop at the government rate."

He stopped talking and quickly scanned the streets. In a whisper, he added, "Times have been tough the last year. I don't know what they need so much fruit for. Sending it off to the territories and colonies where they can't grow things, I suppose. And now they have their own government farms. They're bringing labor in from all over the Caribbean, and everyone says they barely pay their workers. Anyway, it doesn't do to talk too much about all of that." He gave a sidelong look, searching for agents, that we all knew well. I'd heard people call it the "New York glance," but the truth was that we did it everywhere because BNDL agents were everywhere. I could see a few of them standing watch in the marketplace, their telltale black uniforms out of place amid all the color.

"Let's go this way," Coleman said suddenly, and he took a quick turn into an alleyway. We followed him out the other end, and then we all took another quick turn into another alley, making a big circle and coming out near where we'd started.

"Sorry," he said. "Thought I saw someone."

"An agent?" I asked.

"No, no. Not an agent. Come on. Follow me. Here's the market."

I turned and looked behind me. It may have been my imagination, but I thought I saw a flash of black, someone who had been watching and then ducked out of sight.

We looked around at the people standing in line to get into the market. They were carrying baskets filled with mangos, bananas, breadfruit, and piles of the bright-green Ribby fruit. Others were carrying baskets filled with fish and giant lobsters. The soldiers stopped them and inspected the baskets, then sent them on their way into the stalls.

Coleman led us into the market, and we wandered for a few minutes while he bought fish and vegetables for dinner. M.K. found a stall that sold gadgets and engine components, and she bought some bolts and wires of different sizes for Amy. Zander and I looked at the shells for sale.

"That's a Carib Cowrie," Zander said. "And these I've never seen before. This looks like a whelk, but it must be a newly discovered species." He bought a handful, and I bought a little cowrie shell suspended on a silver chain, thinking maybe I'd give it to Sukey, if I ever got the chance.

Zander and I walked by a row of stalls displaying exotic animals. Pucci had been sitting on Zander's shoulder, but now he hopped along the line of cages, poking his head in to look at the birds and mammals and reptiles inside.

"This is awful," Zander said. "That's a Reingold Leopard. It shouldn't be in a cage. And that's an Oopala Pheasant. Someone should do something about these traders." We stopped and looked at the beautiful bird. Its scarlet tail feathers drooped sadly.

Coleman came and we walked with him along the crowded, noisy streets until he stopped in front of a big, robin's-egg-blue house looking out over the harbor.

"Here we are," Coleman said. "Welcome to my home."

Inside, the house was even bigger than it looked from outside. At one end of the living room a huge wall of glass windows looked out on the sea, which stretched out away from the coast, toward points unknown. We'd be sailing out that way in just a few days.

After he showed us our rooms, I took a steaming-hot bath in Coleman's giant tub, looking out over the water and feeling the warm breeze coming through the open windows. The breeze smelled of flowers, and I felt almost recovered from eleven days at sea. When I came out, the others were getting dinner ready. M.K. was setting the table, and Zander was pouring fresh coconut water into glasses at each place setting. The dining room was decorated with paintings of St. Beatrice and other Caribbean islands, and there were more of the beautiful shells everywhere I looked.

"Coleman, what are those?" I pointed to the shell pendants hanging from nails on the wall. They were made from all different kinds of shells, some pink or pale yellow, some made of shimmery mother-of-pearl. Some were carved to look like flowers, some like animals or fish.

"Those are a traditional St. Beatrician art form," he told me. "They're whistles. Each one has a different sound—they're in different keys and have different numbers of finger holes. The fishermen play them as they come into port at the end of the day so their families know they're back. Listen." He took one off the wall and blew through one end, then placed his fingers over the little holes to play a tune. I recognized it as "Spanish Ladies," an old sea chantey that Dad used to sing.

Coleman grilled fish and vegetables on the terrace, and we sat down and dug into the best meal I could remember in a long time—since Dad's disappearance, at least. The fish was crisp and brown on the outside and flaky white inside, tasting of lemon and herbs. Coleman had bought excellent bread in the market and I sank my teeth into a tender slab, my mouth filling with the fresh taste of salt and yeast. The coconut water was pure and cold and a couple of sips made me forget all about the warm, brackish water we'd had to drink on the SteamShip.

Coleman offered a toast. "In the words of the St. Beatrician sailors, may you find calm seas and fine weather. Now, tell me all about this expedition."

We hesitated.

"Well," said Zander. "It's actually Lazlo Nackley's expedition. He thinks we can find oil out there."

"The underwater black waterfalls," Coleman said. "He believes that old story, does he?"

"You don't?"

"There are a lot of stories about what's out there." He winked. "Maybe three or four of them are true."

I hesitated. "We're a bit more interested in the shipwrecks in King Triton's Lair," I said. "You and Dad went looking for them, didn't you? What do you remember about the expedition, Coleman?"

He leaned back in his chair. "I've been trying for a long time *not* to remember. It was that expedition that convinced me I didn't want to be an Explorer. That's why I left the Academy. The shipwreck

haunted me. Better to follow my father into farming." He took a long
sip of his coconut water. "I remember a few things. What do you
want to know?"

"Where had Paul Mirkopoulous heard about King Triton's Lair?
How did he get interested in coming here?"

"It wasn't Paul. It was your father. I don't remember why they
put Paul's name on the expedition, but it was Alex's show all the
way." Zander and M.K. and I exchanged glances around the table.
"Your father was the one who wanted to see if he could find the
shipwrecks at King Triton's Lair."

"What happened? Mr. Wooley said a storm came up and the
ship sank."

"Children growing up in this part of the Caribbean are told in
the cradle not to go near King Triton's Lair," Coleman said grimly.
"When I was a young man, I heard stories about what happened to
sailors who strayed too close. Your father convinced me to go along
on the expedition. I don't know why I agreed. Pride, I suppose.
I didn't want them to think I was a coward. But now I wouldn't go
near it for all the Ribby Fruit in the world. We sailed out for a day or
so. Your dad and Paul had some coordinates they'd found and we set
a course. But before we got very close, we ran into a terrible storm."

Coleman described almost the exact series of events that Mr.
Wooley had, right down to being rescued by the fishing boat.

"It's a miracle your father survived. He didn't say much about
what had happened during his time on that raft, but it must have been
awful. I've known a few fishermen who survived shipwrecks, who spent

time on pieces of their boats at sea. They never get over it. The sharks. And there are stories about other, more terrible things. . . I don't know why you want to go there. I don't know why they'd let you."

"So you really don't think there's oil out there?"

"There may be oil. But whether you can get to it without killing yourselves is a different question."

He took a deep breath and pasted a smile on his face. "Now, let's talk about something happier. Have you ever tasted Ribby Fruit cake? No? Well, you are in for a treat."

Twenty-four

"Look at her. She's a beauty!" M.K. squealed.

Zander whistled. "She sure is. Wow."

We all stared up at the catamaran's huge mast, the mainsail a mosaic of colored sailcloth forming the image of a mermaid staring with placid confidence out to sea. The boat's two broad hulls were made of gleaming dark mahogany, each big enough to contain berths and common space for an even bigger crew than ours. The St. Beatrice boatbuilders were renowned for their expert craftsmanship. Based on traditional multihulled boats, catamarans were faster and more stable than single-hulled vessels. The Beatrician fishermen and seal hunters used them to sail out into the deep waters of the northern Caribbean, precisely where we'd be heading in a couple of days.

Bright red letters painted on the front of the hull spelled out her name: the *Fair Beatrice*. There was a large covered cockpit at the center of the bridge and painted wood mermaid figureheads mounted on each of the hulls.

"*Beauty!*" Pucci squawked. "*She's a beauty!*"

Jack greeted us on deck. He wore bright white pants and a white jacket, a green silk scarf tied around his neck.

"I wouldn't wear that getup if I were you, Jack," M.K. said. "Someone might accidentally spill engine grease on you." He stepped back, a protective hand over the front of his shirt.

Joyce, wearing her navy canvas sailing jacket, Njamba perched on her shoulder, laughed. "Come on," she said. "I'll give you a tour."

Everything was shining and new belowdecks, a roomy galley for cooking meals and three berths in each hull.

"This is more than a fishing boat," Coleman said, running a hand across the gleaming surface of the mahogany chart table. The top lifted to reveal a deep compartment for the charts we'd use to plot our course. "I've seen a lot of boats, but this is something else. Where'd you find this lovely lady?"

"She belongs to a generous BNDL official," Lazlo Nackley said, coming out from one of the berths. "He only agreed to loan her to the expedition when he heard that I was in charge."

I thought about how much Sukey would have liked the *Fair Beatrice*. She was a pilot, after all, and even though she wasn't a glider or a plane, the boat would have been right up Sukey's alley.

Coleman inspected her carefully. "She looks sound enough," he said. But his forehead was creased with worry as he looked around.

Joyce showed us the stern hatch through which you could climb back up on deck, then led us up the companionway back to the cockpit. Mr. Wooley sat in a chair on deck. He still looked ill, his face pale, his hands shaking.

"Can't believe they convinced you to sign on again, Cam," Coleman said. "I wouldn't have thought you'd want to go out there for anything."

"Let's just say . . . it wasn't my first choice, but I am an instructor at the Academy for the Exploratory Sciences and I'm willing to do my duty." He sounded like someone was holding a gun to his back, forcing him to say the words.

Leo Nackley smiled.

Coleman raised his eyebrows. "There's got to be more to that story, but I won't squeeze it out of you. Good luck with your work today." He told Zander, M.K., and me that he'd pick us up at the end of the day.

We spent the morning loading provisions onto the *Fair Beatrice* while Lazlo sat on deck and directed us. With the help of some fishermen Mr. Wooley had hired for the job, M.K. installed stern davits, metal arms usually used to hold and lower lifeboats, on the back of the boat, and secured Amy for the voyage. When we were ready, we could easily lower her into the water. While the rest of us stacked rice and dried pasta and salted meat and barrels of water into the hold, she tinkered with the submersible, making sure she was ready. Once the provisions were loaded, we helped to get the rest of the equipment on board, stowing the drills and pumps and containers Lazlo had brought to take oil samples back for BNDL.

While Joyce continued inspecting the boat, Zander and I offered to get lunch for everyone. We slowed our pace as we walked along the harbor, enjoying being away from Lazlo and feeling the sun on our faces. Pucci and Njamba flew above us along the quays, surprising the gulls looking for fish scraps by dive-bombing them and knocking them into the water.

"I thought Lazlo was going to throw Joyce overboard," Zander said, smiling. "But she knows how to handle him. I'm glad she's along."

"Me too."

We walked in silence for a little while, watching the two birds harass the poor unsuspecting gulls. "What are we going to do once we're out there, anyway?" Zander said. "Do you think there's any way we can look for the shipwrecks with Lazlo obsessed with finding the oil?"

I thought about the Explorer with the Clockwork Hand. "We'll have to find a way," I told him. "I've been thinking about it, and Lazlo is our only problem. Jack doesn't really care and I think Mr. Wooley will be willing to look the other way."

"So what? We'll get into Amy and just escape? How long did M.K. say she could stay underwater?"

"I think she said four hours."

"And then what?" He frowned. "Do you really think Lazlo is going to just let us get back on the boat after we abandon his expedition?"

"You're right," I said. "We'll have to do it at night, without him knowing. Maybe we can do it when Joyce is on watch. I don't think she'd give us up."

"I don't think she would either, but it just seems risky, Kit."

"It's the whole reason we're here," I said. "We have to find whatever it is that Dad wants us to find in the shipwrecks. It's something big. Something important. The Explorer said that everything could depend on us finding the shipwrecks. If you had talked to him, you'd know what I mean."

Zander stopped. "But I didn't talk to him, did I? No one but you has ever met this guy or even seen him."

We stared at each other. Pucci swooped down and landed on Zander's shoulder for a moment, then flapped after Njamba again, cackling loudly.

"You think I'm making it up?" I asked.

"No, of course not. I just don't see how we're going to pull this off."

If I was being honest, I didn't either, but I didn't say anything. We continued down along the harbor, which was ringed with palm trees and brightly painted shops and warehouses. We listened to the fishermen sing sea chanteys about whale hunts and mermaids beneath the sea. Dad had loved sea chanteys and Zander and I stopped to listen to the hearty voices singing in unison as the men scrubbed and painted their boats and repaired their nets.

'Twas Friday morn when we set sail
And we had not got far from land

When the captain he spied a lovely mermaid
With a comb and a glass in her hand

Oh, the ocean waves may roll
And the stormy winds may blow
While we poor sailors go skipping aloft
And the landlubbers lay down below, below, below
And the landlubbers lay down below

"You the boys going out to King Triton's Lair?"

We jumped.

An elderly man was sitting outside one of the little shacks by the harbor, working away on a big fishing net made from small sticks and rope. "You the boys?" he asked again.

He was very old, his skin wrinkled and folded like old cloth. His eyes were watery and unfocused as he looked up at us.

"We're on an expedition from the Academy for the Exploratory Sciences," I said.

"Idiots," he replied.

Zander and I glanced at each other. "What do you know about King Triton's Lair?" I said.

"I know a lot." He snorted and went back to his fishing nets. "Why do you want to go there?"

I decided we didn't have anything to lose by being halfway honest with him. "We're hoping we can find the shipwrecks and maybe the oil," I told him.

"That's why I wanted to go, too," he said. "And I almost died. The storm came out of nowhere. I barely knew it had started to blow before the ship went under. My cousin who was with me that day, he died in the sea."

I took out a map of St. Beatrice and the surrounding ocean that I'd scrawled on a scrap of paper. "Where was your boat when you sank?" I asked him. "Can you show me?"

He looked up at me again and pointed to a place on the map and I marked it down. I could figure out the coordinates later, but it looked to be near to the location of King Triton's Lair on Dad's map.

I thanked him.

At first I thought he wasn't going to say anything else, but as we started to walk away, he muttered, "You won't find the oil. It's just a story. But King Triton's Lair is out there, the weather is out there. There is a song that the fishermen sing that goes:

Don't go down below, boys
Don't go down below
For if you go with Triton
You'll never come up no more

I turned back and met his eyes. "If you try to go there, you are as stupid as all the rest." He was finished. He resumed his work on the net.

Zander and I were silent as we approached a little stall selling fried fish and Ribby Fruit cake. We bought enough for everyone and brought it back to the *Fair Beatrice*.

Coleman met us at the end of the day, and after we'd said goodbye to the others, we told him and M.K. about our conversation with the old man.

"That's Papa Madigan who you met. And he's right, you know," Coleman said. "I've been thinking about it all day, and this is crazy. I don't know why the Academy is letting you do this. I don't know why Leo Nackley is letting his son risk his neck. And I don't know why I'm helping you. I agreed to Raleigh's request to have you stay with me because of your father, but if something happens to you, I'll never forgive myself." Suddenly, he looked over his shoulder and said, "Quick, follow me."

He steered us into an alley. We followed his lead and pressed ourselves against the wall. Coleman looked out, but no one walked by. "Okay," he said. "This way." We ran down to the end of the alley, took a quick left onto a busy street, and then ducked into another alley. "Out here and . . ." he stopped and looked back down the alley. "Okay, I think we lost him."

"Lost who?" I turned around but didn't see anyone.

"The man who was following us," Coleman said. "I think he followed us the day you arrived too, but I can't be sure."

"But who is he?"

"A BNDL agent, a spy—who knows?"

"What kind of spy?" Zander said.

"St. Beatrice is full of spies," Coleman answered. "Indorustans, government spies. Pirates who want to know the details of Ribby Fruit shipments so they can seize them. Could be anyone. It could be me they're following, but I think someone is interested enough in your expedition to be following you. I'll say it again: I think you're crazy. Why did they put you on Lazlo's expedition, anyway? He doesn't trust you. It doesn't make any sense."

"Why would they follow *you*?" Coleman was just a farmer. A fairly successful farmer who had spent two years at the Academy for the Exploratory Sciences, but still.

"I am involved in certain political activities that make me a target," Coleman said. "There are good people on this island who don't like the things being done in their name." Something about his face stopped me from asking any other questions.

We walked the rest of the way in silence.

We spent the next two days working on the boat and getting ready to go. The night before our departure, Coleman told us to be home early for dinner because he had a surprise for us.

"I bet it's another Ribby Fruit cake," M.K. said as we made our way through the bustling marketplace. "I love how it's all crisp on the outside and then the fruit stays kind of gooey, like jam. Mmmm."

"Maybe he'll send some Ribby Fruit cakes with us for the expedition," Zander said. "After seeing all that salt cod and rice in the hold today, I'm starting to think we shouldn't ever leave Coleman's."

We found him in the kitchen back at his house.

"Now for my surprise," Coleman said, smiling mischeviously.

"I'm actually quite amazed that we managed to pull it together. But . . . well, you'll see. Follow me."

We didn't so much follow him out to the terrace as push and run past him when we saw the lone figure standing at the far end of the railing, looking out over the water.

She turned around.

"You didn't think I was going to let you have all the fun while I rotted away with the Snow Deer, did you?" Sukey grinned and wrapped M.K. in a huge hug. "You guys think Lazlo will let me tag along?"

Twenty-five

"We only heard five days ago," she explained, once we were sitting at Coleman's big dining room table eating the fish he'd grilled out on the terrace. "We were sitting in Reykjavik, waiting to go get the gliders, when we heard that a volcano along our route was erupting and sending all this ash into the sky. They decided it was too dangerous to go ahead, so they assigned the rest of us to other expeditions. I got Delilah to pull a few strings with Maggie so I could be on this one. I caught a ride on a cargo airship."

I'd forgotten how her eyes crinkled up at the edges when she smiled. "I just can't believe you're here," I said.

She grinned. "Me either."

We sat down to dinner and updated her on everything we'd learned.

"I'm with Papa Madigan," Coleman told her. "I think it's crazy, but I know you Explorers. You won't listen to anyone. It's dangerous out there. There's the weather and then there are the pirates."

"I'm not worried about pirates," Zander said. "You said all they want is Ribby Fruit."

"If they've heard that you're going looking for something that's worth money, they may decide it's worthwhile to follow along, just in case. There have been rumors about the government wanting to find oil out here. The pirates would like to find it first and charge the government a nice price to get it out."

"How would they get to the shipwrecks or the oil anyway?" Sukey asked Coleman. "They don't have diving equipment. They don't have M.K."

"They have their ways. Those Neos—" He smiled at Sukey. "They may have technology we don't know about." He leaned back in his chair and said, "Do you know what else the fishermen down at the harbor say about the ships that disappeared in King Triton's Lair?"

We watched Coleman's face for the answer.

"They say that they were snatched from the sea and taken up into the sky by The Others. That anyone seeking the ships won't find them because they're no longer . . ." Coleman put his hands together and leaned forward, widening his eyes and lowering his voice. "On Earth."

"What, like extraterrestrials?" I asked. "That's ridiculous."

"Perhaps."

"Maybe the extraterrestrials will take the Nackleys away," M.K. said. "That would be nice."

I laughed. "Coleman, why did Leo Nackley hate Dad so much?" I asked him.

"Leo always wanted to be the best at everything. The problem was, your dad was always the best. He was the first at everything he tried. Leo hated him for that. But . . ." He hesitated.

"But what?"

"Well, there was always something mysterious about your dad. He would disappear at night sometimes, though he only got caught slipping back into the boys' cabins once that I can remember. He was good." He smiled. "I think he was meeting his girlfriend. I considered your father a great friend, but he did like his secrets. I think it drove Leo crazy that he could never figure out what your dad was up to. They were friends once too, but then . . . I never understood it, but then one day they were enemies."

We were all quiet. We could hear the water lap at the shore below us through the open terrace doors.

Pucci had been drowsing out in the evening air and suddenly he squawked. *"Someone there! Someone there!"* We rushed out on to the terrace just in time to see a black-suited figure vaulting over the edge of the balcony.

"Stop right there!" Coleman called out, but the figure was gone.

"Who was that?" Sukey asked.

"Who knows," Coleman said. "A spy, an agent, a pirate. Whoever it was, he was standing right here listening to us. But let's not talk about such things on your last night. Who wants some more Ribby Fruit cake?"

"You don't really believe any of that stuff Coleman was saying about extraterrestrials, do you?" Sukey asked me later that night. M.K. was inside watching Coleman and Zander play chess. I'd come out to look at the night sky and Sukey had followed me, bringing one of Coleman's little carved shell whistles with her. As she tried playing a melody, the notes skipped across the water, which reflected a sky full of stars. There was a nearly full moon, and its image broke apart in the water and danced across the waves. I felt happier than I had felt in a long time.

"No," I said. "Of course not. I don't know what's out there, but I'm pretty sure it isn't extraterrestrials. What I am sure of is that my dad wanted us to come here."

"So he can leave you another map?" Sukey asked.

"Maybe."

She played a quick little "What Will We Do With the Drunken Sailor" on the whistle.

"You're good at that," I said. "I had no idea you were so musical."

"Delilah made me take Deloian flute lessons when I was ten. I didn't practice enough, but I wasn't bad. I can still pick out a tune or two."

She played a few more little songs I didn't recognize, and then we just stood there in comfortable silence, looking out over the water.

"I don't think Zander understands," I said after a few minutes.

"We have to do it. We just have to. It's going to be really hard with Lazlo watching our every move, but we need to do everything we can. At least we'll be rid of his father."

The side of Sukey's face shone in the candlelight through the windows and I watched her profile, the now-familiar shape of her nose and cheekbones, the curve of her neck. "I never met your dad, Kit, but there must be a reason he's doing this, that he's leading you to whatever it is," she said.

"I wish he'd told us what it is."

"No, I mean *you*, Kit," she said softly. "I think he's trying to lead *you* somewhere."

I started to tell her about what the Explorer had said, but for some reason I stopped. I watched her fingers drum out a little rhythm on the railing, and remembered what it had felt like to hold her hand, that cold night in Arizona.

Without really thinking about it, I reached out for her. But she was already stepping away from the railing, and I was left standing there with my hand out as though I was waiting for someone to walk up and shake it. Sukey yawned. "We have to be up early," she said. "I'm going to bed."

"Okay, goodnight."

I stood there for a long time after she left, listening to the tiny splashes of fish jumping out in the silvery ocean, the words I hadn't said stuffed uncomfortably in my mouth.

After I confronted Captain Girafalco about the real purpose of our expedition, he explained that we would be traveling to a strange region of the Caribbean where many ships had sunk and where sailors had long reported seeing sea monsters and mermaids. He told me that we would be investigating the strange phenomena reported there. "As you deduced," he said, "it is my theory that the unusual conditions reported in the area may indicate that it is the site of a deep ocean trench. These trenches may represent points of entry to the very interiors of the earth, and I mean to explore them."

Twenty-six

By noon the next day, we were ready to go. Coleman said he'd see us off down at the harbor. The mood was tense and silent as we passed the marketplace. I looked behind me and caught sight of a black-suited agent following us at a distance. I nodded toward him and Coleman frowned.

"I wish you weren't going. If anything happens to you . . ." Coleman said.

"We'll be fine," I said. "We've planned well. We have an excellent boat, Joyce is about the best captain we could ask for, and we're not going to do anything stupid. If it even starts to get rough, I'm sure we'll head for safer waters. Mr. Wooley won't let us get hurt."

"I know, I know." But he still looked worried.

We had almost passed the market when an old woman, walking the opposite direction and carrying a basket of Ribby Fruit on her head, knocked into me, hard. Both of us fell to the ground, and as I reached out to help her up, she grasped my forearm and leaned in, whispering, "Saylor's Spice Stall. North end of the market. Now."

Then she smiled apologetically, collected her Ribby Fruit, and went on her way.

"You okay, Kit?" Coleman asked.

"Yes, fine," I said. "But I just thought of something I have to get from the market. I'll meet you at the boat."

"What is it?" Coleman looked confused.

Zander and M.K. were up ahead, but Sukey was standing next to me and I whispered in her ear, "The Explorer. He wants to see me. Now. I'll be there as soon as I can."

Bewildered, she nodded, then mouthed, "Be careful."

I took off through the nearest alleyway. I was pretty sure that I could get to the market through one of the small alleys that ran behind the big houses lining the street. I ducked through, then stopped, pressing myself to the wall, to see if the agent was still following me.

It took a couple of minutes, but sure enough, two black-suited agents came slowly past my hiding place. I pressed myself into the wall and prayed they didn't come down the alley. I counted to sixty before peeling myself away from the wall and running further along. I turned right, then left, following the sounds of the voices, and pretty soon I was in the marketplace. People crowded around me, laughing and talking and singing. I could smell rotting fruit and spices and flowers from the stalls. I went along as quickly as I could in the thick mass of people, looking for Saylor's Spices, and finally found it next to a fruit stand at the far end of the row of stalls. I assumed the Explorer would meet me there, so I pretended to browse the packets of red and golden powders stacked along the table and was surprised when the scarf-wrapped old woman standing behind the counter lifted her eyes and said, in the Explorer's voice, "They followed you. We don't have much time."

"I know," I said, barely moving my lips as I looked at the spices, mother-of-pearl whistles, and little trinkets on the table.

"I wanted to tell you good luck," he mumbled, adjusting the scarves wrapped around his head and busying himself straightening up the piles of spices and things while I pretended to consider the little packets. "Are you ready? Do you think you can do it? Do you think you can get away?"

"I don't know. Lazlo will be the problem, but with the four of us, I think we can figure something out."

"I heard a rumor that they've got someone inside the expedition, to keep an eye on you and your brother and sister. Lately, I've been wondering about . . . well, watch Kemal Asker carefully. And BNDL may not be content with a spy. They may send someone to follow you."

"Kemal?" He nodded. I searched the market for agents, and then I met his eyes. They were pale, blue, watchful. "I'm worried," I said. "Everyone keeps saying how dangerous it is."

"I guess we just have to have faith. In your father. That reminds me. Here's something for you to take with you. A good luck charm,

I guess. Don't lose it. It was Alex's. He asked me to give it to you. If you got this far." He took a beautiful mother-of-pearl whistle, carved into the shape of a sea turtle, down from a nail on the wall. I felt the cold metal of his clockwork hand as he handed it over. I could hear it click and whir faintly as it moved. The whistle was bigger and more beautiful than the ones I'd seen at Coleman's. I hung it around my neck and tucked it beneath my shirt. He looked up quickly. "There they are. Get down to the boat. Now. This is goodbye for a little while, I think." He pulled the scarf up over his face and turned away. "Go. Good luck."

On my way back to the water, I took the whistle out and held it, rubbing my thumb over the carved designs, feeling the cool smoothness of the ocean. It felt heavier than the ones at Coleman's house and the surface was soft and dense, like soap. I tried it out, blowing a single, clear note as I went.

I reached the harbor to find everyone standing around on the dock. "Sorry," I panted. "She spilled Ribby Fruit juice all over me and I had to go clean up."

I scanned the group, confused. "Where's Mr. Wooley?"

M.K. hoisted her backpack onto one shoulder and met my eyes. "He isn't coming. He's too sick, and he said it wouldn't be safe for him to be in charge when he can't stand to be up on deck."

I turned to Sukey. She just nodded, looking grim.

"It's true," Zander said.

"So who's coming with us? Who's our chaperone? They wouldn't let us go alone, would they?" I felt panic wash over me.

We'd come all this way. We were ready to go. And now they were going to cancel the expedition because Mr. Wooley couldn't keep his lunch down.

There was a long silence. Suddenly, I knew the terrible answer.

Leo Nackley, wearing a white linen suit, a black scarf tied jauntily around his neck, was standing on the quay, ordering around a group of fishermen who had been hired to help get the last of our gear loaded. In the bright tropical sun, his black hair shone, his mustache gleaming like obsidian. When he heard my voice, he turned around and gave me a triumphant grin.

"I was so sorry to hear about Mr. Wooley's difficulties," he said. "But I was more than happy to step up to the plate. After all, it is my duty as an Explorer of the Realm to help the new generation of Explorers seek out their own discoveries." He rubbed his hands together and put an arm around Lazlo. "Aren't we all going to have fun?"

Twenty-seven

'Twas Friday morn when we set sail
And we had not got far from land
When the captain he spied a lovely mermaid
With a comb and a glass in her hand

Oh, the ocean waves may roll
And the stormy winds may blow
While we poor sailors go skipping aloft
And the landlubbers lay down below, below, below
And the landlubbers lay down below

"Is he ever going to stop?" Zander whispered. "I think he has the worst voice in the world."

"Not as bad as Lazlo's," I whispered back. We were checking lines for Joyce on deck, listening to Jack and Lazlo singing sea chanteys in the cockpit. Even Leo Nackley looked a little annoyed.

"Oh God," Sukey groaned. "They're starting on 'Spanish Ladies.' They're gonna ruin it for me forever."

"Well, this is Jack we're talking about, isn't it? Anything with ladies in it and he'll be singing for hours." I checked to make sure no one was nearby before saying, "This is a disaster. There's no way we're going to be able to slip away with him on board."

"Maybe I can knock him out or something." M.K. grinned.

"No!" Zander, Sukey and I all hissed at the same time. "No knocking people out."

"What if we do it at night? When everyone's sleeping?"

"Kit, they'll hear us lowering Amy into the water," Zander said dubiously.

"Maybe not," M.K. said. "The way I have her attached to the davits is pretty neat. We just have to loosen the ropes and ease her in slowly. We might be able to do it. I tried it when we were in port and it's possible with two of us. And even if they do hear something, we'd be gone before they were up on deck."

"Okay," I told them, thinking out loud. "We may not be able to talk again, so we need a code word. How about *Coleman*? When we think we're close enough, say something about *Coleman* and that will be a sign that we should meet out here at 2 a.m. They should all be soundly asleep by then."

"Except for Joyce, who will be on watch," Zander reminded me.

I'd forgotten Joyce had offered to take overnight watch duty. "Amy's off the stern. The cockpit is on the bridge. If she's looking toward the bow and we do it quickly, we should be okay."

"You guys, this is crazy." Sukey dropped a coil of rope onto the deck with a loud thump. "If we get caught trying to escape, with *him* on board, do you know what will happen to us? I kind of like it at the Academy, even if you don't, Kit."

"We don't have any choice," I told her firmly. "If we wait until we reach the place where King Triton's Lair is supposed to be, there's no way Lazlo will let us go down in Amy by ourselves. And then it's all over."

"Where are you keeping the maps?" Zander asked me suddenly.

"Where do you think?"

"What if he searches you?"

"What choice do I have? He might find them. He might not. That collar pocket is pretty safe. But this is why we have to get away as soon as we can."

"Okay," Zander said. "We'll look for an opportunity."

"I'll check Amy out," M.K. said, "and make sure she's ready."

We all looked at Sukey. "Okay," she said finally.

"Oh, and keep an eye on Kemal," I told them as we finished with the lines. "The Explorer thinks he might be spying for BNDL."

"Are you kidding me?" Sukey asked, an edge to her voice. "Kemal of all people? Do you know what they put him through, Kit?"

"Maybe they offered him a deal. Anyway, he *is* Indorustan. I don't trust him."

Sukey scowled at me. "Well there are people who would say I shouldn't be trusted because I'm a Neo."

I met her eyes. "I'm not one of them."

We stared at each other before she said, "Fine, we'll keep an eye on him. I'm going to see how it's going in the cockpit."

There was good wind all day and we made good time, heading east toward Ruby Island, where we'd decided to drop anchor for the

216

night. It was brilliantly sunny, and in spite of myself, I started to relax, enjoying the wind on my face as the *Fair Beatrice* skimmed across the waves. It was completely different from being aboard the huge bulk of the *Deloian Princess*. The sea wasn't the brilliant turquoise it had been in the shallow waters close to St. Beatrice, but a deeper, darker sapphire. Dolphins leapt beside the boat and gulls and terns dove and raced across the sky. Pucci and Njamba tormented them, swooping crazily. We could hear Pucci cackling evilly high above us.

Joyce adjusted the mainsail and she laughed as the wind ran into it, bowing it out with a wonderful rippling sound. "We're running now! Isn't it a beautiful day?" She had tied a blue-and-white bandanna over her head and another around her neck and she looked happier than I'd ever seen her.

"You look just like a sailor!" Zander tipped his head back, watching her with a huge smile on his face.

"That's because I *am* a sailor, you landlubber!" she called back, laughing.

The sun had come up bright and strong, and the *Fair Beatrice* felt nimble and light as we skipped across the ocean.

Ruby Island came into view in the late afternoon and everyone came out on deck to watch as we approached. The seal-fishing boats were moored out in the little harbor and a line of shacks ran along the shoreline. Ruby Island had been claimed by BNDL not long after St. Beatrice was first explored. It had become economically important to the U.S. because of the large populations of monk seals that used it as their breeding grounds. The seal oil was used for lamps and some people loved the meat. We could see smoke rising from the chimneys of the rendering plants and the air was filled with a terrible odor.

"It's the seal fat," Jack said. "My mother used it in a lamp once. I remember that smell."

"Ugh, it's awful," M.K. said, wrinkling her nose. "Kind of like Zander's hiking boots."

We all laughed, but Zander didn't. "What's awful is what they do to the seals," he said quietly. "They wait until they're asleep, sunning themselves on the rocks, and then they kill them with spears or clubs. The seals are getting smart, so now they have to go out in boats and chase them. If they're not careful, they're going to kill every last one."

Leo Nackley was standing behind him and he snorted. "Don't be alarmist, Mr. West," he said. "Those things are like insects. They're everywhere. The U.S. and its allied nations need the oil and the meat. We have every right to take it."

"And when we kill them all, what will we do then?" Zander's voice was tight and angry.

"We'll find more," Leo Nackley said.

Zander started to say something, then thought better of it and went to stand alone at the stern. Sukey watched him go but left him alone.

Joyce gently touched me on the shoulder, breaking the tension. "Kit, can you come and look at some of these charts? I'm setting our course for tomorrow, but I have a question for you."

I followed her to the cockpit where she had her charts laid on the chart table. She had one, issued by BNDL, showing roughly the same part of the ocean as Dad's map.

"What's up?" I ran a finger over the dotted lines she'd drawn on the chart.

"You told me that we want to set a course for north-northeast from Ruby Island because we don't have the coordinates. That's what I've done, but when I look at those old maps you gave me, there's a huge range of locations given for the strange weather phenomena. Do you have anything more specific?"

I tried to keep my voice nonchalant. "No, not really. But I'm pretty confident that if we sail north-northeast we'll reach the part of the ocean where all this stuff happens."

"Kit," Joyce said seriously, her brown eyes meeting mine. "There's something strange going on here. Don't think you're putting anything over on me. Right from the beginning, this has been the strangest expedition I've ever been on. Lazlo doesn't know a thing about it. It's like he lifted someone else's proposal." I tried not to blush and she raised her eyebrows at my silence. "I get that there may be information you can't share with me, but you have to understand that we're all risking our lives out here. If you can't tell me why, at least tell me that it's for something more important than gold or oil." I didn't know what to say, but something made me trust her.

"Thanks, Joyce," I said. "I can't tell you why, but it *is* important. It *does* matter. I would tell you if I could."

"Okay," she said. "north-northeast it is."

But *was* it important, whatever it was we were going to find?

219

I didn't know. Dad had asked me to do it and the Explorer with the Clockwork Hand had said that it might be a matter of life and death, but I still didn't know why Dad had sent us on this crazy treasure hunt.

As I came out of the cockpit, I caught Kemal standing there. He'd been listening to me and Joyce. When he saw me, he bent down and pretended he was tying his shoe.

"Were you listening to us?" I said, keeping my voice down. "Were you spying on me?" I felt a strong urge to punch him.

He stood up. "I wasn't spying," he said. "I heard what Joyce said, though. She's right. We're risking our lives out here. I just want to know what for."

"For the glory of the country, Kemal, or didn't you know that?" I brushed past him, leaving him standing on deck.

Zander and Jack and M.K. fished off the stern as the sun reddened and sank below the horizon. They caught a dozen orange fish that Zander identified as striped roughies, and they were delicious when they came out of the galley kitchen fried up with a lemon sauce. Jack, who was on supper duty, received a sincere round of applause.

"You know what I always say," he said as he basked in our appreciation. "The surest way to a woman's heart is through her stomach." He grinned at Sukey, Joyce, and M.K., who just kept on eating their fish, ignoring him. "That's why I learned to cook so well."

"Give me seconds and I might agree with you," Sukey said as he jumped up to get her more fish.

I looked out across the water, gray now in the dusky light.

Tomorrow, if my calculations were correct, we'd have another day of sailing before reaching the approximate coordinates of King Triton's Liar.

If my calculations were correct. Joyce was right. The course I'd asked her to follow was vague. We could get lost. We could easily miss our target.

I hadn't been able to look at Dad's map since we'd been on the boat and I was suddenly seized by the feeling that I had to see it right now, that it might reveal something important. But it wasn't safe. There wasn't anywhere I would be alone.

"You okay, Kit?" Sukey asked.

"Fine." I took another bite of my fish. "Just thinking."

I took out the turtle whistle the Explorer had given me. I'd told the others that I'd bought it at the market. "It's a good-luck charm," I'd said, repeating the Explorer's words. Now I thought about them. Dad hadn't believed in good luck charms. *You make your own luck. You don't wait for it to come to you. You create luck by making connections. By putting things together. It only looks like luck on the other side.*

I finally realized what it was that had been bothering me about the whistle. Dad never would have given me something and called it a good-luck charm. The whistle must have some other purpose. But what? I blew a few notes, then held it in my hand, trying not to attract too much attention to it. When I tucked it away under my shirt it felt smooth and cool against my chest.

I went to check on Amy before going to bed. In the darkness, she seemed almost alive, her eight utility arms ready for action, her chrome head shining in the moonlight. "Good girl," I whispered, patting her drill arm. "We're almost ready to see what you can do."

I still had the sense that he was keeping something from me and I watched him carefully for any sign of what it might be. However, the only thing I noticed was that he spent a lot of time alone in his cabin and the few times I had entered the chamber, he had slammed down the cover of a red-bound book on his desk. It was a

Twenty-eight

We stayed out on deck in the sun most of the next day, watching the dolphins leap joyfully out of the water as they raced alongside us.

Leo Nackley seemed relaxed and happy, looking out over the water and even smiling at the sight of the dolphins. I overheard him tell his son that it was all but certain they'd find oil, and that they should start thinking about where they would have the party honoring Lazlo for his find.

Late in the afternoon, Joyce, Lazlo, and I spent some time going over the charts. At dinner Joyce announced that we'd be nearing our target by early the next morning.

"That's great. I'll make the first trip down in the submersible device," Lazlo said. "My father and Jack will come along and Miss West will pilot it. Any questions?"

Zander, Sukey, M.K., and I didn't need to look at each other to know we were all thinking the same thing: We'd need to make our move tonight. "Sounds good to me," I said. "Though I do wish we were back on St. Beatrice. I wonder what Coleman's doing right now?"

"I wonder too," Zander said. "Maybe he's already in bed."

"Oh, I don't know." I tried to keep my voice casual. "It will probably be hours before he goes to bed. He's such a night owl. He often stayed up until 2 a.m. when we were staying with him."

Lazlo and Kemal gave me strange looks.

I lay in my berth that night, listening to the sound of the waves lapping at the starboard hull next to my head, fighting to stay awake. I could hear Zander's even breathing below me and I wanted to say something, to make sure he didn't fall asleep, but I couldn't risk it with Jack and Kemal in the berths across the way. Finally, at ten minutes to two I slid out of my berth and hoisted myself up through the stern hatch. Joyce was on watch in the cockpit, so I couldn't use the companionway to get up on deck. I hoped the others would remember to use the hatch, too.

I crept carefully back toward the stern. When I turned around, I could see Joyce on watch in the cockpit. Her back was to me, and as long as we didn't make too much noise lowering Amy into the water, I thought we could get away without her knowing. The Nackleys would probably blame her for letting us escape, and I felt a pang of regret. I hoped she wouldn't get into too much trouble. I knew I was probably deluding myself, though.

The water was a little choppy and the wind had come up. The sails flapped and the masthead fly rippled noisily at the top of the mast. It was a strange wind. I couldn't tell what direction it was coming from and it seemed to keep reversing course. Because of the double hulls, the *Fair Beatrice* didn't rock the way a regular sailboat would in high wind. Instead it jerked back and forth with the waves. I could feel the water tug at us, the wind pulling the catamaran this way and that. In the cockpit, Joyce moved around, checking charts, using her binoculars to examine the water.

When I leaned over the stern, I could see Amy crouched below-decks in the moonlight.

We had to get her into the water.

I checked to make sure the lines secured to the stern davits were ready. I checked my watch: 2:05. *Come on, Zander. Come on, M.K. Come on, Sukey.* I checked the lines again.

"Planning a trip, Mr. West?"

I spun around. Leo Nackley leaned against the railing on the other side of the stern. He'd been waiting, watching me from the moment I'd come up on deck.

I froze, trying to think of a reason why I was awake.

"Do you have somewhere else to be?" he asked me.

"No, no. I was just checking on the submersible. I couldn't sleep. I thought I heard a crash and just wanted to make sure."

The *Fair Beatrice* rocked abruptly, the waves and wind pulling her one way and then the other, and I reached out to grab the railing.

"I don't believe you," he said. "I actually don't believe

anything you say. I think you're a liar." He stepped forward and the moonlight caught him full on the face. His eyes were narrowed and angry. I didn't say anything. I was pretty sure this was it. I'd been caught. He would get Dad's map, and I would be kicked out of the Academy—maybe worse. Any second now, the others were going to come up on to deck, and then they would be caught too. I felt terrible about Sukey. We had forced her into this, and now she'd pay the price for our mistake.

Suddenly, the boat tipped up on to one hull, throwing me back against the stern and knocking Leo Nackley off his feet. I could hear the main mast creaking, and then the other hull hit the water with a loud *slap*. Amy slammed against the stern and I heard a sickening screech of metal on wood. Nackley hauled himself up. "You know," he said. "I was talking to someone at the Newly Discovered Lands Museum recently. He was very suspicious about that gold Lazlo found in Arizona. He said it didn't have enough—what was it? *Sediment*. For gold that had been sitting in a cave for hundreds of years, there wasn't enough sediment. He said that he thought the gold had been moved."

"Really? That's odd." The boat had really started moving now, jerking to and fro on the waves. I grabbed the deck railing to steady myself as I was almost knocked off my feet again.

"It is odd. What's also *odd* is that your brother proposed an expedition to the exact place that your father visited on his expedition when he was a student. I remember that expedition. He almost got the whole team killed. He disappeared for nearly a week. And when he came home, everyone talked about what a hero he was."

He took a step toward me. "I think you have a map that shows the exact location of the oil. I think you wanted to find it and keep it all for yourself so you and your brother and sister would get the credit—and the money. Just the way your father and his friends in his secret Mapmakers' Guild wanted to keep everything to themselves. Now you're going to give it to me."

He lurched forward, his hands out in front of him.

I looked around desperately. I could see Joyce in the cockpit. She still had her back to us, but if I yelled she might hear, even over the wind. But what could Joyce do? If Leo Nackley wanted my map, he was going to get it.

"I don't have anything," I said lamely. "I swear."

"Oh, come on." He was almost at my throat. There was nowhere to go but into the water.

"Kit!"

Zander, Sukey, and M.K. came up on deck just as Leo Nackley reached me, taking me by the arms and slamming me against the railing.

"What's going on?" Zander asked, Pucci clucking at his shoulder. "What are you doing, Mr. Nackley?" He strode over, ready for a fight. I'd never been so glad to see him in my life.

"Zander," I said quietly, my eyes on Leo Nackley as he squeezed my arms even tighter. "He thinks I have some map of Dad's or something. I don't know what he's talking about."

"Oh, for godssake, hand it over!" Leo Nackley shouted, spinning me around and grabbing my vest.

Just then the *Fair Beatrice* tossed onto one hull and righted herself again, throwing Zander and Leo Nackley off their feet. Nackley sprawled on the ground, swearing and furious.

I reached down and helped Zander up.

"What was that?" he asked.

"Hey!" we heard Joyce shout. "All hands on deck! Now! There's something really strange up ahead!"

Leo Nackley gave me a final poisonous look and then made his way up toward the bow. Joyce was using her binoculars to look into the moonlit darkness. I hung on to the railing, pulling myself hand over hand up to the bow.

Joyce scanned the horizon. "There's something up ahead." Her voice was tight and scared.

"Is it a storm?" Lazlo and Jack and Kemal had rushed up on deck, and Lazlo grabbed the binoculars, peering through them at the horizon ahead.

I got my spyglass out of my vest and focused it on the sky. "I don't think so," I said. The sky looked clear, but when I tipped the glass down, the ocean was disturbed, the surface boiling and churning like soup in a pot.

"It's coming from underneath," I said. "This is what everyone's talked about. It's like it's some kind of gas, coming up from the bottom of the ocean. Look at that."

"It must be the oil." Lazlo grabbed the binoculars. "It has to be the oil. We've found it!"

"That's my boy," Leo Nackley shouted. "We've done it!"

"Have you ever seen anything like that?" I asked Joyce.

"My father told me about something like this on the Bosphorus once," Kemal said behind me. "It was some strange phenomenon where sturgeon were feeding in huge numbers because of the full moon. Any chance it's a large school of fish, some kind of sea life?"

Joyce held up the binoculars again and looked. "It's too dark to see. I can't make out anything but water," she said. "You're right, though. It's bubbling, like there's a storm. But I can't see a storm. We'll have to get closer."

"It's King Triton's Lair," I whispered.

This was it. Dad had led us here. Maybe now we'd figure out why.

"Get the sub ready," Lazlo called out.

"I don't know," M.K. said. "Are you sure? I don't like the looks of this. I haven't tested Amy in these kinds of conditions. Shouldn't we wait until it's light?"

The boat spun again, knocking M.K. against the railing.

"Do it," Leo Nackley said. "Let her down."

M.K. and I looked at each other. The wind was whipping her hair across her face.

"Mr. Nackley," Zander said. "M.K. says it's too dangerous. She built the submersible. She knows what it can handle."

Lazlo pushed him aside.

"Don't tell my father what to do, Zander West. This might be it. If an oil discharge is causing the turbulence, then we can't miss this opportunity. I'm the leader of this expedition. You have to do as I say. Now, is it ready? Will we be able to see anything?"

"The solar cells are all charged up. She'll have lights for three hours at least," M.K. said. "But—"

"It's why we're here," Lazlo said coldly. "We've got a ship that can handle it and it's what the submersible was engineered for. I'm the expedition leader. The decision is mine. I don't think you want to fight me on this, do you?"

"Okay," M.K. said. "You're in charge, Lazlo."

"All right," Lazlo called out. "Everyone to their posts. Sukey and Kit, you're navigating. Joyce, you have the ship. M.K., you and Zander and Kemal get that thing ready for submersion."

We were moving quickly now, the high wind suddenly filling the sails.

"We've got to get out of this storm," Joyce called out. "Lazlo, Jack, ease out the mainsail sheet! Now!"

But Lazlo just stood there, frozen in place.

"For godssake!" Joyce came out of the cockpit, yelling to Sukey to take the wheel.

"I'll help him," Zander shouted. "Lazlo, ease it out!"

"There's too much wind behind us!" I shouted, seeing how the unfurling sail was driving us straight into the worst of the bubbling water.

"We don't have any choice!" Joyce shouted back. "Zander, do it!"

Now the wind was up all around us, so loud we could barely hear each other. Between the wind and the lurching, it was becoming harder and harder to stand. Sukey was trying to reach us by crawling on all fours along the deck, hanging on to the railing.

"What are you doing?" Lazlo screamed. "Get the submersible ready!"

"He's right," Leo Nackley screamed up at Joyce and Zander. "Get down here and help him!"

The boat lurched violently again. I could see the water swirling, and it did indeed feel like a huge whirlpool was sucking us down from below.

"We have to turn away!" Kemal shouted. "This isn't safe!"

"I'm trying!" Joyce called.

Lazlo ignored him. "Get the submersible out!" he shouted. "We've got to see what's going on under there!"

I exchanged a glance with Sukey. This might be our only chance. If we had reached King Triton's Lair, then we needed to act fast. But how were we going to look for the shipwrecks without Lazlo knowing what we were doing? If only we could get him to stay behind on the ship.

Zander must have had the same thought. "Lazlo, don't you think you should stay on board? You're the expedition leader, after all."

"No way. If we find oil, I'm going to be there," he shouted back.

The boat gave another shuddering lurch and he was knocked off his feet as we heard M.K. screaming, "We're going to lose Amy! Someone help me untie these ropes. We've got to get her up on deck. Someone help me!" She yelled a string of not very polite words.

"Is that rain or just mist?" Kemal called out.

"I don't think it's raining," I shouted back. "But it's awfully windy. And I can't see anything. There's some kind of fog."

The air had suddenly become so foggy that even with the

moonlight and the light from my vest, I couldn't see more than a few feet in front of me. I could hear Joyce shouting from up near the cockpit, but I couldn't see a thing.

Sukey and I clung to the railing. The boat spun around and around and M.K. and Lazlo struggled with the ropes keeping Amy secured.

"We're going to lose her," M.K. shouted.

"We've got to help them," I told Sukey. She held on to me as we tried to get back to the stern.

From somewhere out of the mist, we heard Joyce's voice.

"Everyone, put on your life vests," Joyce shouted. "Head for the lifeboats. We may need to abandon ship."

"No!" Lazlo yelled at her. "We're not abandoning ship!"

"Lazlo's in charge!" Leo Nackley screamed.

And suddenly, we were tipping up on the starboard hull. I reached for my life vest, but it slid away and washed overboard. Another huge wave washed over us all and the boat rolled nearly onto her side before righting herself again.

But the water just kept coming over the railings and we just kept spinning.

"She's breaking apart," Zander yelled.

Time slowed as the boat twirled and spun. I could hear yelling, M.K.'s voice and Zander's screaming orders and Leo Nackley yelling something about the main mast.

Then I heard a crack. When I looked up to see where it had come from, I could just barely see the sky, obscured by the blanketing veil

of mist. Through the strange grayness, the main mast was falling; it
had snapped in two and half of it was crashing down onto the deck.
I heard it fall behind me and then the boat was splitting in two, half
the deck attached to one hull, the other half to the other. The sea was
next to me, the surface of the water rising up like a huge opening
mouth. I heard Pucci and Njamba shrieking overhead. Then there
was another crack and I felt a sharp pain in my head.

The wind blew.

The ocean rose up.

I was in the water.

It felt like needles on my back and limbs. My head throbbed
and my arms and legs didn't seem to be working the way they were
supposed to. Everything was happening very slowly. My Explorer's
vest filled with air.

I thrashed my arms and legs, trying to swim; my vest was
tugging me toward the surface of the water and keeping me afloat,
but something strong was pulling me down. I reached for Dad's
whistle around my neck and blew as hard as I could, trying to attract
someone's attention. I reached down and felt a rope around my right
foot. I tried to slip it off, but it was taut, the water too dark for me
to see what was on the other end. Then Sukey was there, pointing to
my feet. I tried to tell her that I knew, but I couldn't get it off, and
I flapped my arms uselessly and just kept sinking under the surface.

This was it, I told myself. I felt sorry that I hadn't done what
Dad had wanted me to do. I felt sorry that I'd put everyone else in
danger. I was sorry I was going to die. And then I didn't care about

anything. I needed oxygen and I felt that my chest was going to burst if I didn't open my mouth.

I sunk down, the desperate urge to breathe leaving me, replaced by a sense of peace.

And then things got weirder. I saw a strange glow in the water, a yellow light, like a huge eye blinking at me, warming me, keeping me safe.

I could feel myself sinking through the water and then a voice in my head told me to let go, that everything was going to be okay.

I stopped struggling.

I saw Sukey up ahead. I reached out for her, but she was too far away and something was keeping her from me, as though a pane of glass was between us in the water.

But it was okay. The eye loomed in front of me. I felt peaceful and safe.

Sukey was there. The water felt almost warm now.

And then, slowly, as though the moon was sliding over the surface of the sun, the yellow light faded away.

On our twenty-second day at sea, we experienced our first stretch of bad weather, a nasty storm that followed us all the way from Bermuda down to the coast of Florida. I have been so ill I have not been able to write. I pray this weather ends soon.

Twenty-nine

I awoke to pain in so many places on my body that I wasn't sure where one ache began and another ended. Eventually, I was able to separate out the throbbing in my head from the stinging on my shins from the rawness on my hands on the sand beneath me.

"Ow." I wasn't sure if I said it out loud.

"Kit?" My eyes were already open, I think, but it took a minute for the dark blur to resolve itself into Sukey's face, red and panicked. The images came back to me slowly: the churning water, the *Fair Beatrice* lurching and twisting, the feeling of sinking through the cold water. The strange dream of the yellow light in the water.

I squinted up at her. The sun beat down on us from overhead.

When I took a breath I could feel a deep ache in my lungs, as though I'd inhaled fire.

I pushed Sukey aside, got up on my knees, and looked around.

An expanse of beach, palm trees. An island.

I looked down at my vest. Dad's whistle still hung around my neck and my vest was still slightly inflated. I scanned the beach, then looked behind us at a high, cone-shaped mountain. Its ridged sides rose steeply toward the sky, the black soil covered with thick, green vegetation. The jungle ran almost down to the beach, which was ringed by palm trees and some kind of low-growing plant blooming with white flowers. We were all alone.

Sukey looked terrible, her face bright red, her hair a mass of tangles, her flightsuit torn and dirty, and a long scratch bisected her forehead. I was willing to bet I didn't look much better. I could feel grit in my mouth and eyes. I probably looked like M.K. after she'd been working on an engine.

I jumped up, searching the beach, trying to ignore my headache. "They're not here," Sukey said, reading my mind. "A least not on this part of the beach. But they could be on the other side. They could have been rescued."

I felt a hard ball of fear rise in my throat and tears spring into my eyes.

"I know," she said, following me and reaching out to touch my hand. She was crying too.

I took a deep breath. "Maybe they got into the lifeboats. Maybe they got into Amy and saved themselves."

We leaned together, Sukey's arm around my shoulders. My head still hurt, but not as badly as it had when I'd first come to. I was thirsty, though. I knew that we needed to put away our fears about

Zander and M.K. and the others for a bit and figure out how we were going to survive.

"We'll find them," I said. "But first we need to figure out where we are."

"Could it be Ruby Island?"

I checked the chronograph utility embedded in my vest. I was glad to see it was still working and I wound it, silently thanking Dad for his superior craftsmanship. "I don't think so," I said. "It's nearly noon. We went down around, what 2:30, 3:00 a.m.? I don't think there's any way we could have ended up all the way back at Ruby Island. It's too far."

The sand beneath us was black and rough. "It's a volcanic island, anyway," I said, picking up a handful of sand and letting it fall through my fingers. "As if that giant volcano over there didn't already tell us that." Suddenly I remembered the maps, and I stripped off my vest. Sukey watched as I hurriedly unzipped the pocket and stuck a hand down inside to feel the paper. "They're okay." The waterproof lining had done its job and kept the maps and the key to the secret room dry and safe. The rest of my gadgets seemed to have survived too. I focused my spyglass on the horizon and searched for any sign of land or ship, but all I could see was the brilliant turquoise water, stretching out in every direction.

"Your whistle made it," Sukey said, pointing at the whistle.

I told her about the Explorer giving it to me. "He said it was a good-luck charm. But Dad never would have said that. So he must have wanted me to have it for some other reason." I put it to my lips and blew, covering different holes with my fingers to make different notes. "I'm just too dumb to figure it out."

"Thank God he made your vest inflatable," Sukey said. "I think it must have saved our lives."

"That means that Zander and M.K.'s vests inflated too," I said. "Maybe they made it. Maybe they were able to help the others."

"I hope so." Sukey looked worried.

We walked down the beach until the sand disappeared. We couldn't get around the cliff of ropy, black volcanic rock. There didn't seem to be anywhere else to land on the island. The beach where we had washed ashore appeared to be the only inlet on the island. But of course we couldn't know that until we'd climbed high enough to see over the top of the volcano.

"We're lucky," I said. "Anywhere else and we'd have been crushed against those rocks. But somehow, we washed up at the one place we could . . . I still don't understand how we made it here."

A strange look came over her face. "It must have been the tides. They must have just washed us up. I've heard of it happening before. But what was that last night?" she asked. "Was it a storm?"

"It didn't seem like a storm. It was like it was coming from underneath the water."

"Girafalco's Trench?" she said.

"Maybe."

"We need fresh water." Sukey said with a crack in her voice. "I'm really thirsty."

"We should split up and see what we can find. Sometimes islands like this have hidden springs or even streams." I wasn't sure that was even true, but I wanted to make her feel better.

"I don't want to split up," she said in a small voice, looking towards the dense jungle. "We don't know what's out there."

I was glad she'd said it. "Okay. You're right. Let's stay together."

"What about coconuts?"

"That's a good idea." I searched the ground underneath the palms, but there wasn't any fruit that I could see.

"No coconuts, but look." Under the trees were a bunch of palm leaves that seemed to have come down in a high wind. "It must have rained not too long ago." There was still a little bit of water collected on some of the leaves and Sukey and I dropped to our knees and drank as much as we could before she said, "We should save some. Put the other leaves over it so it won't evaporate as fast."

But we were so thirsty we couldn't stop ourselves from drinking all of it. When we were done, we went back to the shoreline, feeling a little better.

"We need to make a plan," I said. "Remember what we learned in Wilderness Survival? 'Make a plan accounting for all known facts and assessing all known assets.'"

"Yes, sir," Sukey said. "What's your plan, sir?" It was the first time I'd seen her smile since we'd woken up and I couldn't help smiling back.

"Come on. This is serious."

"I know, I know. Let's go back down to the beach and come up with this brilliant plan."

Thirty

I used a stick to draw a circle in the sand and wrote "Sukit Island" underneath.

"Sukit Island?"

"Well, can you think of a better name?"

"Okay, okay. Go on."

I drew an X on one side of the island. "Here's where we are. The sun came up over there, so that's east. We came from the west." I made a long line stretching out from the other side of the island and then drew another X. "I've been watching the way the tide comes in. I can't be sure, but I think the shipwreck must have been somewhere out here."

Sukey picked up a stick and drew another circle directly west of the X I'd made for the shipwreck. "So that must be St. Beatrice Island. Which means . . ."

I drew another circle. "We're definitely not on Ruby Island."

"We found an uncharted island?"

"Looks that way."

"So if we could make a raft or a boat, we could go this way and avoid King Triton's Lair and make our way back?" Sukey asked, drawing the route in the sand.

"Yeah. But we can't do anything stupid until we know we got the map right. We need to get up high. We need to be able to see more than we can see from here."

We both looked up at the volcano.

"Okay," Sukey said. "But we should wait until tomorrow morning. We don't know what's up there and it would be better if we don't have to spend the night. And we should get something to eat. What about those fish Zander caught on the boat?"

"What about them?"

"Do you think we could catch some fish?"

"With what? Did you bring a fishing pole I don't know about?"

"No, but that's not the only way to catch fish. Doesn't Zander catch them with spears or something?"

"Hold on!" I dug around in a pocket of my vest and came out with the spearfishing utility M.K. had given me. "Let's try this."

I held it over the surface of the water, waiting until one of the fish swam directly underneath me, and pushed the button. It took a couple of tries to get the hang of it, but finally I pulled up the spear by its wire and found a wriggling fish pierced by the tip. I caught a few more while Sukey looked for firewood.

There wasn't much—everything was fairly damp—but we built a little fire of the few dry palm fronds and branches we found, lighting them with my firestarter utility. "Is that M.K.'s?" Sukey asked when I took it out.

"No, she made me my own over the summer. Zander too."

"Well, maybe they're using theirs to start a fire somewhere else," she said.

The palm leaves didn't burn very hot, but it was enough to cook the fish through so we could eat them. We used my knife to bone them and ate our fill. The flesh was flaky, white, and sweet.

"This is delicious," Sukey said. "We should catch more."

We caught a few more, and by the time we had cooked and eaten them, our spirits had brightened. We sat on the sand in a comfortable, exhausted silence for a long time, watching the water, feeling the sun on our faces.

She reached up to wipe sweat off her forehead. "God, it's hot. I'm going for a swim."

She ran down the beach and jumped into the water, swimming out a couple hundred yards and then racing back with a perfect crawl stroke.

"Aren't you coming in?" she called back.

I hadn't thought I'd ever want to be back in the ocean after almost drowning the day before, but it was so hot and the water looked so cool and peaceful, turquoise and still in the little bay. I stripped off my vest and shirt and boots, used the knife to cut off my leggings at the knees, and ran down to the water, diving cleanly under the surface and hovering there for a moment, feeling the lightness of my body. When I opened my eyes, I almost gulped a mouthful of seawater in my astonishment. The island was fringed by a huge reef of coral that seemed to stretch out as far as I could see, adorning the undulating waves of the ocean floor. There were amazing things under there, pink coral and green sea anemones and purple fish and turquoise starfish. I came up for air and yelled to Sukey, "Have you looked under the water? It's incredible. It's a huge coral reef!"

Sukey pinched her nose and went under and I swam to meet her, pointing out striped fish and snails and coral formations and fish shaped like ribbons and huge purple crabs before we both had to go up for air again.

"I've never seen anything like it," I told her. "There must be at least a hundred new species. Can you imagine what's out there, beyond the reef?"

When we'd had enough, we lay down on the sand and stared up at the cloudless blue sky. I must have dozed off and when I woke up, the sun was low, sinking towards the horizon. Sukey was sleeping too, and when I nudged her gently, she opened her eyes, smiling at me before she remembered.

"It's okay," I told her. "We fell asleep. It's getting late, though, and we're going to need more water." I thought of something. "Why didn't we see any coconuts anywhere? Those are coconut palms, I'm sure of it."

She sat up and looked around. "I don't know. Maybe it's not coconut season. Maybe something . . . ate them?" We exchanged a look.

"Maybe there's some other kind of fruit here," I said.

We hunted around the beach. We found a beautiful pink conch shell and some dead crabs and fish skeletons on the sand. There wasn't any fruit anywhere. We'd try again tomorrow. There was only one route up the sides of the volcano that we could see, a sort of path that wound up through the ground cover, but it would be hard climbing up that slope and the jungle was pretty thick. I had a knife in my Explorer's vest, but what we really needed was a machete. I thought of Zander cutting the path for us on the Derudan challenge back at the Academy. It seemed like a long time ago.

My vest had a couple of thin tarps that could be used as sun shades and Sukey and I lashed them to two palm trees at the back of the beach to make a shelter.

It would keep us protected if it rained at night and it would keep the sun off us during the day. We sat on the beach, watching the sun disappear down into the water as it washed the wispy clouds in peach and yellow light. Soon it was dusk, and the purple-black sky settled down against the dark line of the water. I switched on my vestlight and we huddled together in the cold air, not wanting to leave the beach. We listened to the little splishing sounds of fish jumping out in the shallows.

"Well, I guess we figured out what happened to your dad's expedition," Sukey said. She leaned into me and the whole length of her arm felt hot, as though it was burning a mark into my skin. I didn't want her to take it away, so I stayed very still, my back cramping.

"And Gianni Girafalco's ship too. And I guess we figured out why there are all those stories about sea monsters and aliens and everything. Whatever that was that brought the ship down, gas or an earthquake, well, if you didn't know better, you'd think it was some sort of monster, wouldn't you?"

"Do you think anyone's looking for us?"

"Once BNDL realizes that we're missing, I'm sure they'll send someone to look for us."

"But how long will that be? And if they do send a boat, how will it find us?"

"They might send an airship," I said.

"But you told me yourself that airships had gone down over this part of the ocean. Whatever was going on back there seems to prevent anyone from reaching or even seeing this island."

"It's going to be okay, Sukey."

"No, it's not. We might never leave this island. Don't you understand? We're going to be stuck here forever. We're going to die here, of thirst or hunger or —" She looked over her shoulder at the jungle rising up the sides of the volcano. "Something else." She was crying now.

"Look," I told her. "We can't get ahead of ourselves. Let's just get through tonight. We'll get some sleep. We have food and water— for a little while, at least. Tomorrow, we'll take stock and figure out what to do."

"You're right," she said softly. "I'm so tired all of a sudden."

"Dad always said everything looks better in the morning."

The sun was gone now. It was almost completely dark. "Delilah says that too." Sukey started to get up and then she pointed at the water. "Kit—look!"

I saw it too: lights, shining out in the darkness of the bay.

The lights got brighter and then, in an instant, there were more. They dotted the surface of the water, moving languidly, like bubbles of air in oil.

"It's beautiful," Sukey whispered. "It must be some kind of animal, something that's bioluminescent, right?"

"They look like jellyfish." I watched the strange, otherworldly blobs dance in slow motion. The darker it got, the brighter they became. Pretty soon we could see that they were different colors: red and orange and purple and pink and green.

We must have watched for an hour, even as the air grew colder and the wind moved through the palm trees behind us.

"Whatever happens," Sukey said, turning to look up at me, "I'm never going to forget that, as long as I live. That was amazing."

"Me neither."

We looked at each other for a long moment. I could just make out the expression on her face and I liked the way she looked at me, as though she was trying to find my eyes in the darkness, trying to figure out what I was thinking.

"Do you think . . ." she said, turning away from me to look at the jellyfish again. "Do you think your father was here? On this island? Do you think he came here when he made the map?"

I didn't say anything. I didn't know.

"You're sure there isn't a code on the map? Something telling you what you're supposed to find here? A secret message?"

"Sukey, I've tried everything I can think of. Maybe you can figure it out."

I took off my vest and got the map out, unfolding it and spreading it on the sand. I shone my vestlight on it and Sukey leaned over to examine it.

While she looked at it, I took off my whistle and tried playing "Twinkle, Twinkle, Little Star."

"Very nice," Sukey said. "I give up on the map, though."

We sat there for a few moments just looking out at the bobbing lights.

But I was thinking. *You create luck by making connections. By putting things together.*

What could I put together? What had Dad given me? The map and the whistle. So . . .

I lay the whistle down on the map, holding my breath, then moved it back and forth a couple times, rubbing the domed surface of the turtle's shell across the paper.

"What are you —?"

"Sukey," I said, my voice shaking. "Look."

There were new lines and decorations across the map. They glowed in the dark, and the sea horses sprinkled across the ocean were glowing too.

"What are those?" Sukey said. "They look like compasses."

"They are. They're compass rose lines and compass roses!"

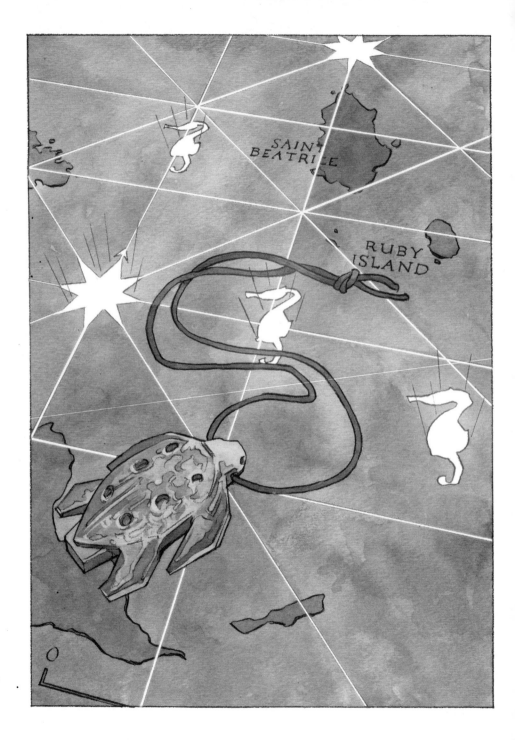

I leaned over the map, tracing the glowing lines. "Mariners used to use them for navigation. See, the lines relate to the cardinal directions. North, south, east, and west, and the intermediate points, too. They were called wind rose lines because they corresponded to the winds they used to navigate." I ran a finger over the glowing lines. "This is incredible. It must be some kind of bioluminescent ink that's only revealed when it touches the whistle. I remember Zander talking once about how bioluminescence sometimes depends on the animal being near particular bacteria that react to the bacteria in the animal's own bioluminescent ink organ. I don't understand it, but it's why Dad gave me the whistle. I had to put them together!"

"So what do the lines mean? Were they supposed to show us how to get to King Triton's Lair?"

"Maybe." I studied the lines and decorations for a long time, but I couldn't make any sense of them. I could feel Sukey waiting beside me.

"Kit?" she said finally.

"I don't know! Obviously he went to a lot of trouble to keep it secret. You can only see them in the dark. You can only see them when they're in contact with the whistle. He made sure no one would find it by accident. But why? What's the code? It's so frustrating!" I felt like throwing something.

"We've got to be missing something," Sukey said. "Did you try substituting letters or numbers for the little pictures? Maybe just the ones with the invisible ink."

"Of course I did! I told you I did. That's the simplest code there is!"

"Fine," she said. "I'm just trying to help."

I picked up the whistle and looked at it. Then I held the map close to my face, studying the luminescent lines. "It's a whistle, Sukey. It activates the ink but it's also a whistle. Obviously he wants me to play it, but what should I play?"

Sukey just stared at me, confused.

I traced the wind rose lines carefully with a finger. There were five compass roses, five horizontal lines. And all along those lines . . .

"The sea horses!" I shouted, jumping up and pulling her up with me.

"What about them?"

I grabbed Sukey's hand, squeezing it, and laughed. "The sea horses are notes! I can't believe I didn't see it before. It's a musical code. He's telling us how to play the whistle!"

I will never forget my first sight of a Caribbean harbor. We arrived in St. John's Harbor on the island of Antigua on May 23rd. My first impression was of a riot of color, the green of the palms, the blue of the water, the bright pink of the climbing flowers that seemed to cover nearly every surface. The markets on the island are noisy and colorful and I bought many shells to take home with me. The ladies in the

Thirty-one

"I can't believe we didn't see it," Sukey said, pointing to the little sea horses distributed across the blue ocean, some on the horizontal lines and some in between them. "Five compass roses. Five lines in a musical staff. It's a piece of music."

I was already trying it out, blowing through the mouthpiece and pressing my fingers over the little holes. "Coleman said that each one is different. You can play different tunes by covering the holes, like a flute or a recorder. It must make a song. Maybe the song is the message to us. Anyway, we'll figure that part out." I blew. "It's not really coming back. What note is that?"

"Give me that," Sukey said impatiently. "We have to figure out what key it's in so we'll know how to play the music." She covered all the holes and blew. "That's the lowest note. It's D. So now let me see the map. She covered one hole and blew again. "B," she said. She covered two holes. "A. That's E." In a couple of minutes she'd figured out how to play the whistle. "All right. So the song goes like this."

She played it.

"Does that sound familiar?"

"No," I said. "It's not even really a song, is it?"

"Here, you try." She handed it to me and I played the little sequence of notes. "Nope, doesn't sound familiar to me either."

I played it a few more times, but now I was pretty sure I'd never heard it before.

I felt suddenly dejected. I was so sure I'd had it.

"That has to be it, though," Sukey said. "That has to be the code on the map."

"But if I can't figure out what the song is," I said. "What good does it do me?"

"We'll get it. We're just so tired. Our brains aren't working right." She sounded exhausted. Already, the lines and notes on the map were fading and I put the map back in the pocket of my vest and the whistle back around my neck.

We sat there silently, staring out at the ocean, when Sukey said, "Kit? Is there something down there? On the sand?"

"What do you mean?" I stood up and looked down toward the shoreline. It took a couple of seconds to see what she meant. Something *was* moving on the sand.

"It looks like a fish," I said.

"It's coming up on the beach, though." Sukey backed up a little, looking alarmed. "It's . . . slithering. That's not a fish."

Whatever it was, it was hard to see in the darkness, but when I turned on my vestlight, I saw that the things were wriggling up all over the beach, lots of them, coming out of the water and moving from side to side like snakes. Except they weren't snakes.

Sukey scrambled backward as they came toward us, struggling to climb to her feet.

I couldn't stop staring at the strange creatures. There were about a hundred of them, writhing along the sand. They were each about two feet long, slimy, shiny black, with a sharp red fin running along the tops of their heads to their backs. They twisted and turned, their muscular bodies rippling over the sand. I stood transfixed until one got so close that I could see its mouthful of sharp white teeth, and I came to my senses.

"They're eels," I said. "Hundreds of them. And they're coming up the beach! Run!"

We sprinted up the beach, the beam from my vestlight bobbling on the sand, and found our shelter, climbing in and pressing our backs against the trees. I dug through the pockets of my vest, coming out with a knife and the spearfishing tool. I handed the knife to Sukey and held the spearfishing utility out in front of me, ready to shoot the first eel that came over the threshold.

"I can't look, I can't look," Sukey whispered. "Are they coming? Are they coming?" She was hiding behind me, trying to burrow into the tree.

"Uh . . ." The truth was that I didn't want to look either. I was terrified. But I pointed my vestlight out at the darkness. They moved in a wriggling mass. I could hear the wet sound of them slithering up the beach, but they weren't coming our way. They were heading for the trees.

"I think they're climbing," I whispered, poking my head out of the shelter. "I think they're climbing . . . up the trees."

The eels *were* climbing, like tree snakes, and pretty soon we heard a crunching sound coming from the tops of the palms.

"They must be eating the coconuts," I told Sukey. "We wondered why there weren't any on the beach."

"Can all eels come out of the water like that and climb trees?" Sukey whispered.

"I don't think so. Maybe they've evolved to be able to come up on land. It must be an unknown species. But at least they don't seem interested in us."

"This is crazy," Sukey said. "A new species of eel. Bioluminescent jellyfish. Zander would have loved this."

"Yeah, he would have."

We were both silent, thinking of Zander.

"Kit," she said, after a minute. "It's going to be okay, isn't it? We'll find them. We'll get off this island."

I didn't know what to say, so I just pulled her into a hug and we sat there like that for hours, leaning against into other and listening to the eels chewing on the coconuts up in the trees. At some point, we must have fallen asleep, because the next thing I knew, it was very early morning, the sun staining the sky pink as it rose.

Sukey was still fast asleep and I carefully got up so as not to wake her. I walked down to the edge of the water. There was no sign of the eels now, and the waves softly lapped at the shore, the breeze salty and gentle on my face.

I walked for a while, following the shoreline as far as I could before it ran into the sharp rocks of the cliff. I still felt frustrated by Dad's map. I had figured out the musical code. That should have been it. And yet there was some other mystery to discover. I felt suddenly angry. What was Dad thinking? We'd almost died and he was playing games, teasing me with maps and clues.

Except I couldn't quite believe he'd do that. If what the Explorer had said was true, that Dad was leaving these clues for me and me alone, then these puzzles must have some purpose. I was missing something.

I pulled the whistle out from under my shirt and put it to my lips. I'd memorized the notes, and I played the piece through a couple of times, but no melody emerged. I wracked my brain for songs that Dad had sung to us, tunes he whistled while he worked, ballads he liked to sing in the bath, but nothing matched the notes on the map. I was about to turn away and head back down the beach when something made me look out at the water.

And look again.

The sun was very bright now. I wondered if I was hallucinating.

Emerging from the sea and onto the beach was a sea turtle as big as an elephant.

We stayed on the island of Antigua for two weeks, during which time we conducted more research into the local legends about King Triton's Lair. It seemed that the local legends centered on the existence of sea monsters or giant fish in the area where most of the ships had gone down. Captain Girafalco and I spent our days talking to fishermen and a few of them spoke of a mysterious part of the ocean where ships often foundered. Captain Girafalco said the stories indicated something was hidden there and that he believed that emissions of air from the deep ocean trenches could cause the water to bubble and boil, the shapes of the waves seeming to resemble a monster or even an island.

Thirty-two

It had a huge head and beak, its skin a shiny, pearly green. I knew it must be a sea turtle, but it was unlike any sea turtle I'd ever seen. Its shell, instead of being flat and ridged, was domed and perfectly smooth, made of a pearly but transparent glasslike substance. There were shiny metal fittings all along the edges of the shell, hinges and screws and gadgets. Its flippers were each as big as a rowboat. The right one had a long scar on it in the shape of a check mark.

When it blinked its giant golden eyes at me, I knew this was the creature I thought I'd hallucinated under the water. The creature that had saved my life and brought us to the island. The turtle blinked again and waved its right flipper, the one with the scar, insistently, making a reedy chirping sound that sounded very much like Dad's whistle. I considered: If Dad's map had been a musical code, a code

that was meant to summon the turtle when played on the whistle—
well, then, why? Why did Dad want me to see this fantastical turtle?

And then something happened that I couldn't explain: I heard a
voice inside my head.

Not my own mind's voice, the one I had been hearing for as long
as I could remember, the voice that told me I'd said something stupid
or the one that told me to be careful or that sometimes said things
like *No one likes you* or *You have no idea what you're doing* or *That's a
good map!*

This was a completely different voice. It was a voice that came
from somewhere else, that said, in a low whisper that seemed familiar,
Get inside. Come with me.

I stepped back so quickly that I tripped over a bit of driftwood on
the beach. "Was that . . . was that *you?*" I said out loud once I'd gotten
up, before I realized how crazy it was. A turtle who could somehow
make me hear what he was thinking? It was impossible.

His mouth didn't move, but I heard the voice inside my head
again. *Yes. I hear you think. You hear me think.*

Like this? I thought, trying to direct the thought at the turtle's head.

Yes, said the voice. *Come with me.*

With an audible click, the front of his shell opened, and again,
he waved his flipper insistently. I didn't know what else to do—the
whole thing was so crazy that if I thought about it for more than two
seconds, I was going to run screaming down the beach—so I stepped
inside and sat down on a little ridge in the turtle's shell that served as
a bench. The shell slowly lowered and clicked shut.

263

I was inside an airtight dome, but I found that I could breathe without any trouble at all. When I put my hand over a row of little holes down near the floor, I felt cold air coming out of them. The whole inside of the shell was made of a shiny, transparent substance that gleamed and glittered. It smelled of the sea, a fresh salty smell that surrounded me.

And then he was using his flippers to scoot us along the sand and into the shallow waters off the beach. We sank silently below the surface in a rush of air bubbles and as soon as we were away from the beach, the turtle took off, speeding through the clear turquoise of the sea. We sped up and slowed down. The coral reef stretched out around the island. The turtle wove in and out of the reef so I could watch the colorful fish and anemones moving peacefully among the seaweed.

Look.

I did. And everywhere I looked, there was color. A huge yellow parrot fish swam by, inspecting me through the clear shell. A purple octopus flew up from the ocean floor amid a cloud of black ink. I saw a few of the coconut eels swimming dreamily down toward the ocean floor. A pack of bright yellow manta rays flapped by and we saw a fuchsia eel baring its teeth at the turtle from underneath a rock. All around me were amazing fish I had never seen before, fish I was pretty sure no one had ever seen before, and I felt a pang of sadness again, wondering if Zander would ever get to see them.

And then we were beyond the reef and in the open water. The ocean floor fell off quickly and the turtle began descending, maybe ten feet every couple of seconds. The ocean grew darker as less light filtered through and it became harder and harder for me to see anything outside the shell. For the first time since he'd come up on the beach, I felt afraid, and I thought about Sukey, all alone, wondering where I'd gone. I shouldn't have left her.

We must have been traveling for nearly an hour when I saw the turtle wave his flipper again, and I heard the voice say, *We're almost there.* I looked up to see something emerge from the murk, a huge dark field of shapes rising from the ocean floor. At first I thought they were trees, but as we got closer, I could see that they were the masts of sailing ships.

The turtle swam slowly, letting me see the shipwrecks heaped on the ocean floor.

As we came around, the words painted on their hulls, though worn away by time and water, stood out against the sand.

The *Mary South.*

The *Adelaide.*

The still brightly painted hull of the *Fair Beatrice.* The turtle swam down so I could see that there weren't any bodies in the wreck, just the broken half of the boat that had brought us here.

This was the final resting place of Gianni Girafalco's ship and of many others, as well. And perhaps it was the final resting place of their treasure.

Was this what Dad had meant for us to find?

I was still staring at the ghostly ships when the turtle started moving again, darting and circling and dropping though the now murky water. It got darker and darker as he swam, but his flippers began to glow like the jellyfish and I recognized the white light that had surrounded me in the water after the wreck.

We were in a different part of the ocean now. No sunlight filtered down from the surface and I could see only because of the turtle's luminescent flippers. There were no colorful fish or coral here, only small, amoebalike creatures, tiny shrimp, an odd-looking spiny fish that stared at us for a moment before moving on. The turtle swam deeper and deeper and the ocean floor sloped down steeply into the blackness.

As the turtle swam along the bottom of what seemed to be an underwater canyon, I suddenly realized why I had a nagging familiar feeling that I'd seen this before. As I looked at the walls and curves of the canyon I realized I'd seen this exact topography described in lines and shades on paper.

We were swimming through Girafalco's Trench.

I scrambled for the map and followed our route along what seemed to be the eastern slope of the trench, keeping an eye on my compass. We kept going, down into the narrowest part of the trench. The lights in the turtle's flippers illuminated the walls as we reached the bottom. We flew along the ocean floor. Then the turtle slowed, turned, and soon we were speeding through a narrow tunnel of rock into what looked like a giant undersea cavern.

And suddenly, it was even lighter. Light poured from the walls of the cavern, pearly, creamy light from no source I could see. It seemed to respond to our presence, getting brighter as we got closer, dimming once we'd passed. The walls seemed to be made of the same substance as the whistle.

We're almost there, the turtle said.

Where?

There. The turtle pointed its flipper into the water ahead.

At first, I was only aware of a huge presence, of something taking up a lot of space. As we got closer, the presence resolved itself into the outline of thousands of buildings sprouting from the ocean floor, some very tall and skinny, some short and squat, some with rounded dome roofs that looked almost like the turtle's shells, pearly but translucent, and in the very center, a huge, ornately decorated structure that reminded me of a church, with soaring towers and minarets and a dome rising above all the others.

It was a massive underwater city.

The turtle slowed and we approached a huge arch that seemed to mark the entrance. I had been staring so hard at the buildings that I hadn't noticed two other turtles—not quite as large as mine—hovering at attention next to the gates. They chirped something at my turtle, who chirped back, and we went on through the arch.

All across the ocean floor, there were thousands of structures, made of the same mother-of-pearl as the turtle's shell. The tall, wide walls of the buildings were a rich, creamy white. The huge sheets of shell material were joined together with shiny metal rivets, the doors and windows made of translucent glass. And decorating the sides of the buildings were thousands and thousands of colorful seashells, pink and red and blue, forming incredible murals, just like the ones on St. Beatrice.

There were other objects set into the sides of the buildings too, I realized as we swam more closely—shining gold coins and

gemstones and pottery, the treasure from the ships, salvaged and used as decoration.

The turtle wove his way through the streets.

My mouth must have hung open as I stared at the incredible sights all around me.

And then I heard the turtle's voice in my head.

Welcome to King Triton's Lair.

Thirty-three

There were more turtles inside the city. Some swam like guards around the perimeters, circling around and around the glimmering structures. We wove in and out of the grid of streets, my turtle slowing down in front of the murals so I could see that many of them were maps like the ones on St. Beatrice.

Who lives here?

The voice took a moment to answer in my head. *The Men of the Sea. But they are gone. We keep the city safe.*

Where did they go?

We do not know.

Except for the turtles, the city was deserted. The turtle was too big to enter the buildings, but he hovered near the windows so I could see into the rooms. Most of them contained furniture, couches and beds and tables made of coral and mother-of-pearl, decorated with seashells, some of them turned over as though whoever had lived there had left in a hurry. There was something timeless about the scenes in front of me. The Men of the Sea, whoever they were, could have left yesterday. Or a hundred years ago.

When we'd been through the whole city, the turtle glided over to a central domed structure, a temple, I decided, and we swam inside through a huge window that seemed to have been made for him. We found ourselves in a cavernous hall, with the seashell murals decorating the walls and tables and chairs in rows. They were made from the same mother-of-pearl as the buildings. At one end of the hall was a huge throne, beautiful and empty, constructed from red coral and decorated with seashells and gold coins and gemstones.

"King Triton's throne," I whispered to myself.

Yes, the turtle answered. *Now I will take you to the place.*

Which place?

The place you were told to go.

You mean my father? Do you know my father?

The turtle didn't send any response, and I had a moment of doubt. This was crazy. What was I thinking? Of course Dad hadn't been here. It was ridiculous. If he had discovered the city where King Triton lived, if he had discovered a race of giant turtles who could communicate without talking, if he had found the ships' graveyard, well, we would have known about it, wouldn't we?

But we had thought that about Ha'aftep Canyon. Maybe this was a place like that, a place that Dad had wanted me to know about, a place he didn't want to reveal to the world. Because like Ha'aftep Canyon, it would be destroyed if people knew about it. I imagined tours through the city streets, gift shops selling shells plucked from the buildings, the turtles placed in cages for viewing.

The turtle made his high chirping sound, and a door in the wall behind the throne slowly swung open, revealing a winding tunnel lined with the pearly, light-emitting substance that surrounded the city. We swam through and the doors closed behind us.

We were now inside a long tunnel. Waiting for us at the end was another turtle, standing sentry before a small, rectangular room. This turtle was bigger than my turtle and his face had a wizened, wrinkled look to it that made me think he was very, very old. He warbled in a high reedy whistle and my turtle warbled something back before settling down on the floor of the cavern. I waited, but he didn't offer any explanation. I walked around the inside of the shell, trying to figure out why he'd brought me here and what I was supposed to do.

The walls of the room were covered with more of the shells, arranged in shapes that reminded me of hieroglyphics. At the far end, an entire wall was covered with tiny white stones and shells. They had been set into its surface, forming lines that radiated out from a central circle in imitation of the rays of the sun. Was that it? A picture of the sun? Was it another code? Clearly this is what the turtle had wanted me to see.

I stared at the pattern until the lines of shells blurred together and I had to stand back to see the design made by the winding lines.

And then, finally, I knew what it was.

This was the next map. Dad had been leading me here all along.

I tried to imprint it upon my brain, to take a mental picture of it so I would remember later, but it took me a while to get oriented. Before I could try to match this map to the maps in my head and figure out what it was, my turtle looked up sharply, as though he'd heard something, and whistled to the other turtle, who started to move around as though he was very agitated, churning up a lot of sand in the chamber. My turtle chirped and wheeled around, swimming back out through the tunnel, his flippers rowing through the water. I couldn't see anything now, just the white of the churning water as we flew away from the map I'd come all this way to see.

"No! No!" I pounded on the shell, not trusting my inner voice and yelling out loud at the back of the turtle's head. "We can't leave! Go back! I didn't memorize it yet!"

But he didn't respond. We swam out of the throne room and then out of the city, very quickly now, up through the trench. Frantically, I took out my compass and kept track of our direction so I'd be able to find my way back. We sped through the dark part of the ocean and then into the shallower, lighter waters, filled with all that bright sea life.

What's wrong?

Danger.

What kind?

No answer. The turtle seemed scared, swiveling its head back and forth to search the ocean around him.

We raced up toward the surface once again.

I closed my eyes and tried to picture the map. But I hadn't looked at it long enough. It was the most frustrating kind of work, trying to remember something I'd hardly seen.

This time, the beautiful fish and bright-red coral held no fascination for me. I shut my eyes and tried to remember, but all I could come up with was a mosaic of shells with no logic or order.

The water around me became lighter and lighter and then suddenly, the door was opening and I was tipped out into the shallow water. Before I knew what was happening, the turtle had disappeared and I was standing on the beach, warm turquoise water up to my waist, blinking up at the bright sun as though nothing had happened.

Thirty-four

"There you are!" Sukey called. I looked up and saw her running down the beach toward me. "Where were you? Did you go swimming?"

"I—I—I—" I stammered. I looked behind me to make sure the turtle wasn't still there, but the water was calm, smooth as glass. We were alone. I stood speechless. She looked sunburned, her freckles not as stark as they usually were against the now-pink skin of her cheeks and nose. I was shaken. My legs were weak. I was worried I was going to pass out. I wanted to tell her about the turtle, but I didn't even know where to begin and my brain was racing. The turtle's thoughts had made their way into my brain and mine had made their way to his. Could it happen again? Did Sukey know what I was thinking? Would I be able to hear her thoughts? Had she been able to hear what I was thinking last night as I'd held her on the beach?

I shivered just thinking about it, then shook my head, trying to clear it. Of course she couldn't hear my thoughts. I kept staring at her.

"Are you okay?" She pushed a stray curl back into her ponytail and leaned forward, peering at me quizzically.

"I got worried," she said, talking too fast. "I didn't know where you were. I woke up and you were gone and I thought something had happened to you. I started hiking up the volcano a bit, to see if I could find you, and I couldn't see you anywhere."

I found my voice then. "I'm sorry, Sukey. I went for a swim and—"

"It's okay, it's okay." She waved my explanation away. "What I've been trying to tell you is, well, look. Look!"

She took me by the arm and turned me around, pointing at the volcano.

Just over the top of the mountain, a black smudge against the bright blue sky, was a long, twisting tail of smoke.

She squeezed my arm so hard it hurt. "There's someone else on the island!"

We talked in circles, trying to decide what to do. Sukey was convinced that it was Zander and M.K. and the rest of the team. I wasn't so sure. I still felt shaken by my experience under the water. The turtle had said there was danger, but he hadn't said what kind. We were both weak and thirsty and we didn't really have any weapons beyond the spearfishing utility and my knife. I knew we weren't equipped to deal with someone—or something—that wanted to do us harm.

"It could be the pirates," I told her. "It could be Monty Brioux."

"I don't think it's the pirates," she said stubbornly.

Finally, I gave in. As the morning wore on, a mass of dark clouds moved across the sky above the island, and I knew that if we didn't get going soon, we might not have the chance. We caught some more fish and cooked and ate them as quickly as we could, then set off up the mountain. It was hard going. The path, such as it was, ended after a few hundred yards and we had to resort to tramping through the thick undergrowth. The foliage was odd, not like a rainforest but a dense mat of trees and low bushes, all covered with white and pink flowers. I recognized their sweet, spicy scent from St. Beatrice, and for just a moment I let myself remember what it had been like, lying in the bathtub at Coleman's, feeling the warm breeze waft through the window.

It took us much longer than we'd thought it would take to cover even a small amount of ground. By 2:30, we were only halfway up, and the face of the volcano ahead looked even steeper than the section we'd just covered. We could still see the curl of smoke on the other side.

We kept climbing. The sky got darker, and we felt the first raindrops only a few minutes before the sky opened and the rain clattered down on us, instantly soaking our clothes. I didn't think I'd ever heard a rainstorm as loud. It pounded down out of the heavens, creating instant rivers that ran down the slope toward the sea. We tilted our heads up and opened our mouths to drink our fill of fresh, cold rain.

I pushed the button on the back of my vest that released the umbrella gadget. It kept us out of the downpour, but I found that it made it impossible to walk through the trees on the narrow path. We decided to sit down under the umbrella and eat our lunch.

I had wrapped a little bit of the cooked fish in some palm leaves and Sukey and I gobbled a quarter of what we'd brought, saving the rest for later. Dad had always said that the worst thing an Explorer could do was to consume all of his or her food or water. You never knew what might happen to change your plans, he'd say. The fish wasn't going to be good for much longer, but I still thought we should save some.

"Do you really think it's the pirates?" Sukey asked.

"I don't know, Sukey. I don't know anything. I think it's letting up a little. We should get going."

"What's wrong with you? You're acting so strange."

I hesitated, trying to decide if I should tell her. But how would I even start? *This morning, a giant telepathic turtle took me to a magical city under the sea.* "I'm fine," I said. "We should go."

I folded the umbrella back into my vest and stood up abruptly, setting off up the trail again. The rain was now coming in slow droplets and I could hear her calling after me.

"Kit! Kit! Wait!"

I kept walking. I just wanted to get to the top of the damn volcano, but it was raining even harder and my feet kept slipping on the path.

"Kit!" Sukey called from behind me. And then I felt a hand on my arm and she was spinning me around. Rain was dripping from her hair down along the side of her jaw and she reached up to wipe it off.

"Where were you this morning? You were gone for hours." Her eyes were dark, suspicious in the low light. "Is it something to do with the Mapmakers' Guild, something you can't tell me? Something you don't trust me with?"

I'd never seen her look at me like that before, her eyes hurt, guarded.

We stood there for a long moment, staring at each other, panting, the rain running down our faces. "You'll think I'm insane," I told her. "If I tell you, you'll think I'm completely insane."

"I won't."

So I told her.

When I was done, her eyes were wide and she was looking off into the distance, thinking.

"See? You think I'm crazy," I said. "Or that I'm making it up. I keep wondering if I could have eaten or drunk something without knowing it—"

"You're not crazy," she said, still staring off into the distance.

"But it's so strange. I mean, the thinking thing. Telepathic turtles? Who ever heard of that? It's nutty."

"Listen," she whispered, her eyes meeting mine now. "I might be crazy too, but after the wreck, when we were in the water, I saw something, this sort of light and a giant head. I was so scared but as soon as I saw that light, I was okay. I knew we were going to be okay. And then I must have blacked out."

"I think they put us into their shells and brought us to the island. There's no other explanation."

"But why? I don't understand it. Why would they save

us? None of the other accounts of ships sinking said anything about turtles."

I thought for a moment. "I blew the whistle as the ship was going down. I was trying to get someone's attention, but maybe the turtles heard it and somehow they knew that—well, that I was meant to find the city."

Sukey watched me. Finally she said, "And they saved us. They brought us here." The rain was running down her face and I wanted to reach up and brush it from her eyes, from her cheeks. But I didn't touch her. She smiled at me, a smile I'd come to know so well I could see it when she wasn't there. "If you've gone crazy, then I have too."

While we were at sea, Captain Girafalco had taken to capturing a wide variety of the unusual creatures we saw. Most of these he examined and returned to the water, but one day I came upon him dissecting one of the large squid that we caught in our nets. He told me that the creatures seemed to spray a glowing substance from their bodies when threatened. He had encountered other creatures that produced an ink that emitted light only when placed near other creatures with similar capabilities. He used his dissecting knife to slice open one of the creature's tentacles and showed me a gelatinous substance housed within.

"This is fascinating," he told me. "Many of these creatures have ink sacs that contain the miraculous liquid, but this fellow seems to produce it in his tentacles." He explained that the substance had bioluminescent qualities that

Thirty-five

The last hour was the hardest climbing yet, but it finally stopped raining as we approached the top of the volcano. The clouds blew quickly across the horizon, followed by blue skies. I could finally see the trees in front of me start to fall away and I knew we were nearing the top.

Panting, my vest and cutoffs still wet from the downpour, I stumbled out onto a little plateau.

"What is it?" Sukey called from behind me. "What do you see?"

We had come out into a clearing the size of a football field, the ground covered with the flowering bushes that filled the air with that wonderful scent. It ran right up to the edge of a steep cliff.

Far below we could see a beach. The water was pristine and the contours of the coral reef fringing the island were clear from above.

Sukey caught up to me and took in the view. The sun was

dropping down toward the water, filling the sky with rosy smudges. It wouldn't be light for much longer. The golden clouds looked lit from within, shot through with the sun's rays. I felt like we'd walked into some Italian painter's idea of heaven.

I could see the ocean in every direction I turned. Not a bit of land to be seen anywhere.

We were all alone—except for whoever was down there, at the source of the plume of smoke curling up toward the sky.

"I think it's them," Sukey said as she held her hands over the little fire we'd managed to get going in the low brush. I'd been worried about setting the whole mountain on fire, but everything was still so wet from the rain that there wasn't any danger of that. The fire we did get going was pretty pathetic, but we sat very close to it and warmed our hands and faces.

"It might be, but we shouldn't get our hopes up," I told her. "Think of how it's going to feel if we get down there and it's not them." My voice caught a little and she turned to look at me.

"I know," she said. "I'm sorry, Kit."

The fire sputtered and a weak spark floated up toward the star-filled black of the night sky, disappearing among the bright points of white.

I tucked my vest under my head, pulling the reflective blanket I'd taken out of one of the pockets around my shoulders.

"Look at all those stars," Sukey said. "Think of how many people out there are looking up at these same stars. "We're just two of them. We hardly matter, when you think of it that way. If we never get off this island, how many people are going to actually care about me?"

"I would care," I said.

Sukey laughed. "You idiot, if I don't get off this island, you're not getting off either."

"Right."

"Kit, you're not mad, are you? I just meant . . . It's true. Whatever happens to me is probably going to happen to you."

Embarrassed, I threw another wet branch on to the fire. "We should go to sleep," I said.

As soon as the sun was up, we started back down the other side of the mountain, making our way quickly down a narrow, muddy path toward the source of the smoke. The plume was much smaller, as though the fire had gone out overnight, but a thin line of gray still snaked its way up toward the wispy white cloud cover.

"We'll stop when we get about halfway down," I said. "We need to figure out who it is before we get too close. If they're dangerous, we need to be close enough to the top so we can run."

It wasn't more than an hour before I whispered, "Okay, let's stop here." We could smell the smoke in the air and I thought I heard a faraway murmur of voices. We stood very still for a moment, just listening.

"Did you hear that?" I asked, taking out my spyglass and switching on the sound utility. I pointed it in the general direction of the smoke and listened. All I could hear was a rhythmic banging sound, as though someone was swinging a large metal object at a rock. I didn't like the sound of it. Other than that, I could only hear the waves, amplified by Dad's gadget.

"What is that?" Sukey asked, listening to the banging over the spyglass.

"I don't know. I'm going to get closer and see if I can see anything more. The trees are too dense here. Wait here. I'll be right back."

"Why should I wait here? I'll go down with you."

"But what if something happens to me? At least this way you can head back to the other beach."

"All right." But she looked annoyed.

I made my way down the path, going slowly and quietly as I could. Finally, I came to a little promontory and trudged through to the end of the thick vegetation. I was looking down onto a little beach. I could only see one end of it. The smoke was coming from the other end, but I could see that someone—or something—had been digging in the sand. There was a very large hole in the center of the stretch of beach.

I leaned out as far as I could and directed the spyglass down toward the beach. All I could hear was the same rhythmic banging sound. Nothing else.

I decided to go a little farther along the path and see if I could see the other end of the beach. I had only walked a couple of yards, though, when I heard a piercing scream from behind me.

Sukey.

I turned and ran back toward where I'd left her.

But I didn't have to go far. She'd followed me and I found her slumped against a tree just before the promontory. Wrapped around her neck was a huge, green eel, just like the ones we'd seen coming out of the ocean, but much, much larger. It was speckled and nearly six feet long. She was gasping for breath, but the eel was only squeezing tighter and tighter.

I got the knife out of my vest and started stabbing the eel, but it didn't seem bothered at all, and I could see from her face that Sukey was having trouble breathing. The eel was hissing and baring its sharp teeth at us, switching its tail back and forth.

I looked for a stick I could use to pry the eel away when suddenly, a whir of black went by my head and I heard a loud squawk. *Eel! Eel!*

I looked up in astonishment.

Pucci attacked the eel with his metal talons, squawking *Eel, Eel!* again, as Zander, holding a sword and followed by Joyce, came crashing through the underbrush.

"Did someone say eel?"

Thirty-six

I was so astonished to see Zander alive that I barely noticed he had put the sword on the ground, dropped to his knees, and started humming, in a low, steady voice, in the vicinity of the eel's head. Even more remarkably, he was stroking it along its back. But then I saw Sukey's eyes roll back and heard her gurgle as she fought for breath.

"Zander, it's killing her!" I shouted.

"Don't worry," Joyce called back. "He knows what he's doing."

Already, I could see that the eel's constricting muscles had loosened. It let go of Sukey and started moving away, and then it slithered off into the bushes.

Sukey took a couple of long, ragged breaths. Then she struggled to her feet and hugged Zander fiercely around his neck, gasping, "You're alive!" I hugged him too, and Pucci flew around our heads, squawking *alive, alive!* We hugged Joyce and then Zander again, dancing around as Pucci squawked and chortled from my shoulder.

Sukey was still breathing hard and rubbing her neck but she seemed to be okay.

"Is M.K. all right? What about everyone else?" I asked.

"She's fine. Everyone's fine. I'm sure they're wondering what happened to Joyce and me. I don't know if they heard the scream from down on the beach." Zander was bare-chested, wearing only his Explorer's vest and leggings. He was very tan and he had a piece of his T-shirt tied around his forehead. Joyce had ripped the sleeves off her blouse and was wearing her green bandanna tied around her head pirate-style.

"What did you do to that eel?" I asked Zander.

"Oh," he said. "I just sang to him."

"Sang to him?"

"Yeah, we discovered it the first night on the island. Those things are everywhere. There are vegetarian ones that just eat the coconuts at night, but these guys are nasty. I'd been thinking about our old friend Petunia and then I remembered something I'd learned about this new species of island boa constrictors in the South Pacific. They hate low tones. All you have to do is hum at 'em and they get away as fast as they can. Who knew it might work for constrictor eels as well? I'm glad to see you two, I'll tell you that. But come on down to the beach. We'll show you the camp." He picked up the sword, tucked it into one of the loops at the bottom of the Explorer's vest, and put an arm around Sukey, who was still taking deep, rasping breaths, as we started down the path toward the beach.

They had all made it off the *Fair Beatrice* before she sank, Zander and Joyce told us. M.K., keeping her head about her, had remembered the inflatable raft in her vest, and she'd deployed it just as they'd all abandoned ship. It had been a tight squeeze, but they'd fit Zander, Joyce, M.K., Kemal, and the Nackleys into the raft. Then she'd rowed over to retrieve Amy. The submersible had floated free of the stern. Her boilers had been damaged and wouldn't run, but she was buoyant, and they had tied her to the raft and paddled away from the site of the shipwreck.

"We looked for you as long as we could," Zander said. "But the water was still bubbling and boiling away and we needed to get out of there. It was so dark. Leo Nackley hurt his leg in the wreck, but he had us take turns paddling and sleeping through the night, and early the next morning, we saw this island. We managed to get Amy ashore on some rocks and then we explored a bit and found a sandy beach nearby. That's where we set up camp."

"Where did you find the sword?" I knew I'd never seen the jewel-encrusted scabbard and sword before.

"On the beach," Zander said. "There was a bunch of stuff, pieces of a wooden boat, some old silver cups and pottery. At first we thought there might be someone else on the island, but the stuff is pretty old. Maybe it was from one of the shipwrecks."

"The raft made it?" Sukey asked. "So we have a boat?" I could see the hope flash in her eyes.

Joyce shook her head. "It was ripped by a piece of the ship. By the time we got here, we were having to bail her constantly to stay afloat. Besides, Lazlo's dad doesn't think she's big enough, even if we could repair her. The seas are too rough and it's a long way to St. Beatrice. He says we're better off staying here and waiting to be rescued by BNDL." A worried look crossed her face. "I sent Njamba out with a note tied to her leg yesterday."

"Joyce was awfully brave about it," Zander said, glancing her way. "Pucci couldn't make the long flight over water, but we think Njamba can do it. We figure it might take her a couple of days to reach St. Beatrice. M.K.'s been working away on Amy's engines to see if she can get them going again, though she probably doesn't have the range, and we just decided that Kemal and I are going to climb the volcano tomorrow."

We told them about how we had ended up on the other end of the island—minus the part about the psychic turtles—and about what we'd learned of our location at the top of the volcano.

"There's nothing around. We're all alone out here in the middle of the sea," I said. Zander searched my face, trying to figure out if I'd figured out anything about the map, but of course he couldn't ask in front of Joyce.

"I'm really happy to see you," he said to Sukey, slinging an arm around her shoulders again and pulling her in for another hug. "I don't know what I'd do without you, Suke."

Sukey blushed and I felt something give way in my stomach, an unpleasant little shift. I'd never heard him call her that before, but it sounded familiar, something he'd used more than once.

"Well, here we are," Joyce announced, as we came out of the trees and onto a wide, black-sand beach ringed with palm trees, almost exactly like the one on the other side of the island. "Camp Castaway!"

Thirty-seven

"Hey, everyone! Look who we found!" Zander shouted as we came down onto the beach.

Kemal and Jack were the first ones to see us emerge from the trees and Kemal shouted, "M.K.! Someone go get M.K.!" and then ran toward us, grinning.

"You're okay," he said in a quiet voice. He surprised me by throwing his arms around Sukey and then me. I was so happy they were all alive that I hugged him back.

"We thought you were dead!" Jack exclaimed, hugging Sukey and hanging on just a little too long. "Your hair smells really good, by the way."

"Okay, Jack," she said, pushing him away. "That's enough."

"It's just so good to see you," he sighed. "You guys, too." He was still wearing his white suit, but the pants had been torn off at the knees and the sleeves ripped off the jacket and it was now the color of dirt.

"We found them up on the side of the volcano, being attacked by one of the eels." Zander told them.

"Did you sing to it?" Kemal asked.

"Zander did," Joyce laughed. "It was beautiful. His best performance yet."

And then M.K. came running down the beach, holding her wrench, a funny hat made of woven palm fronds shielding her face from the sun. The hat fell off when I grabbed her and picked her up to hug her and I think Sukey stepped on it when she hugged her too.

I hadn't seen M.K. cry since we'd gotten the news about Dad, but her eyes were wet now and she clung to me whispering, "We thought you were dead. We really thought you were dead." I felt my throat tighten and my own eyes filled with tears. I quickly brushed them away.

"Well, we're not dead," Sukey said, hugging M.K. tightly. I think she was crying too.

They'd only been there two days, but they'd been busy. The inflatable raft had been supplied with the same thin tarps that were in my vest, and they'd made some tents at the back of the beach. Someone had been collecting palm fronds; there was a big pile of them next to the tents. For the first time in what seemed like months, I let myself relax a little. We were all okay. I had gone for a ride in the shell of a giant turtle who had shown me an underwater city, and I had failed to figure out the map Dad had left for me there, but at least we were all alive.

"Did you find water?" I asked her.

"We found a little bit in some leaves and we were able to collect some that condensed on the underside of the tarps last night, but there are a lot of us. We need a source of fresh water and we need it soon." She lowered her voice. "We wanted to take a vote on what we should do, but Lazlo's being impossible. He keeps trying to say that we're in a state of emergency and as the expedition leader he's like the king of the island or something."

"Where are they?" She knew I meant the Nackleys.

"In the tent. Mr. Nackley's resting. His leg looks kind of nasty. I'm worried it's infected but he won't let anyone touch it."

"Hey, Lazlo," Joyce shouted as we walked across the beach to the tents. "Look who we found. You didn't lose a single kid!"

Leo Nackley was lying in the middle tent, his right leg propped up on a pile of palm fronds, his face pale and tight with pain beneath his dark beard.

"You're okay," Lazlo said, eyeing us coldly. "I didn't think you would be." He was very sunburned, his pale skin an angry shade of red, his nose peeling. He was thinner, but I guess we all were.

"Well, we're sorry to disappoint you," Sukey said cheerfully. "Hi, Mr. Nackley."

He nodded at her, then looked up at me. "Where have you been?"

"We washed up on the other side of the island," I said. "Two days ago. It looks pretty much exactly the way this side of the island looks."

"They climbed the volcano," Zander told him. "And we're alone out here. No land or ships in sight. So I think we need to—"

"We'll talk about it later, West," Lazlo said. "Can't you see my father's resting?" Leo Nackley glared at me.

We left them alone and went back down to the beach, where Jack was sitting on the sand and trying to comb his hair with a stick. "How's he doing?" he asked, looking worried.

"He looks like he's in pain," I told him.

"Yeah," Jack said in a low voice. "I think Lazlo's worried too."

"Well, something's making him act like he's the Emperor of the Indorustan Empire," M.K. muttered.

"He's under a lot of pressure," Jack said. "It's not his fault."

"Yeah, right. Keep telling yourself that. I'm going to go work on Amy," M.K. said, marching off down the beach.

We spent the day swimming and sitting around staring at the ocean or sleeping in the sun. Joyce kept checking the sky, and I knew she was worried about Njamba.

By five o'clock, we were all hungry and starting to think about dinner. The fire had mostly gone out and Kemal said he was going to try to get it going again. I offered to help. They had managed to pile some palm fronds on top of the fire before the storm arrived and when we took them off there were still a few embers at the bottom. I helped him bring over some dry branches he'd stored under a tarp. "Where'd you find these?" I asked. "We had a terrible time finding stuff to burn on the other side of the island."

"There are some trees that grow up the slope," he said pointing. "Your brother thought they might be related to mangroves. Anyway, they burn really well." He cupped his hands and got down low, blowing on the embers. We watched as a small flame shot up to catch the crumpled palm fronds he'd used for tinder. He piled some more on at just the right moment and the fronds caught fire.

"You're good at that," I told him.

"I should be." He smiled. "Besides the thousands of dollars the Academy's spent on teaching me how to build fires, I got lots of practice when we were escaping from Ottomanland. We camped in the desert for twenty-three nights before we arrived in Simeria. The desert gets cold at night. There are wild dogs, snakes, other things. My parents had to hunt for food." He gave me a small smile. "I got good at building fires. Get me a few pieces of that wood." He pointed to the pile of debris they'd found on the beach. There wasn't much, five or six boards from what looked like a lifeboat, broken pieces of pottery. They'd already removed the few bits of silver, a cup and a few spoons, and were using them for cooking. There was something eerie about the little pile. Had any people washed up with it? If so, what had happened to them? I pulled out a couple of the boards and tossed them onto the fire.

The damp wood hissed and steamed as the flames licked at them.

"So what do you think?" Kemal said in a low voice, as we watched Zander and Sukey walk toward us, talking and laughing. "Do we have a chance of finding the shipwrecks?"

He was trying to sound casual, but he hadn't quite succeeded. "You mean the oil?"

"Yeah, I mean the oil. I thought . . . I mean, well, what you and Joyce were saying." He blushed.

Zander interrupted us. "How's that fire? Suke and I are going to try to rustle up some fish for dinner."

"Zander says he's got some new method that works better than the spear!"

"I found this little net, all folded up in my vest," Zander said. "Dad left it for me. It works great."

Kemal and Jack and I set up a little platform of sticks for cooking over the fire, and and it wasn't long before Zander and Sukey came running up the beach, laughing and holding a makeshift palm frond basket filled with fish.

When the fish were cooked, we laid them out on rocks and sat around the fire, watching the sun go down. Leo Nackley came to eat with us, limping down the beach and wincing as he lowered himself to the sand.

Once we'd all eaten, he raised a hand and announced, "Now that we know we all survived the shipwreck, Lazlo and I think we have to address the fact that the strange conditions in the water back there indicate something's there, under the water. Lazlo thinks it must be the ocean trenches that we've been seeking. They were letting out oil, and that's what caused the shipwreck. He wants to repair the raft and use the diving equipment from Miss West's . . . machine to see what's there. Don't you, Lazlo?"

"Yes," Lazlo said nervously. "I think that may be the source of the oil. I'm going to go tomorrow and I'm taking Jack and, uh . . . Zander with me."

"Are you joking?" Joyce asked him. "You want to go back there?"

"In a leaking raft?" Zander asked. "I won't go."

"It's not up to you," Lazlo said. "I'm the expedition leader. You have to do as I say. Miss West is going to fix the raft."

"With what?" M.K. asked him. "Don't you think that if there was a way to fix that boat I would already have tried it?"

"Everyone says you're such a good engineer," Lazlo told her. "You shouldn't have any problem. Besides, it's not your, uh, job to question." He glanced at his father. "I'm the expedition leader!"

"But we're shipwrecked," Kemal said. "There is no expedition anymore, Lazlo. The expedition was a disaster. Don't you see that? You can forget about Mr. Mountmorris's gold."

Lazlo rose up to his full height and turned on Kemal. "The expedition is not a disaster, Kemal. I am going to find the oil and I am going to win the prize."

Leo Nackley had been silent, listening to us argue, but now he raised a hand and said, "Lazlo is in charge. He will make the decisions about how we are to proceed. I, for one, feel that we are in good hands. And now I'm going to rest my leg." Lazlo helped him up and watched his father limp back toward the tents.

"Lazlo," Sukey said once his father was gone. "We'll be lucky if we get off this island alive. You can't do it. Zander, don't go with him."

"I decide who goes and who stays," Lazlo said.

They kept arguing but I didn't say a word. I was too busy panicking. If Lazlo went out in Amy looking for the trenches at the site of the shipwreck, he might find the underwater city.

But I didn't think the turtles would let that happen. They would probably sink the lifeboat and Lazlo—and Jack and Zander with him.

Once it was dark, we all sat there watching the jellyfish light up the water off the beach and listening to the eels slither up the coconut palms.

"What do you think everyone else is doing right now?" Sukey wondered. "How do you think Mr. Wooley's feeling? And where do you think Maggie is?"

"Maybe she's giving Mr. Foley a foot massage," I suggested. Everyone laughed except for Lazlo.

"That's not a very respectful way of talking about your headmaster. Or the director of the ADR," Lazlo said. "Someone tried to kill him at the Kickoff Dinner, or have you forgotten?"

"Oh, come on," Kemal said. "Nobody tried to kill Mr. Foley. Everyone knows it. They set that bomb behind the elephant. They staged the whole thing. If that had been real, do you think they would have let all the guests leave before they figured out who it was?"

We all stared at him in surprise, even Lazlo.

"But why would they do that?" M.K. asked. "Why would they pretend?"

"Why do you think?" Kemal asked bitterly, and suddenly I remembered what Joyce had said about those two days she was being questioned.

I leaned forward to poke the fire. "Because they wanted to be able to search us, to put the extra agents on campus. They wanted an excuse to know exactly what we were up to. Because they wanted to be able to ask Joyce and Kemal for the names of their friends and families."

"He's right," Joyce said quietly. "It was pretty clear when they were questioning us that they weren't trying to figure out who put the bomb there. That was just the pretense."

"I don't have to listen to this," Lazlo said. "This is ridiculous."

Zander leaned forward and poked the fire too. "I knew they were low when they let you steal our proposal, Lazlo. But I didn't realize they were quite that low."

"I didn't steal it," Lazlo said.

"Yes, you did."

"No. I didn't." He glanced over his shoulder to make sure his father hadn't come out of his tent. "They . . . they *gave* it to me. Said I had to turn it in and that if I did I would be chosen as leader. They said it was an old one. I didn't know it was yours."

"He's telling the truth," Jack said. "He really didn't know it was yours."

"But why?" Joyce asked.

Lazlo looked at Zander, M.K., and me. "Because you're hiding something. My father thinks you have a map that shows exactly where the oil is. He's not going to stop until he finds out what it is. We need it. The country needs it."

"That's ridiculous," Zander said, but he didn't sound very convincing.

I didn't say anything; I didn't dare.

"It's so cold," Sukey said, trying to change the subject. "It's so hot during the day that it seems hard to believe it could cool off so quickly at night." Zander put an arm around her shoulders and pulled her into him.

"I'm going to work on Amy," M.K. announced. "If you find any rubber cement or durable composite patching material, you let me know, Lazlo. I'll get right to work on that raft."

"I'll go with you." I jumped up and followed her along the dark path through the trees to the little rocky beach where they'd managed to get Amy up on dry land.

"How's it going?" I asked her as she started tinkering, using her vestlight to illuminate the parts of Amy's engine and boilers.

"Pretty good. I'm almost there, but don't tell Lazlo. I need to reconnect the internal steam filter to the exterior pressure gauge, but I don't have any extra wire. I'm using the first-line plugs to make the connection and . . . you have no idea what I'm talking about, do you?"

"No, but it all sounds good."

M.K. looked up at me. "Do you believe Lazlo? That he didn't know?

"I think so."

"So what do you think about Dad's map now that we're here? Was that King Triton's Lair back there? The waves or whatever it was that sunk the ship?"

I'd never lied to M.K. in my life, but suddenly I heard myself saying, "I don't know. It might have been," and she was giving me a strange look.

"Are you okay?" she said. "Did you find something on the other side of the island?"

I shook my head. "I'm just tired. I need to get some sleep." I made my way back along the path to Camp Castaway. Hearing

Zander and Sukey's laughter rising from the circle around the campfire, I went straight to my tent and got under my reflective blanket. I listened to them all talking and laughing.

It was so strange. I was relieved to know they were all okay, and yet I was filled with regret that it wasn't just Sukey and me on the beach anymore. I felt suddenly and deeply alone and I remembered the Explorer's words: *And you should know that it isn't about your brother and sister. I was directed by your father to give the book to you. Just you. Not to Zander, not to M.K. To you, Kit.*

I knew now why Dad had sent us here. I knew why he'd given me the map, why he'd given me the whistle. But I didn't know how I was going to get back to the secret map at the bottom of the sea before BNDL arrived.

It was a long time before I fell asleep.

noticed that Captain Girafalco had become quite secretive. Anyone entering his cabin was made to knock and I noticed that he had taken to locking his charts away in the safe box under his bed. I also noticed that he had taken to wearing a strange piece of jewelry, a carved shell bauble that

Thirty-eight

The next morning, after we'd eaten fish for breakfast, M.K. and Zander started work on a contraption for collecting drinking water. They had made a number of baskets out of palm leaves and put them around the beach to collect rainwater, but we had discovered that they leaked and hadn't collected much at all from the rainstorm.

While they tried to repair the baskets, I emptied my vest pockets to see if there were any gadgets or utilities we could use to collect drinking water. The spearfishing utility had been in the upper right-hand pocket and I remembered a few other things in there that I hadn't recognized.

"What are those?" M.K. asked as I spread out three large circles of fabric, coated with a smooth substance. "There's some kind of marking on them."

She was right. A little cartoon diagram showed a stick figure digging a hole in the ground, then placing a cup in the bottom of the hole, and then placing the circle of plastic over the top and weighting down the edges.

"It's a condensation device!" M.K. exclaimed. "Look at the picture! Help me dig some holes. The fabric will make them airtight, and when water condenses on the inside, it will drip down into the cup. Quick, Kit, see if you can find some palm leaves that we can twist into a better cone receptacle."

We got busy and pretty soon we had the three water condensers set up on the beach.

When we were done, I announced that I was going for a walk.

"Take a sword with you," Zander said as I was leaving. "That's the rule we made after we discovered the eels." He showed me how to attach a scabbard to one of the loops on my vest, and I set off up the path toward the top of the volcano, keeping an eye out for the constrictor eels and trying to figure out what to do. If all had gone well, Njamba may have already reached St. Beatrice. It would probably take BNDL another day or two to reach us, if they could. Lazlo might try to go out in the raft and force Zander and Jack to go with him. I knew that I needed to get back to the city to warn the turtles. But how? The Nackleys were already suspicious. If I disappeared for too long, they would try to come and find me, and I couldn't risk them seeing the turtle as he came up on the beach to get me.

I caught movement in the sky and looked up, shielding my eyes against the bright sun. Far off, coming from the west, a small black dot resolved itself into a bird. At first I assumed it was a gull, but something about the way its wings moved made me look again. It seemed heavier than a gull and as I watched, another black form— Pucci—rose up from the beach below me to meet it, calling out *Njamba! Njamba!*

I ran back down the slope, bursting out onto the beach just as Njamba swooped down onto Joyce's shoulder. She let her rest there for a moment and stroked the bird's head while Zander ran to get her some fresh water and fish. Joyce waited until she'd finished drinking to remove the bag tied to her leg.

"It's a note," she said, taking out a rolled slip of paper covered with typed words and reading, "'Arriving as soon as possible. BNDL.'"

"Hurrah!" Jack shouted. "We're saved!"

Joyce looked relieved and M.K. allowed herself a little cheer. But I met Sukey's and Zander's eyes and saw that Kemal looked downcast too.

"By the time they get here, I will have discovered the oil," Lazlo announced. "It will be perfect. How's that raft repair coming, M.K.?"

"What's the matter?" Jack asked me. "You don't look very happy, Kit."

"You're all forgetting what happened to us just a few days ago," I told them. "The . . . whatever it is that brought down our ship is going to bring theirs down too."

"He's right," Kemal said. "I don't know why you all don't see it. We're never getting off this island." He smiled grimly. "Better get used to fish, everyone." Maybe he was just being sarcastic, but

I almost had the sense that he didn't care, and I remembered what the Explorer had said. If Kemal was BNDL's spy, maybe he wanted us stuck on the island as long as possible so he could try to get the map from me.

"You don't know BNDL," Lazlo said. "They'll be able to do it. They have ships, machines, things you can't even imagine. Zander, Jack, make preparations for our expedition tomorrow. And M.K., you'd better get those drills going for when we find it. We're going to be waiting here with good news for them when they arrive." He looked over at me. "Don't worry, Kit. They'll get here soon enough."

Thirty-nine

I fell asleep that night almost as soon as I closed my eyes and dreamed that I was back in the underwater city. I swam through the streets, following a beautiful mermaid with red hair who was smiling and leading me toward King Triton's throne in the temple. The turtles were there too, and we all made our way toward the throne. As we reached the end of the tunnel, I saw a figure seated on the throne, but before I could see who it was, I woke up to darkness. It was still the middle of the night. I heard the sound of the waves and the wind and Zander's snoring. I snuck out of the tent, listening to make sure that no one else was up.

Lazlo had told M.K. to try patching the raft with the rubbery substance from the trees, and from the looks of it, the repair had worked. Dad's raft was sitting on the beach, tied to a tree and fully inflated. I was betting Lazlo would want to set out at first light.

I didn't have much time.

I made my way along the path to the beach where Amy was sitting, gleaming dully in the moonlight, and I walked into the water, letting it wash around my boots, soaking the leather. Then I took out the whistle and played the song once through, as quietly as I could so I wouldn't wake anyone.

Nothing happened.

I tried again. I knew I had it right. I waited for twenty minutes and he still didn't come. I kept at it for nearly an hour, playing the song softly every few minutes before I accepted that he wasn't going to show up.

I sank down onto the sand. Was there nothing else I could do? I had come so close to finding the next map that Dad had left for me, and it seemed impossible that I would fail now. But the turtle wasn't coming and there didn't seem to be any other options. Once BNDL arrived, it would all be over. They'd find the city and the map.

I looked out over the water. There *was* one other option. There was Amy. M.K. had said that she was almost fixed. But I couldn't operate her on my own. M.K. and I wouldn't be able to get her into the water without help. I ran back to Camp Castaway and went quietly over to the tents.

"M.K.," I whispered. "Wake up."

"What?" she asked, a little too loudly. I put a hand over her mouth and she sat up. I nodded toward the beach and she grabbed her vest and followed me.

"I need you to wake up Sukey," I told her. "Meet me on the beach where you've been working on Amy."

Good old M.K. She didn't ask any questions. She just nodded and I headed for the tent Zander and I were sharing with Kemal. I shook Zander awake and put a finger to my lips, and he slipped on his shoes and followed me out onto the beach. We waited silently for M.K. and Sukey, Pucci sitting on Zander's shoulder and nuzzling his ear.

When they appeared, I pointed and they all followed me along the path to the other beach.

"Okay," Zander said. "What's going on?"

"We have to get Amy going," I told them. "Right now. Can you, M.K.? It's really important."

"I'm close," she said. "I was going to try my fuse trick from the Derudan challenge next."

"Kit, what the—" Zander started.

"I know I'm asking a lot," I told him. "I'm sorry, but I found something under the water. I can't explain now, but we have to get there before BNDL arrives. If they get here first, it could be disastrous. M.K., what do you say?"

She fiddled with one of the wires in her vest, then went over to Amy and knelt down on the sand, working on the engine in the light from her vest.

"Damn it," she said. "I need a finer wire. Anybody have anything?"

Zander and I searched our vests but came up empty. She kept fiddling. Finally, she stood up. "Okay," she said. "I think that should do it, but we won't know until we start her up."

"Let's try starting her in the water," I said. I was hoping that would muffle the sound of the engine so the others wouldn't hear.

We each took an arm and slowly, with a lot of effort, pushed and pulled her along the beach until we could ease her into the water. Zander told Pucci to wait for us, and the bird gave us each a little nuzzle before he flew up to perch in a palm tree. Then we waded into the water and climbed into the cockpit, shutting the hatch and settling into the four seats. I checked that the diving suits were there.

"Okay, let's try it," I said.

M.K. pushed the engine's starter button.

Nothing happened.

She did it again. "Come on, Amy. Come on," I said.

The engine coughed once and was silent. "Please, Amy," M.K. whispered.

She tried once more and the engine came to life.

We all clapped and gave M.K. high fives.

"You're amazing, M.K.," I told her. "Absolutely amazing."

"Thanks very much." She switched on Amy's lights and eased the throttle forward. The submersible scuttled along the sand and out into the deeper water of the bay, but this time I couldn't see much of our descent. We gazed out into the dark water. I felt a rush of panic as we went out farther and farther. It had been different when I'd been in the turtle, but even though I knew Amy was solid and sea-worthy, I felt vulnerable and couldn't help remembering the cold water pressing in on me after the ship sank. If something went wrong, we were all dead. The look on Sukey's face told me she was thinking the same thing. We sped up and I got my compass out and gave M.K. some directions. "North-northeast until I tell you differently," I said.

"Whoa." Sukey was staring out the window at the illuminated murkiness. Every once in a while, a fish or small eel would cross our path, but Amy's lights didn't reach the reef or any of the marvelous things I'd seen the last time I'd been here. "We're actually under the water."

"We are under the water," said Zander. "And I for one wish Kit would tell us what we're doing here under the water. What is it we *have* to see before BNDL arrives?"

"It's not going to make any sense to you until we get there," I told them. "I just want you to see it."

"Kit," Zander said. "You can't do that to us. We're risking our lives under here."

In the dimly lit cockpit, I glanced at Sukey. She nodded.

"All right." I took a deep breath. "It sounds crazy, but there are these giant sea turtles. And one of them took me under the water in his . . . shell. There were more of them and—"

"His shell? Kit, what are you saying?"

"Did you eat any strange berries before you found us?" M.K. asked me, turning away from Amy's controls and gauges for a moment.

"No. I'm completely serious. Just forget it. You'll see what I mean." I held my compass out and kept my eyes on it. "Keep heading due east now, M.K. That's good."

"You have to tell us *something*," Zander said. "We could die under here. If Amy malfunctions, if something attacks us, that's it."

316

"Amy won't malfunction," M.K. grumbled. "I can't believe you said that."

Zander turned to me and the scowl on his face scared me a little.

I hesitated, unsure of where to begin. "The code, on the map, well . . ." I glanced at Sukey again. "Sukey and I figured out that it's a series of musical notes. The Explorer with the Clockwork Hand gave me a whistle from Dad and we tried playing the music, but nothing happened. I think it was because the turtle was waiting until I was alone. Anyway, the next morning I tried again and this turtle came up on the beach and his shell opened and I was able to ride in it—I know, I know. Just listen—and he brought me under the water, just like this, to a city, an underwater city. I saw the shipwrecks too. The treasure from the wrecks is in the city."

There was a long silence. Amy's engine made a deep rhythmic chugging sound.

"Kit, do you know how crazy that sounds?" Zander said. "Turtles? That you can ride in? An underwater city?"

"He's right," Sukey said. "I know it sounds crazy. But I saw them too."

"You went under the water with him?" Zander said.

"No, but I think they saved our lives after the wreck. I think they brought us to the island."

"And that's not even the craziest part," I added. "They're telepathic. I was able to communicate with my turtle without talking."

The ocean was dark, the path ahead illuminated only by Amy's lights.

"Kit," Zander said. "That's impossible."

"I know, I know. But just wait."

We traveled for another twenty minutes in silence and I was starting to think I'd made a navigation error when all of a sudden we saw the shapes of the shipwrecks up ahead, the masts reaching up from the ocean floor.

"It's the ships," I told them, pointing. "This is where they all came to rest."

Zander stood up. "Aren't we going to go explore the wrecks?" he asked. "This is incredible. There must be millions in treasure here."

"We have to get to the city," I told him. "If BNDL gets there before we do, they'll find the map, and everything Dad worked for may be lost."

He didn't say anything, just kept watching through the window as Amy motored by the ghostly shapes. "Keep going straight, M.K.," I told her, watching my compass as we traveled. "It won't be long. This is Girafalco's Trench."

The walls of the trench sloped down steeply into blackness. "It looks so cold," Sukey said. "It seems hard to believe that anything could survive down here."

"Just wait," I told her. We traveled for another thirty minutes before I saw the walls of the cavern up ahead.

"Oh my god," Sukey gasped. "Look at that. The walls. They're glowing. I can see everything."

M.K. maneuvered us through the cavern and then we were at the end of it, just outside the city, looking down into a wide valley of light and rippling seaweed.

Are you there? I tried sending my thoughts out to the turtle, but I didn't get any reply.

"Look," Sukey said, pointing. "*Look!*"

We were approaching the entrance to the city, and in the near distance the shimmering panorama of buildings became suddenly visible.

"I didn't believe you," M.K. said to me. "But . . . it's real."

"My God," Zander whispered. "I never would've believed you until I'd seen this with my own eyes."

"It's beautiful," Sukey said, gazing through the window at the spires and minarets and domes. "It's the most beautiful thing I've ever seen."

I saw movement up ahead. "There's a gate into the city up there," I said. "Keep going. I think I see the turtles."

We saw fifty or more turtles just outside the city gates, but instead of guarding it, they were swimming around frantically. As we got closer, we saw that their movements were kicking up sand and eroding the walls of the city.

"They're destroying the buildings!" I said, watching as the pearly structures seemed to shatter in the wake of the turtles' efforts.

"Why would they do that?" Sukey said, staring out the window at the maelstrom.

The turtles ignored us as Amy chugged past them. Inside the city, many more turtles were all using their flippers to crush the buildings to sand.

I watched as spires and domes crumbled and fell across the city.

"When I was here, the turtle told me he sensed danger. They must know that BNDL is coming, and they're destroying the city so it won't be discovered."

"How do they know BNDL's coming?" Sukey asked.

"They must have turtles who act as scouts. And they can sense thoughts, feelings. Remember, whenever a ship came near the city, they created the whirlpools, the storms."

"But what is this place?" Zander asked, still staring. "What is it that they're destroying?"

"It's an underwater city," I told him. "It was abandoned by the people who lived here. The turtle called them the Men of the Sea."

Zander stared at me. "People? What, like mermen, merpeople? Are you telling me there's such thing as mermaids?"

"I don't know, Zander. Maybe. They're not here now. The turtles are the guardians of the city. They stayed to keep the secret, even after the Men of the Sea left. So no one would see it."

"But why? Why can't anyone see it?"

"And why are they destroying the city?" Sukey asked.

I thought for a minute. "I'm not positive, but I think the reason that no one can see it is that there's a map here, the map Dad wanted me—us—to see. That's the turtles' job. To protect the map."

"Why don't they just sink the ship like they did with us?" She was right. Why didn't they just sink the SteamShip that BNDL was coming in?

Zander was staring out the window now. "I don't understand any of it. The size of their shells. It's incredible."

We were silent, taking it all in. I remembered the way to the temple the best I could, directing M.K. along the streets, where the turtles were now busy destroying the beautiful buildings, crushing the murals and stones and shells to dust.

"It's so sad," Sukey said, watching the turtles work. "This beautiful place. All destroyed."

We were almost to the temple when I saw him.

It was my turtle, up ahead, working away with the other turtles, crushing the walls of the buildings. I recognized the scar on his right flipper.

You're here, he said. *I'm glad. I couldn't come.*

Yes. I'm here. Why are they destroying the city?

Someone's coming.

Who?

The Men of the Land.

I knew he was talking about BNDL. *Can you take me to the map?* I asked. *Can you take me to the old turtle again?*

Yes. Follow me.

"Kit?" M.K. asked me. "Are you okay? We lost you for a minute." "Did anyone else hear that?" I asked, searching their faces. "He was talking to me. He said someone's coming and that's why they're destroying the city, so it won't be discovered."

"I didn't hear anything," Zander said. "Who are you talking about?"

"That turtle." I pointed. "Follow him, M.K. We've got to follow him. BNDL's coming."

M.K. and Zander exchanged a worried glance, but she did as I said. We followed the turtle along the streets, toward the huge domed roof of the temple.

They were quiet as we entered. It hadn't been touched by the turtles yet and everything was still in place, the lovely murals and the coral throne.

"They'll have to destroy this too," Sukey whispered. "All these beautiful things. All because we brought BNDL here. It's our fault."

I hadn't thought of it that way, but I knew she was right. If we hadn't written the proposal, they wouldn't have given it to Lazlo and we never would have come here. Dad had wanted me to come and find the second map, but had he known the turtles would destroy the city?

There wasn't any way we could go back and change things. The only thing I could do now was what Dad had wanted me to do. I had to find the next clue. The next map.

"The map is in a chamber behind the throne," I told them. "I don't think Amy can get to it. The turtle will take me. I'll put on a diving suit." I also didn't think the turtles would let the others through.

"I'll go with you," Zander said. "Let me get into a suit too." He jumped up and started putting on the other diving suit.

"No," I said. "I think I have to do it alone."

"What are you talking about? Are you trying to act noble or something?"

"I need to do this alone. I don't think they'll let you in. I think the turtle can only take me."

And then the turtle's voice entered my head. *Only you. You are the one he sent.*

Who?

The man. Your father.

"Kit?"

"I'm sorry, Zander. Just . . . believe me."

"What do you mean? If Dad wanted us to do this, I'm going too."

I looked right at him. "Dad wanted me to do it. Just me, Zander."

"What? How do you know?"

"I just know."

Sukey put a hand on his arm. "Zander. Let him go."

He looked at her for a long moment, then nodded.

M.K.'s diving suit was tight against my skin, made of a thick synthetic material that was supposed to keep me warm in the frigid water. Once I had the helmet on, I signaled that I was ready to go out through the diving hatch.

Sukey touched my arm and I met her eyes and smiled. It was strangely silent inside the helmet. The only thing I could hear was the rasp of my breathing apparatus. I waited a moment before opening the hatch to the air lock. I waited there for a moment until the door to the outside opened and I swam out into the freezing water.

I started to panic, remembering the shipwreck, with the cold pressure on my body, the terrifying inability to breathe, the feeling that my lungs would burst. I took a deep breath.

It was okay. This was different. I could breathe inside the helmet. And the turtle was here. He swam alongside me and his shell opened enough that I could swim inside. It shut again and I took off my helmet as the water drained out and I found myself once again in the cool, glowing quiet of the turtle's shell.

I waved to Zander, M.K., and Sukey. Their astonished faces got smaller and smaller as the turtle swam into the passage to the chamber behind the throne.

Now, he said. *It is almost the end.*

Why? Why are you destroying the city? I asked him.

No one can see. It is one of the places.

What places?

Not now. Now you must see the map.

In a few minutes, we'd reached the map room. The elderly turtle was there, hovering before the huge mosaics, with the map in the center and the panels with their strange hieroglyphics all around it.

I hadn't tried to communicate with the old turtle before, but now I stared at him, directing my thoughts into his huge head.

What is this? I asked. *Who left it here?*

It doesn't matter who left it. It matters that you found it. You are the one. You were chosen. His voice sounded different in my head from the other turtle's—older, raspier.

But why? What do I do with it?

I don't know. But you must remember it. So someone will know. So you can carry it.

I studied the map with everything I had. This was it. This was my one chance to remember what Dad had sent me all this way to see.

I stared and stared, working to imprint it upon my brain, taking snapshots, the way Dad had taught me. "Work across the map," he'd said. "One square at a time. Create pieces of a puzzle in your brain, pieces you can put together later to recreate the whole."

For what must have been an hour or more, I stared at the map and the panels, closing my eyes and testing myself to see if I could still see it.

Finally, I had it.

It's okay, I told the old turtle. *I'm finished.*

Goodbye, he told me. *Now carry it.*

I took one last look at the map I'd come all this way to see. Each tiny stone and shell was perfect on its own, the shapes and colors completely unique. Together they created something else, something I didn't yet understand, a map of some yet unknown place, a place I couldn't even imagine.

Forty

We found the temple mostly destroyed, the throne and murals crushed to sand. Through the gaping holes in its side, I could see the ruined city and the dark water beyond. It was empty except for Amy.

You must go now, my turtle told me. *They have all gone. The men of the land will be here soon.*

I looked back at the passage. *What about the map? We can't let them find it.*

He will destroy it.

I looked at Amy. I thought of the old turtle, his flippers tired, his raspy voice. *We'll help*, I told him, putting on my helmet. *We'll help you.*

The shell opened and I was back out in the frigid water, murky now with sand and debris. M.K. maneuvered Amy over to me and

I made my way through the hatch. It was a relief to be back inside Amy and out of the helmet.

"What happened?" Zander said. "Did you do it? Do you know what the map shows?"

I held up a hand. "I'll tell you later. They say BNDL will be here soon. We have to help them, M.K. Can we get the drill to work?"

She raised her eyebrows. "I don't know. Zander, flip that switch and then use these levers to control it."

He did as she said. There was a grinding noise and the tentacle with the drill on the end stretched out, the huge bit on the end spinning powerfully.

As M.K. guided Amy close to the passage and the walls of the temple, Zander used the lever to bring the drill up and out. It hit the mother-of-pearl wall with a terrible rasping. What was left of the temple began to crumble away.

My turtle just watched us, a sad look on his face. *Thank you*, he told me.

The other turtle, I said. *He needs to come out now. This is all going to go in a minute.*

He didn't say anything. Amy kept drilling, and what was left of the walls of the temple and the passageway kept falling. Soon we'd reach the map chamber.

I was determined that if Mr. Mountmorris and BNDL made it to this part of the ocean they would find nothing more than a few mounds of cracked shells covered in sand.

The water around us suddenly darkened.

"What's that?"

M.K. turned around. "I don't know."

"There's something coming out of the cracks! See that black stuff?" A black ribbon, thick and viscous, was seeping out of the fissures in the rock. Thousands of dark ribbons curled through the water.

"It's the oil," Zander whispered. "The stories were right."

"We've got to get out of here!" M.K. yelled. "I can't see anything!"

Suddenly, the rest of the walls crumbled away in a rush of black.

"I'm pulling us out," M.K. yelled.

"The turtles!"

"There isn't time. They'll follow us!" M.K. spun Amy around and throttled us out into the streets of the city, slamming against piles of debris as she tried to maneuver through the water, which was densely clouded with the black oil.

I concentrated as hard as I could, trying to send my thoughts back to the turtles. *Come out. Quickly. The oil will hurt you.*

They didn't answer.

"It's oil," Zander whispered. "All that stuff about the black waterfalls. They were right. There *is* oil here."

"A lot of it, by the looks of things," Sukey said. "Look how fast it's coming!"

"We've got to stop it," Zander said. "It will kill everything it comes in contact with. We've got to stop it."

I watched. "How can we? We need equipment. We need something that can block it."

330

Zander was silent. Finally he said. "We've got to get help. We've got to get back to the island. Where are those turtles?"

"They must be coming out," I said. "They must be."

Come on! I tried to tell them. *You'll die if you stay there.*

Nothing.

We sat there watching as black snakes of oil kept slithering toward us. The turtles never appeared.

Forty-one

"**Z**ander's right," I told M.K. "The only way to stop the flow is to get BNDL to bring down pipes and equipment."

"This is awful," Zander said angrily. "Do you know what we've done? Do you know how many animals, how many fish and birds may die because you wanted to protect that map? There are species here that no human being has ever seen. And now no one will ever see them because they'll be gone."

With a rush of air bubbles and black silt, another huge chunk of the city disappeared

"Go," I told M.K. "Go now!" Amy was making terrible grinding and wheezing noises.

"Is she going to be okay?"

"I don't know." M.K. worked away at the controls, checking pressure gauges and pushing buttons to release more steam, trying to figure out what was going wrong. She eased the throttle forward, but we barely moved. M.K. flipped a few more levers and after a few minutes, Amy sounded a little better. We seemed to be moving with more power.

And then we heard a *boom* and saw, in the distance, a huge cloud rise up from the ocean floor as what was left of the city collapsed down into the trench, disappearing in a swirl of sand and dark water. "Go!" I shouted to M.K. "It's coming down! It'll bury us!"

"I'm trying!" M.K. shouted as she flipped a lever. She pushed the throttle all the way up and Amy shot forward, up, up, away from the oily cloud of sand rising from the trench.

"I can't look at it," Sukey said. "Why do they have to destroy it?"

"They don't want the city to be discovered," I whispered.

"But why?" Zander asked me. "They destroyed the map."

I thought about it. "I think it's about something even bigger than the map, but I don't know what it is. I think that they don't want anyone to know about the city. They're willing to destroy it in order to keep it a secret. But I don't know why."

We chugged back the way we'd come, out of Girafalco's Trench and up into shallower waters. Up ahead, we saw the ghostly shapes of the shipwrecks rising out of the darkness. They were like dead trees, the broken masts bobbing gently with the current. Zander and Sukey and I pressed our faces to the glass.

"Amy's not happy, but she's running," M.K. said. "We've got to get back up as soon as we can. Kit, look . . ."

Sunlight was now filtering through the water, and beyond the wrecks we saw undulating fields of seaweed and hovering anenomes. We made our way slowly through the water.

But something was wrong.

"Where are all the fish?" M.K. said.

The sea stretched all around us, empty of life. The anemones and coral remained, but the fish were gone.

"Do the fish know?" Sukey asked. "Do they know that BNDL's coming?"

Zander watched the empty void. "I don't know. But they're all gone. Nothing's there. Not a single fish."

And then suddenly, there were thousands of fish swimming past us in huge schools. We couldn't tell where one began and another ended.

"They're swimming away from the oil!" Zander said.

"Look at that one," M.K. said. "And that one . . ." I followed her gaze.

Some of the fish were slowing down, then sinking, unable to swim.

It's killing them," Zander said. "But I don't know. . . . They're all going the same direction."

It was like standing in a field on a blustery day and watching as a rain cloud blew by, leaving blue sky behind it. The waves of fish went by and then we were all alone again in the silent ocean.

And then we saw it, wriggling up slowly toward us out of the deep, a giant black form twisting through the water. It was, I realized with horror, a gigantic version of the eels on the island, its white teeth gleaming, its mouth opening to attack Amy.

"What is that?" M.K. asked, fumbling with the controls.

"It's an eel," Sukey said. "It's a really giant eel."

"Dive!" I shouted. M.K. steered Amy into a dive. Through the side windows, I could see the eel following us through the murk, and M.K. pulled us up again. But the eel kept coming. "Here it comes. Get us out of here, M.K!"

"It's huge," she shouted. "I don't know if I can get away."

"It's coming!" Zander said.

It swam up slowly, its body twisting, one eye staring at us through the cockpit glass. M.K. pushed the throttle all the way up and Amy shot ahead, but the eel followed, curious about this strange octopus. It kept pace with us easily, twisting through the water.

"How far are we from the beach?" M.K. asked.

"I don't know." I checked my compass to make sure we were going in the right direction.

M.K. kept Amy moving quickly through the water and I thought we were going to get away, but when we tilted up toward the surface, there it was in front of us again, rising up, its enormous mouth open and ready for attack.

Sukey screamed. She reached for the tentacle controls and swung the pincer arm at the eel, but it barely noticed what must have felt like nothing more than a tap on the back.

"Try the hose," M.K. said.

But before Sukey could engage the hose arm, the eel struck the glass with a terrible bang and we watched in horror as a thin crack appeared on the windshield.

"Come on, Amy. Come *on*." I could feel Amy go a little faster. But not fast enough. The eel seemed to be maddened by the fact that it hadn't been able to get us, and it reared up once again.

We all watched as its body grew rigid and its huge eye fixed on us.

"Oh god," I whispered.

But just before it attacked, it hesitated, its body rippling as it turned its head toward some far-off sound or smell.

"What is it? Is it the turtles?" M.K. asked.

I couldn't see anything through the dark water.

The eel looked at us again, and then it was spiraling away toward the bottom of the ocean.

I peered through the water and then I saw a cloud of thin black curls easing toward us, twisting through the water.

"It's the oil," I called out.

"I'm taking us up," M.K. said. "We can't let it get into the engine."

We sped away from the oily cloud through the water. "I think we're almost back to the island," M.K. said. "There's the coral reef."

Up ahead, the reef still buzzed with life, fish and small eels swimming over the sandy floor, the sunlight filtering through the gentle waves and casting shimmering patterns on the floor.

I felt the tension leave my body, but Zander was becoming more and more agitated. "It's a disaster. It's going to kill everything in the ocean. Why did you have to do that? Why did we have to destroy that map? If you hadn't destroyed the map, that never would have happened."

"We had to," I said. "You know that. The turtles were destroying

it anyway. The oil would have come out when the city crumbled."
I tried to convince myself.

"But we're killing off hundreds of species. We're destroying an
ecosystem that doesn't exist anywhere else on earth. And for what?
A map? A map only you're allowed to see? I don't know what you
think Dad intended to happen, but it can't be this. You don't even
know what it's a map of. You don't know if you'll ever find out. And
down here, there are hundreds, maybe thousands of species of fish
and animals, and we've made them extinct before anyone can ever
see them!"

"Dad wouldn't have told me to—"

"Dad! Dad! I'm tired of you talking about Dad as though you
have some secret line of communication to him. Where is he? If he
wants you to do this so much, then where is he? *Where is he, Kit?*"
Zander grasped my shoulder so hard it hurt. His eyes were furious.
I'd never really been afraid of him until now.

"Stop!" Sukey yelled. "This isn't the time. We're back at the
island. What are we going to tell them? We've been gone for hours."

Zander let go of me and turned to look out the window at the life
all around us. "We'll figure something out," I said. "It's still early.
Let's leave Amy on the other beach. Maybe we can sneak back and
get into the tents without waking them up."

Amy rose up and up, a white veil of air bubbles covering the
windows as we surfaced into sunlight. M.K. maneuvered Amy up
onto the beach as best she could and Zander, Sukey, and I helped to
pull her up even higher. Pucci was waiting for us in a palm tree, and

he started to greet us, squawking. Zander hushed him and made him stay on his shoulder.

The sun was rising above the horizon now and the sky turned a beautiful pink-orange as we walked through the sparse trees and low bushes in single file, trying to be as quiet as possible. I was in the rear, looking up at the morning sky, and suddenly bumped into M.K., who had stopped just in front of me. Joyce was on the path ahead of us, holding one of the water receptacles we'd made from palm fronds, two swords hanging from a piece of rope around her waist. I checked for Njamba and found her flying overhead. Joyce put a finger to her lips before we could say anything, and then she silently beckoned us to follow her. We walked along the path for another hundred feet before she stopped and pointed.

Through the trees, we could see the bright purple sails of a big sailing catamaran anchored just off Castaway Beach.

Forty-two

ried to tell you, Pucci chortled on Zander's shoulder. *Tried
to tell.*

"Shhh," we all hissed at him.

Joyce put her finger to her lips again and whispered, "I went
to look for water and when I came back, six pirates were storming
the beach and tying everyone up. There are more out in the harbor.
I managed to stay out of sight, and they don't know I'm here."

"Unless Lazlo told them," Sukey whispered.

"Unless Lazlo told them," Joyce admitted. She was wearing her
green bandanna tied pirate-style around her head again.

Zander craned his neck to try to see the beach, but we were still
too far away. He silently pointed up the hillside and then pointed
two fingers at his eyes—we needed to climb higher in order to see
what was going on. Joyce nodded and we all crept up through the

flowering bushes until we were up above the beach, behind a rocky outcropping, with a good view of the camp.

It was Monty Brioux.

I recognized his long red hair and purple cloak. And I recognized his shiny red alligator-skin boots. He had five pirates with him, three men and two women, all of them dressed in leather boots and bright Neo clothes, their hairlights and facelights blinking and flashing.

I counted four additional pirates on the deck of the catamaran out in the bay. I held up ten fingers and Zander nodded. They were ten to our five. Not good odds.

At the back of the beach, Monty Brioux stood before Leo Nackley, whose hands were tied together behind his back. Brioux was smiling broadly and training a huge chrome-and-brass pistol on him. Not far away, the three other pirates guarded Lazlo, Jack, and Kemal, whose hands were tied together like Leo Nackley's. They were all lined up on the sand.

I carefully slid my spyglass out of my vest pocket and focused on Brioux and Leo Nackley, then pressed the button of the listening device. "—would be a fine thing, wouldn't it, to ransom the famous Explorer Leo Nackley." Brioux's voice rang out of the tiny speakers on my spyglass, loud enough for all of us to hear. "I was hoping you had found the oil for me, but a hostage may do just as nicely. I wonder how much money BNDL would pay for you, Mr. N. We'll find out once we sail back to St. Beatrice."

"They're on their way," Leo Nackley said. "In fact, they'll be here any minute and I don't think they'll be very happy to see you."

Monty Brioux let out a loud laugh. "They'll never make it. We'll see them before they see us, and they'll be sorry they ever sailed these waters." He brandished his pistol in the air.

Now it was Leo Nackley's turn to laugh. "You have no idea," he told them, his pale face sweaty and exhausted. "They aren't coming in a fishing boat."

"Well, either way, we're ready for them. You and your son will fetch a tidy sum. Now, sit there and don't move."

The two female pirates were standing closer to us and now Monty Brioux approached them. The first one was a short, wiry woman with spiky blue hair and a blue cape. She looked lithe and fast and had a little dagger tucked into her belt. The other woman was much taller, wearing a long dress that was tattered and dirty at the bottom. She had bright pink hair in tangled braids and a scowl on her face.

"All right," Monty Brioux said in a low voice. "He says BNDL's coming, so we've got to wrap this up. Bluebird: you, Rascal, and Hickory take the Nackleys out to the ship. I'll stay behind to deal with the other two."

"Okay, but what are you going to do with them?" asked the small blue-haired woman. When she turned my way, I could see a pistol holstered next to the little dagger and a Longsword jammed into the other side of her belt. She kept a hand on the pistol while she talked.

"What do you think?" Monty replied. "No reason to let them live. I'll dump their bodies in the ocean and no one ever needs to know. We'll tell the Nackleys we're leaving them behind on the island so they don't get too excited. Now go. Pearl," he turned to the tall pirate with the braids, "you stay with me."

Through the spyglass, I watched Bluebird walk down the beach toward the three male pirates who were guarding Lazlo, Jack, and Kemal near the tents.

"Hey, Rascal. Stop that," she called to a tall man dressed in many shades of green. His kelp-green hair was pulled back in a ponytail, and his aqua leather boots reached up to his knees. He had Lazlo with his back against a palm tree, and held a wicked-looking dagger out in front of him, jabbing it into the tree, inches from Lazlo's neck, again and again. Lazlo's expression of terror seemed to strike the pirate as hilarious, and he laughed hysterically each time Lazlo flinched.

"Monty told you not to be an idiot," Bluebird said, slamming the palm of her hand against his upper arm.

She pulled him away from Lazlo and through the spyglass, I could hear her whisper: "Monty wants to take your boy there and his father out to the ship. The other two are fish food, okay?"

"Okay." He smiled and moved his feet in a happy little dance, as though the idea that he'd get to kill Jack and Kemal had made his day.

"In the meantime, Rascal, don't do anything stupid," Bluebird said. We watched as she stepped over to the other two pirates, who were also guarding Lazlo, Jack, and Kemal. One of them was short and fat, with long red hair hanging loose to his shoulders. He wore glasses with blue lenses and a woven cap that he'd bent into the shape of a captain's hat.

"Morris," Bluebird barked. "You and Rascal are staying here to finish off the collateral once we've made the trade." Then she grinned at the other pirate, a lanky straw-haired boy with a huge pistol strapped across his bare chest. She said to him, "This is your lucky day, Hickory. You and I get to take the most precious cargo out to the ship with Pearl and Monty."

I turned and looked at the others to see if they'd heard everything. The expression on their faces told me they had. We all nodded and made our way back to the far beach to make a plan.

"If it were just the Nackleys, I'd be inclined to let Monty Brioux go ahead and ransom them," Zander said, pacing around. "But you heard what they said about Kemal and Jack. We've got to do something."

"But what can we do?" I said. "There are ten of them and five of us. And they have weapons and—"

We all looked down at the swords that Joyce still had tucked into her belt. She smiled and handed one to Zander. When he pulled it out of its hilt, it gleamed in the early sunlight.

He swung it at the low-hanging branch of a palm tree and it sliced the branch in two with a neat *snick*. Joyce pulled the other sword out of its sheath and got into her fencing stance, holding the blade out in front of her and swinging it a few times to test its weight. I knew it was heavy, but she wielded it gracefully. "Okay, Zander West, how are we going to do this?"

Zander thought for a moment. "We need a two-pronged attack," he said. "From the water and from the woods on the sides of the beach. It's the only way. We might have a chance at fighting them if we can trap them on the beach. Here." He drew a little map in the sand, making an X to represent the zone between water and beach. "M.K., what do you think? Can Amy help us out from the water? She was pretty banged up."

M.K. pushed her bangs out of her eyes and broke out into a big grin. "Of course she can! I may have to make a few adjustments, but I think she'll be fine."

"Great. Now, our only hope is to force them toward the water and then take them out one at a time. Joyce and I are handiest with the swords." Sukey frowned and said nothing, and Zander went on, "It's just true, Suke. If we needed a pilot, you'd be my choice all the way. But right now, we need to figure out how to make it so Joyce and I aren't taking on all six of them at the same time. We need you and Kit to distract a couple of them and draw them away from their friends. This may be the most important part of the plan. There are more of them than there are of us, but we can even things up if we can attack while their attention is elsewhere." He drew a little arrow at one side of his diagram. "Walk out onto the beach here as though you have no idea what's going on, as though you were just out for a walk and you're coming back. At least two of them will go for you. Hopefully they'll just try to tie you up."

"Hopefully?"

Zander waved the stick. "Don't worry. I'm sure they won't shoot you or anything. Once a few of them are occupied with you, then Joyce and I will come down on the other side of the beach and take out the other ones. Then we'll loop back around and rescue you two.

Joyce, what do you think? Can the two of us take on the remaining four pirates?"

Joyce took the stick from him and ran it along the diagram, thinking. "Or if we wait for the woman with the blue hair and the short one and the shirtless guy to get into the boats with the Nackleys, we'll only have Brioux and the other man and Pearl to deal with. But I'm worried that if we wait that long, we're putting Kemal and Jack's lives in danger. Brioux has a pistol—when he sees us coming, he might decide to just get them out of the way. I think you're right— we need to make our move. Zander and I will attack from the back of the beach. If we can drive them to the water, then M.K. can help take them out once she's dealt with their ship. Kit and Sukey, you'll need to untie the Nackleys and Jack and Kemal so they can help us. Okay?" We nodded.

Zander silently traced his stick across the map, making little arrows and lines. I figured that he was weighing the different options for the attack, thinking through all the possible outcomes.

"Okay," he said finally. "It's decided."

M.K. got into Amy and we all helped to push the submersible back into the water. M.K. started the engine and we waved to her through the glass as she disappeared under the surface of the water.

Zander reached out to touch Sukey's cheek, then patted me on the shoulder. "You guys okay? You know what you need to do?" We nodded. I didn't like the way Sukey held his gaze a couple of seconds longer than she needed to.

"All right," I said. "Let's get going already."

We walked silently along the path back to the beach. I was terrified, my heart beating, my hands shaking. When we reached the edge of the beach, Sukey squeezed my hand. "Think of it this way," she whispered. "For the rest of our lives, we'll be able to tell the story of the time we fended off a wicked band of pirates."

Forty-three

Sukey and I crashed through the undergrowth and came out onto the sand, singing and talking and generally making as much noise as we possibly could.

"Hey everyone, we're back!" I shouted, stopping in my tracks and trying to look surprised when I saw the pirates. "Wait, what's going on here? Who are you guys?"

The blue-haired woman and the tall shirtless pirate were untying Leo Nackley's hands in preparation for marching him to the boat. Bluebird looked up and yelled, "Who're they? I haven't seen those ones before. The Indorustan boy said there weren't any more people on the island!"

"Well, we lied," Kemal said, looking up at me, trying desperately to communicate something with his eyes. I shot him a look that I hoped let him know we were in control. "And I'm not

Indorustan," Kemal said, "I'm an Ottomanlander."

"Where did you two come from?" Monty Brioux bellowed. He swung his pistol around, pointing it straight at my head.

"We've been here for days. We just went for a walk," Sukey said. "Who are you? What's going on here? Did you get shipwrecked too?"

Sukey and I started walking down the beach, toward the water. We had to draw them right down to the waterline.

"Hickory!" Monty Brioux yelled to the shirtless pirate. "Don't just stand there!"

"Don't move, you two. Stay right there!" Hickory shouted. He and Bluebird followed us down the beach, walking very slowly, their hands on the pistols at their belts.

"If I waited for you two to handle the situation I'd be here all day!" Monty Brioux strode down the beach to us, sticking his pistol in my face and saying, in a low, controlled voice, "I won't ask you again. Who are you?" Close up, I could see that his long purple cloak was made of Gryluminum chain mail. In addition to the pistol, he had a sword, sheathed in a thick metal belt at his waist. I wished there was some way I could warn Zander about this extra weapon we hadn't factored into our plan.

"You two, get over there with your friends," Bluebird said. "Tie them up, Morris." We put our hands up and the fat red-haired pirate started toward us. But before he reached us, I waved my hands in the air.

"Hey, Morris," I shouted. "Come and get me." I did a little dance on the sand, waggling my fingers and swiveling my hips, all while sticking my tongue out at him. It seemed to make him mad.

"You little brat," he yelled and made a leap for me. I jumped to the side and he fell flat on his face on the sand.

"I love your hair," Sukey called to Bluebird. "Do you dye it yourself or was there some kind of accident?" She took off running down the beach. Bluebird followed.

Two down. Now it was up to Zander and Joyce.

Morris jumped in my direction again, his red hair swinging, his small eyes angry behind the lenses of his glasses.

From the thick vegetation up above the beach, we heard two loud whoops, and Zander and Joyce came leaping out of the trees at the back of the beach, both of them brandishing their swords.

"On guard, Monty Brioux!" Zander shouted.

Monty Brioux whirled around in confusion, holding the pistol out in front of him. We heard a loud *bang*, but instead of a bullet, we saw a long thin stream of light come out of the barrel. I closed my eyes, but it was Morris who fell to the ground in front of me, clutching his leg.

"My leg! My leg! You shot me!"

"Shut up, Morris!" Monty Brioux snapped. "It's just a little burn. Get up and fight!"

Hickory and Pearl, her pink braids swinging, unsheathed their swords and advanced slowly upon Zander and Joyce. The green-haired pirate named Rascal was still trying to untie Leo Nackley's hands, but it looked like he was having trouble.

"Come on!" Zander shouted to Hickory. "I don't think you can catch me!"

Hickory lunged with his sword, which allowed Zander to strike a blow that knocked Hickory's weapon to the ground.

Hickory reached for the pistol slung around his chest. But Zander delivered a quick *conk* to the back of Hickory's head and the pistol fell from his hands. The lanky pirate sank down onto the sand, looking like he would be out for a while.

Meanwhile, Joyce and Pearl were circling each other warily, swords drawn. They were both nimble as they moved carefully around each other. If Mr. Turnbull had been here, he would have shouted, "Engage! Engage! This isn't a dance party!"

Joyce feigned a move to the right and then darted back, bringing her sword down on Pearl's shoulder. Pearl stumbled but came back up, swinging her sword and catching Joyce on her left arm. A thin line of blood appeared on Joyce's bicep and I heard Sukey say, "She got you, Joyce! Careful!"

"I'll get you again," Pearl said, waving her sword in crazy, swooping arcs.

Joyce still looked calm, but I could tell that she was angry. She swung her sword viciously, forcing the pirate back toward the trees.

Morris was still on the ground, rubbing his leg. I looked behind me and saw Bluebird advancing on Sukey, pushing her back toward the water's edge.

The last pirate, Rascal, had his sword out and he was advancing on Zander. Zander waited for him to come for him and then danced away, moving them to the other side of the beach.

Clang. We heard steel meet steel and then turned and saw Pearl sprawled on the sand, her sword a couple of feet away from her outstretched arm. Joyce picked it up and tucked it into her belt. "Stay where you are," she told Pearl and went to Sukey's aid, sprinting down the beach toward Bluebird. The blue-haired pirate whirled around, pointing her pistol at Joyce, who swung at her arm with the sword and knocked the pistol to the ground. Sukey kicked her in the rear end while her back was turned and Joyce forced her down onto the sand and kicked the pistol out of her reach.

"Take the Nackleys to the ship!" Monty Brioux called to Rascal.

"Ahoy! A little help!" He called out to the ship.

"Be careful, Zander, there are more on the boat," Kemal said quietly.

And indeed, the pirates out on the ship had noticed what was going on, and a few of them were getting ready to jump down into the water and wade to shore.

We all watched the little bay. It looked peaceful, the water blue and serene despite the scene on shore.

"Hurry, you idiots," Monty Brioux shouted.

Come on, M.K.

"Now I'm going to deal with you, young man," Monty Brioux said. "Rascal, get him!" Rascal turned his pistol on Zander, inches away from pulling the trigger.

And just then, Amy's egg-shaped head broke the surface of the water with a huge splash, like a giant gleaming sea creature leaping from the depths.

Her tentacles whipped back and forth. We could just barely see a determined-looking M.K. through the glass, her arms working away at the controls.

"What the hell is that?" Rascal said, dumbfounded. In one fluid movement Zander had leaped upon him, tackling and disarming him, then pinned him to the ground. "Whoa," Joyce called out. "Good one."

Zander punched Rascal once. "Stop struggling," he said, then punched him again. The pirate lay back, defeated.

Amy's hose arm whipped back and forth and then, with a great whoosh, it sprayed water at the pirates on the pirate ship. M.K. motored forward to spray them again at even closer range.

The men scurried to the long swivel guns on deck. I hoped that M.K. knew what she was doing.

A deafening boom echoed across the beach and we saw a cannonball shoot out of Amy's eighth arm and blow a hole in the starboard hull. The pirates leapt screaming off the deck. Monty Brioux stood there, dumbfounded, watching as his ship began to sink.

"Monty Brioux," Zander shouted, "you've been beat." He ran toward the pirate, brandishing his sword, and Brioux spun around and pulled his own sword from its sheath on his belt and countered Zander's first swing with his own.

Sukey gasped as Brioux swung again, forcing Zander to jump back.

Zander and the pirate danced across the sand, matching each other blow for blow, their swords clanging against each other.

"Drop your sword, boy!" Monty Brioux shouted to Zander.

Zander grinned as he delivered a wicked blow to Brioux's blade. He swung again and I was sure he had him when Brioux leapt out of the way and then turned his sword on Zander, whacking him on the back of the knees and forcing him to the ground.

"Let him go!" Joyce picked up Bluebird's sword and advanced on Brioux. He looked momentarily panicked and then turned to defend himself, giving Zander the opportunity to pick up his sword again and hold it to Brioux's back.

"We've got you," Zander said. "Now, why don't you drop *your* sword?"

But before Brioux could answer, we all heard an impossibly loud *whoosh* from the bay, and a hulking, dark monstrosity broke the surface of the water.

The giant submarine rose from the water like a city emerging from the deep. It was as long as a city block and shaped like a torpedo, its nose pointing up as the water ran off the hull in torrents.

It looked fit to travel in the world's most dangerous waters, a warship impervious to storms or tides or giant eels. No wonder the turtles had had to destroy the city. They never could have kept this thing away, not with a thousand turtles whipping up waves.

The massive submarine kept rising and finally came to rest on the surface. Loud clanking and whirring sounds added themselves to the whoosh of water running off the metal, and a glass-and-chrome elevator car rose up out of the tower that soared above the deck of the submarine.

A door in the elevator opened, along with many hatches on the deck, and we watched as black-clad figures poured onto the surface. Now we could see the words on the hull: the *Trident*, painted in official white block letters above the BNDL logo, shining in bright red.

There must have been a hundred agents on deck now, leaping into the huge black inflatable boats that sprang out of the railings along the deck, lowering themselves to the surface of the water, and buzzing toward shore on invisible motors. I raised my spyglass and watched as two men, instantly recognizable by their clothes and hair, stepped out of the glass-and-chrome elevator tower, made their way down a ladder on the side of the hull, and were escorted into a swift little speedboat that had appeared below.

Mr. Mountmorris approached in the speedboat, surrounded by agents and dressed in a shiny black suit, his earlights flashing slowly.

"So we have found our castaways at last!" he called out as the boat came up on the beach. Jec Banton leapt out and helped him to step out onto the sand. Mr. Mountmorris's assistant still had his hair dyed blood red and cut into a lethal-looking spike along the top of his head.

Mountmorris's eyes gleamed with something like suspicion as he met my gaze. I always felt he was able to see through me and I had never felt it so keenly as I did now.

"I am very pleased to see you alive and well," he said, his pale blue frog's eyes never leaving me. "Very pleased indeed!"

"Mr. Mountmorris, I'm so sorry," Lazlo Nackley told him. "The storm came up and we did the best we could, but I've failed you. I'm sorry."

"It's not Lazlo's fault," Leo Nackley said in a weak voice.

"I'm really sorry," Lazlo said again. He looked very thin, his shoulders rounded in defeat and his black jacket and pants dull and dirty.

Mr. Mountmorris grinned. "But Lazlo, my boy, what are you talking about? You're a hero!"

"What . . . do you mean?" Lazlo glanced at his father, who looked as confused as he did.

"The oil!" Mr. Mountmorris announced. "You found the oil! We saw it on our way in."

"The oil?" Lazlo asked, turning to us. "Oh, yes, of course, the oil!"

"Do you know what this means?" Mr. Mountmorris asked the group assembled on the beach. We could see agents leading Monty Brioux and the other pirates into speedboats headed for the *Trident*. "It means tanks, it means bombers, it means trains. It means we win the war."

There was a long silence.

"War?" I finally said. "Which war do you mean? Sir?"

Mr. Mountmorris grinned. "Oh, of course, you haven't heard, have you? You've been on a desert island! Ha ha, you've literally been on a desert island! I mean the war that was declared yesterday by the Indorustan Empire in the Simerian Territories!"

A hushed silence fell over the group. "We're at war?" Lazlo asked lamely.

"They're calling it a *military action* now, but yes, we are or very soon will be at war. And you, Lazlo, and your great find will make it all possible. If this oil field turns out to yield even half as much as I think it will, well . . . all of your names may go down in history." Mr. Mountmorris grinned broadly.

"You are all to be commended, of course," he added, turning to us. "And you will see that your work on this expedition will not go unrewarded. After all, not only did you find the oil, but you discovered an uncharted island and you appear to have saved Leo Nackley and his son, as well as your classmates, from a notorious band of pirates. No, your work will not go unrewarded at all." He nodded to Zander. "There are lots of opportunities for such an enterprising and brave young Explorer as you, Mr. West. Miss West, Miss Neville, Miss Kimani, Mr. Asker: I think you will find that this opens many opportunities for you all, and all of you will be rewarded. I think you can count on that! Look, the *Trident*'s airship has already disembarked. We'll get word to the authorities and within a couple of days we'll have twenty ships here to install the drills and pipes."

We all watched the miniature airship lift off from the deck of the *Trident* and bank west, flying back toward St. Beatrice.

"Our expert on the sub says it may be the most important find of its kind ever," Jec Banton said as the red lights in his ears blinked on and off.

I knew Zander felt sick, thinking of the turtles, of the fish—even of the eel. I felt sick too, but there was nothing I could do. At least the map was safe, the lines formed by the stones and shells on the walls of the underwater chamber hidden in the deepest recesses of my brain. I could practically feel it hanging there, a heavy weight I now had to carry.

and the water became very
rough, despite the clear skies and
lack of any wind or rain. As
we looked down at the churning
water, he seemed filled with joy
and said, "This is it. This is
what I have been searching for."

I must now go above deck to
see if I can help. The ship
is pitching terribly. I pray
to our Lord for our survival
and salvation. If I should
not survive and this book is
found, give my most fervent
regards to Miss Mary Jennings
of Southampton and tell
my mother and father that
I love them.

Forty-four

It was a marvel of modern engineering, and there were many people who would have killed for a chance to explore every nook and cranny of the *Trident*, but we spent our twenty-four hours aboard the submarine sleeping and eating, exhausted and barely aware of our surroundings. We surfaced on the second day, and as we steamed into St. Beatrice Harbor, we all went up on deck to watch the island come into view. It was a perfect Caribbean day, hot and sunny, with a slight breeze. We could see crowds of people standing in the harbor and Coleman and Mr. Wooley right at the front of the crowd, waving wildly. Dolly Frost stood next to them with her notebook at the ready.

Sukey stood alone on deck and I went over to her and leaned against the railing so I could look at her. They had found clothes for all of us on the *Trident* and she was wearing a fancy silk blouse in a shade of brown that made her eyes look luminous. I felt seasick, my head pounding, my stomach empty.

"Hey," I said. "Are you okay?"

"Yeah. I think so." She smiled nervously, barely meeting my eyes before she looked away again. I remembered the way she'd looked at me on the beach as we watched the jellyfish. I wished she would look at me like that again.

"So there's going to be a war," I said.

"I know. I think they've known for a while. I told you about the flying squadron I was practicing with back at school. Well, I had the feeling we were training for something. The only question was where they were going to get the fuel."

"But how could they have known?" I asked her. "The uprising just happened."

"I don't think they cared whether there was an uprising or not," she said carefully.

"Well, we know the oil's not a question anymore." I tried to meet her eyes, but she wouldn't look at me.

"You did what your father wanted you to do," she said after an awkward moment. "There's that, at least."

"Yeah, although I still don't understand why. I don't understand what he wants me to do with it. I can't just keep following the maps from one place to another. There must be a reason."

"Maybe—"

"Hey, guys," Zander said, joining us on deck, a troubled look on his face. He stood very close to Sukey and I saw her blush bright red.

363

Still, she leaned into him, just a little, barely enough to notice.

"Are you okay?" she said.

"I feel so guilty about the oil." He looked out across the harbor. "It's a terrible thing we've done. They'll get it under control, but if it ever leaks, if the pipes break . . ."

"It's not your fault," Sukey said. "You know that. You were following the map."

"The map he gave to *Kit*," Zander said, and there was something in his voice that made me look up. His eyes were narrowed in anger. "Not me. *Kit*."

"Zander," Sukey said. "You know it isn't like that."

"Except that it is," he said. "I just don't understand why he would send us on a treasure hunt without telling us what we're looking for. These maps—it's ridiculous. We don't even know what the next one is. We don't even have it. It's just . . . in Kit's brain. And who even knows if he remembered it correctly? Who else is going to get hurt? Who else will get killed if we keep trying to follow them?"

"Zander," Sukey said quietly, touching his arm.

I flinched. "I'm going to get my stuff ready." I left them alone, but when I turned back, Sukey was standing even closer, whispering in Zander's ear and gazing up at his face. Pucci had been flying back and forth between the submarine and the harbor and now he flapped down onto Sukey's shoulder, cawing and nuzzling her neck. Behind them, Leo Nackley was making his way up on deck with the help of a cane. He caught my eye and the look he gave me was so full of hatred that I shivered, even in the hot sun.

Forty-five

We returned to the Academy in the dead of winter. There was a huge snowstorm in the White Mountains just after we returned, and for a couple of weeks, the snow was too deep for us to go anywhere but the Longhouse for meals and the library to study. Zander and Sukey went snowshoeing or skiing nearly every day, sometimes taking Joyce or Kemal with them. Lazlo and Jack had gotten permission to stay in New York with Lazlo's parents until classes started again. M.K. was full of ideas for new gadgets and machines, and she retrofitted a SteamCycle with a small plow so she could clear the path to the workshop. I spent my time in the library, trying to find references to the Mapmakers' Guild, trying to learn what Dad might want me to do with all these maps. Of course, I didn't find anything, and after a week of searching I couldn't believe I'd been stupid enough to think I would. After that, I focused on the atlases, trying to find a match for the mysterious arrangement of lines and angles in my head.

One night, I was walking to the library when Mr. Wooley caught up to me. He had taken the *Deloian Princess* home with us, but I'd barely seen him during the eleven-day voyage and I'd assumed he'd been seasick again. I'd had the feeling he'd been avoiding me since we'd been back at school.

But now he put a hand on my arm and said, "Hi, Kit."

"Hi, Mr. Wooley."

We each gave a New York glance down the path for agents who might be listening.

"How are you?" He didn't look at me and I could see his fingers knotting and unknotting the ends of the neon-green plaid scarf tied around his neck.

"Fine. Cold."

"I . . . wanted to apologize, to you, for what happened on the expedition. I've been feeling terribly guilty about it. I abandoned you. You could have died, and . . ." His pale face twisted with worry, a lock of platinum hair falling across one eye. I turned to face him.

"Mr. Wooley, no one blames you. We all knew that Leo Nackley had you kicked off the expedition so he could come along. They probably planned it from the beginning."

He hesitated. A cold wind blew through the trees and he said, "Well, as it happens, that's not exactly right. I asked to be taken off. I pretended I was sick."

"Because you were scared of going back there?"

He looked surprised. "No, no. Well, there was that. But I'm an Explorer of the Realm. I can deal with fear. No, I didn't want to go because . . ." He lowered his voice. "They asked me—forced me, really—to spy on you. They were convinced that your father had given you a map and they wanted me to find out where you kept it and steal it for them. For BNDL. That's why you were all assigned to Lazlo's expedition. It was all planned out. They set off in the *Trident* before you'd been gone two days."

I stared at him. "*You* were the spy?"

He smiled. "Well, as it turned out, I *wasn't* the spy. But I've been feeling terribly guilty about it and I just wanted to apologize. And to tell you how glad I am that you survived. It's like something out of an adventure story, isn't it? Castaways on a desert island. Well, goodbye for now."

I watched him go. So it hadn't been Kemal after all.

I was still turning Mr. Wooley's words over in my mind as I sat down at a table on the second floor of the library and started working. I couldn't risk drawing the map from my memory, but I'd been drawing pieces of it, which I then destroyed, in order to keep it fresh and to see if it meant anything. I doodled for a few minutes, aware of the sound of my pencil in the silent library, but something was bugging me. It took me a few minutes to figure out what it was.

Castaways on a desert island.

I jumped up and went downstairs to request the books I'd looked through all those months ago, the ones that had led me to Gianni Girafalco. This time Mrs. Pasquale didn't scowl quite as hard. Everyone at school had been nicer to us since we'd returned from the Caribbean.

Back upstairs, I started flipping through them, rereading until I found what I was looking for.

But in May of 1823, his ship disappeared and he was never heard from again. The sole survivor, a boy native to Southampton, UK, described rough and turbulent seas just before the ship foundered. The boy was found floating on a piece of wood by a fisherman.

There had been a survivor. A castaway. Just like Dad. I'd forgotten that detail. I thought about the debris we'd found on the island, the swords, the pieces of a lifeboat.

I went back through the books and found the one with crew lists from important nineteenth-century expeditions. I looked up the lists for Girafalco's voyages. Running a finger down the names for the 1823 trip, I stopped at *James Rickwell. Age 16. Southampton.* Sixteen years old. A boy. Southampton. That had to be it. Rickwell.

Downstairs, I searched through the clockwork card catalog, the cards flipping past me as the engine clicked and whirred, but couldn't find anything by or about Rickwell, James. I took a deep breath and went over to the big desk.

"Here you go, Mrs. Pasquale," I said, handing the books over. I pretended to hesitate and then added, "We don't have anything by a James Rickwell, do we? I checked the catalog. But I think it might be one of the old books in the special collections. A study of, uh, tropical frogs and their eating habits."

She studied me, then turned to the huge card catalog for the special collections behind her desk. "Rickwell, Rickwell," she murmured, flipping through the cards printed with authors' names and titles.

"Nothing about frogs," she said after a few long minutes. "But we do have something by James Rickwell. *Diary of a Caribbean Voyage*. Surely it's not the same—"

"I'll take it," I practically shouted. "I mean, it's the Caribbean. That's tropical. It might contain some of his notes."

She looked at me carefully before slipping a hand into the IronGrabber and reaching high into the stacks to bring down a wooden box. "It's damaged and very fragile," she said, reading the label on the front. "Be careful."

I nodded, my heart pounding, and took it upstairs.

Inside the box, I found a small leather book. The pages were stained and torn, some missing altogether and many others torn in half. I lifted it out very carefully and began to read.

I, James Rickwell, aged 16 years, of the city of Southampton, in the country of England, on this 3rd day of May, 1823, do hereby put down this record of the voyage of the Adelaide, *captained by the mapmaker and explorer Gianni Girafalco, in the hopes that our expedition will prove of historic value to those who come after us. It is my hope that if our expedition is successful, this journal may prove of interest to future generations of explorers.*

It was a diary of a boy on Gianni Girafalco's voyage to discover King Triton's Lair. I started leafing carefully through the entries that were still legible, a sense of déjà vu washing over me. I was reading about the precise voyage that we had just taken.

Rickwell had met Girafalco in Southampton and been taken on board to learn navigation. It sounded as though he'd started to suspect that Girafalco had a secret motive in making the voyage to the Caribbean, but it didn't sound like Rickwell had ever learned of the existence of the underwater city or the maps.

I read the short diary straight through over the course of the next two hours. When I got to the diary's final entry, I read:

> . . . *when the sea started to become very rough, despite the clear skies and lack of any wind or rain. As we looked down at the churning water, he seemed to be filled with joy and he said, "This is it. This is what I have been searching for."*
>
> *I now must go above deck to see if I can help. The ship is pitching terribly. I pray to our Lord for our survival and salvation. If I should not survive and this book is found, give my most fervent regards to Miss Mary Jennings of Southampton and tell my mother and father that I love them.*

There wasn't anything else in the book—just empty pages, torn and stained like the others. I closed the book and stared at the black leather cover.

It had seemed like such a promising lead. I'd been sure that

I would find something in the journal. I flipped through it again. On the outside of the box a small printed label read, "Generously donated from the personal collection of Mr. R. Delorme Mountmorris."

As though I could will words into existence, I flipped through the torn and blank pages after the final entry again. Running a finger over the water-stained pages, I felt a slight texture on the surface. I remembered the feeling of the bioluminescent ink on the map, like a faint scar, barely there under my fingertips.

Was it possible?

I felt my heart race. I was wearing the whistle—it had become something of a talisman since we'd returned and I'd never taken it off. I needed a dark place to look at the book in safety. There was the secret room, but I couldn't risk leaving the library with the book. Mrs. Pasquale was already suspicious, and if I was caught leaving with the book hidden on me, it would draw attention to the map. I looked around. I was completely alone on the second floor. I listened for a moment, then opened the door to the stairway that led to the roof and climbed the stairs as quietly as I could, hoping Mrs. Pasquale didn't have some kind of listening device.

It was cold and blustery and dark on the other side of the door at the top and I stepped out into the night, taking care not to slip on the sloped roof. The book was warm from being inside my vest. I opened to the blank page and passed the whistle over the raised texture on the page.

While I waited, I looked up at the stars, trying to find the constellations Dad had taught us: Andromeda, Ursa Major, Ursa

Minor. He had loved watching the night sky. I felt superstitious, as though the longer I waited the better chance there was that something would appear.

Finally, I looked away from the night sky and down at the journal.

The blank page was now covered with glowing writing.

write these words in fear of my life. Our
ship is now in grave danger and if, as
I suspect, I do not survive this strange
storm, I must somewhere recount
the true nature of my conversations
with Captain Girafalco. I do so in his
invisible ink, in the hopes that my
words will only be found by a member
of our society.

After we reached Antigua, I became
suspicious of Capain Girafalco's true
motives. He admitted that he was
searching for something, but it took
him some days to admit to me what it
was.

I will recount, as best as I can
remember, the words he spoke in his
cabin that night.

"My dear boy," he said as a candle
flickered on his desk, "I had been
watching you for some time before
I approached you in Captain Sibley's

library. I observed you down by the docks asking the sailors about nautical charts and navigation techniques and I made some inquiries of your schoolmasters, after which I learned that you were a talented mathematician and cartographer and that you displayed a passionate interest in maps and codes.

"For this to make sense, I must tell you about something that happened to me when I was about your age. I too had always loved science—geology was a particular interest, along with navigation and cartography—and though it was assumed that I would go to sea like my father, who was the captain of a ship that took goods, oranges mostly, around the world, I harbored a secret desire to study the inner workings of the earth at a great university. One day, I was practicing knots down at the harbor when a man approached and asked if my name was

Gianni Girafalco. I told him it was and he said that he had heard of my interest in geology and that he had something for me. He was dressed strangely, in a black cape and hood, and he kept looking behind him and spoke in a low, furtive way. He handed me a map and said that I was to prepare for a great adventure. He then mumbled something about my being chosen for this task and walked off hurriedly.

"I was to meet the man several more times over the next few years, after I had traveled to England and the University at Oxford, to study geology at that great seat of learning, but my future interactions with him are a story for another day. I will tell you plainly that the man was a member of a secret society of Explorers and that I was inducted into that society on a fine day not long after my seventeenth birthday. Ever since, I have been in service to this society and I have had many adventures as I have sought to carry out its aims.

"I had thought to teach you for many more months before I let you in on my secret and before I gave you the tools to be of service to this society yourself, but everything I have heard while we have been in the islands leads me to believe that my endeavor may be a very dangerous one. And so I show you the map that I was given so that you will understand the true purpose of our voyage."

He then took a large piece of paper from a hidden compartment in the wall. It was a chart showing the waters in which we were traveling.

I looked at it, waiting for an explanation, but Captain Girafalco astonished me by taking a small figure, what appeared to be a turtle carved from a piece of shell, and passing it over the chart.

I was about to ask if he'd gone mad when he blew out the candle on his desk, plunging the room into darkness, and I saw the true nature of the chart. There were now glowing wind roses and lines and little drawings across the blue water.

He explained that he had been given the turtle by a member of the society, and had only just discovered its effect on the map. He had discovered that the ink he had made from the creatures he'd dissected seemed to glow in the dark when in the presence of the turtle and he theorized that the turtle was made of a natural substance that activated the invisible ink. "I don't know what the markings on the map are yet," Captain Girafalco said. "But I mean to find out. If I fail, you must do it, my boy. You must do it for me."

Scrawled on the next page in the invisible ink was a map I had come to know very well, a map of King Triton's Lair, with the wind roses and emanating lines, and the little sea horses dancing up and down along them. It took me a minute to see the difference—this map didn't include St. Beatrice or Ruby Island because they hadn't been discovered yet, but everything else was the same.

I closed the book.

Dad had seen this map. In order to make his own map, Dad must have seen this one. Which meant that Dad had been . . . chosen, the way Gianni Girafalco had been chosen, the way James Rickwell had been chosen.

My mind was whirring. I was thinking about Gianni Girafalco and the map of Girafalco's Trench. I was thinking about Dad's map and the code he'd left for me to find.

Gianni Girafalco had been a member of the Mapmakers' Guild. Just like Dad. Dad had followed Gianni Girafalco's map because like Gianni Girafalco, he had been chosen to do so. Someone had given him the turtle. Someone had pointed the way to King Triton's Lair.

I looked up at the black sky again, filled with the same stars and planets that Sukey and I had watched on the island. The same stars and planets the Explorer with the Clockwork Hand was probably looking at now, wherever he was.

The Explorer with the Clockwork Hand—he'd recognized Gianni Girafalco's name.

And you should know that it isn't about your brother and sister. I was directed by your father to give the book to you. Just you. Not to Zander, not to M.K. To you, Kit.

Forty-six

Classes started up again when the rest of the students returned from their expeditions at the beginning of March. It was actually nice to have everyone back. Every day there was news from Simeria, reports of the terrible things the Indorustans had done to the Simerians who were fighting them. A bunch of ADR agents came to the school and gave a presentation to the students about joining the Explorers-in-Training Academy Corps, an elite group of students who would be trained and ready to join the military when they turned eighteen. Within a few weeks, fifteen or so students, including Lazlo and Jack, had joined. They marched endlessly around campus in their blue uniforms. Maggie had tried to recruit Zander, telling him he would be officer material when he was old enough to join, but he said he wanted to wait.

Sukey didn't have any choice. Her flying squadron was

automatically enlisted in the Academy Corps and she was off nearly every night, training and studying. I hardly saw her. When she had free time, she spent it with Zander.

The snow started to melt in early April and we all thought winter was over. But just before Harrison Arnoz Day, an early spring snowstorm covered the already budding trees and green shoots of leaves with a delicate blanket of snow. Campus was already decorated for the awards ceremony, and the Harrison Arnoz Day Dance and all of the trees outside the Longhouse sparkled with tiny white lights, the chandeliers woven with blue-and-yellow paper chains.

I was trudging home through the snow very late that night when I heard a familiar rustle in the trees next to the path. I stopped, looked around, and then veered off, making my way into the thick trees by the moonlight, very close to the spot where he'd found me the first time.

"Hi," I whispered, and then he was there, appearing suddenly from behind a tree as though it were the most natural place in the world to wait for someone. He was clean shaven now, dressed in desert khakis rather than his Explorer's jacket and leggings.

"It looks like they're getting ready for Harrison Arnoz Day," he said. "The dance is always fun. Good food, you know."

"Is that all you have to say?"

He laughed. "I'm very glad to see you alive, Kit. You had quite an adventure."

I smiled in spite of myself. "Do you know what happened?"

"Most of it. The shipwreck. The oil."

"We didn't want to find the oil," I said. "It was awful. Zander feels terrible about it."

"But you did what you were meant to do? You found what your father wanted you to find?" He sounded like he was trying to keep the hopefulness out of his voice.

"Yes," I said. "A map. Of the next place he wants me to go, though I'm not sure where it is yet."

He smiled. "Good. That's very good. I'm proud of you, Kit."

"Don't be too proud until I figure out what it is."

"You will."

"I did find something," I told him. "A diary that belonged to a boy who was on Gianni Girafalco's ship. It's been in the library all this time. It belonged to Mr. Mountmorris. He must have donated it to the library without knowing what it was."

He turned to look at me, his eyes wide in the moonlight.

"You recognized his name, didn't you?" I continued. "The first time I mentioned it? Well, Girafalco was a member of the Mapmakers' Guild. I know from the diary. This thing, whatever it is, has been going on for a long time. Now will you tell me about it?"

He hesitated. "You seem to be figuring it out pretty well on your own," he said. Far away, we heard DeRosa's dog bark once. He was on patrol. But the Explorer raised a hand and said, "It's okay. I made sure they'd be occupied somewhere else tonight."

"I want you to tell me. You owe me that."

"Why don't you tell me what you think you know."

"There are maps," I said. "Secret maps, of places that must be hidden at all costs. He codes them so they'll be safe if they fall into the wrong hands. There's some element that only I can figure out. He's leaving them for us. For me. Like a treasure hunt. One leading to the next. And it all has something to do with this secret society of Explorers, the Mapmakers' Guild."

"Very good." He smiled and the corners of his eyes crinkled. "You asked me if your father had been a member of the Mapmakers' Guild. He was. I am too. And I believe you're right about Gianni Girafalco. I don't have time to explain everything, but do you know what a cell organization is?"

"No member of the organization knows everything. Each person only knows a little bit, so if someone's caught, they can't give away too much."

"That's right. In order to keep the whole organization safe, each member knows only about his or her own assignment."

"John Beauregard's was Ha'aftep Canyon," I said, figuring it out as I said the words.

"That's right."

"What's your assignment?"

"I'm kind of a special case. My special charge isn't a place. It's a person. You."

"Me? Why?"

He hesitated. "At any one time, there are only a couple of members of the guild who know everything, who have all of the secrets. They're called High Mapmakers. One of these was your father. So was Gianni Girafalco. The rest of the members are there to help the High Mapmaker, to help him or her keep the secret."

I had suspected something like this, but now that I knew it, my head was swimming with questions.

The Explorer's voice was so quiet I could barely hear him against the wind moving through the trees. "I'm not sure, but I suspect that your father is leading you to each of the maps, in turn, so that you will become one of the few, like Gianni Girafalco, like him, now that he is gone. I think something similar must have happened to him when he was your age." We heard DeRosa's shepherd bark again, closer this time. "I can't stay. But I'll be keeping track of you. As much as I can. Good luck, Kit."

"Can't you at least tell me your name?" I said.

He chuckled. "Seems fair enough. Tell you what, you can call me Marek." He buttoned his jacket up around his chin and slipped away noiselessly into the trees.

The woods were cold and silent, the moonlight illuminating an endless stretch of snow and trees. I looked back once and then I hunched down into the collar of my vest and set off into the frigid air.

Forty-seven

"And now, to announce the winner of this year's Harrison Arnoz Prize, I am pleased to introduce the director of the Bureau of Newly Discovered Lands, Mr. R. Delorme Mountmorris." Maggie smiled down on the rows of students and guests lining the festive-looking Longhouse, everyone dressed in their best and most colorful clothing, the Neos' facelights flashing merrily. "Let's give him a warm welcome."

Harrison Arnoz Day had dawned bright and sunny, the new layer of snow sparkling and catching the light everywhere one looked. In the evening the temperature had dropped, though the roaring fire and candles made the inside of the Longhouse warm and inviting. Outside, a few snowflakes had started to fall.

Mr. Mountmorris bounded up to the front of the room, where they had set up a podium decorated with flowers and yellow streamers.

"Hello, hello!" he said, turning to look at the wall above him with an exaggerated expression of fear on his face. "Just checking for elephants." The room laughed, though I noticed that Kemal and Joyce, seated across from us, maintained stony expressions. Dolly Frost had arrived the day before to cover the Arnoz Day celebrations for her newspaper, and she copied Mr. Mountmorris's remarks into her notebook with a little smile on her face.

"I am delighted to be here for this special occasion. As you know, these are difficult times, but thanks to the work of our military and to the Explorers of the Realm, the United States and its Allied Countries are holding their own against the ruthless attacks from the Indorustan Empire."

"Now, as you all know, each year we award the Harrison Arnoz Prize to the young Explorer-in-Training who has most contributed to the well-being and security of the nation. This year, we are honored to have *three* winners!" The room buzzed with surprise. "Lazlo Nackley, Zander West, and Joyce Kimani, please come up to the front of the room!"

Everyone rose to their feet, cheering and clapping, as Lazlo, Joyce, and Zander made their way up to Mr. Mountmorris at the podium. He hung a medal around each of their necks and grinned broadly out at the audience.

"Mr. Nackley is receiving this medal for the excellent leadership and planning he demonstrated in leading the expedition that discovered a new source of oil in the northeastern Caribbean. The oil well that will soon be operational there will allow our country to establish dominance over the Indorustans in myriad ways. Congratulations, Lazlo. I must also congratulate you for being the recipient of the $50,000 in gold that I offered at the beginning of the Final Exam Expedition season. It is well deserved!" Lazlo stepped forward and bowed deeply, smiling around the room at the noisy applause.

"Mr. West and Miss Kimani, you are receiving the Arnoz Prize for your bravery in organizing the attack against the ruthless pirate Monty Brioux and his crew. You surely saved the lives of several of your classmates by acting as you did. You showed yourselves capable of executing a well-strategized plan of attack. Congratulations!"

The applause and cheering filled the room as the waiters brought out platters of lobsters and beef and roast chicken. When those were gone, there were bowls of bright green Ribby Fruits and plates filled with slices of Ribby Fruit cake, but my appetite was gone.

Across the table from me, Joyce and M.K. were discussing an idea Joyce had had for a portable outboard engine that could be carried in a backpack and attached to an inflatable raft.

M.K. caught my eye as I pushed my chair back and stood up. "Where are you going?"

"Library," I told her.

"Aren't you going to congratulate Zander?"

"I don't see him anywhere. I'll tell him later."

Kemal looked up from his food. "You and M.K. should have gotten the award, too," he said. "I know that and so does Lazlo."

"Well, it's not about the awards, is it?" My voice sounded

bitter to my ears, so I tried to smile and added, "Thanks, Kemal. I appreciate that." He smiled back.

As I slipped out of the Longhouse, I ran into Zander and Sukey. They smelled of the cold air, of snow and ice, and they were laughing, their cheeks pink from the cold, snowflakes settling on their eyelashes and lips.

"Aren't you coming back in?" Sukey asked, gripping Zander's arm. "The dance is about to start."

"I have too much work to do," I said.

I felt Sukey watching me as I brushed past them, but I didn't turn around.

I settled into my usual chair on the third floor, opening up a newspaper and reading about the war. I was studying a map of Simer City printed alongside a story about the latest offensive when I heard footsteps coming up the stairs to the second floor. I didn't look up, assuming it was Mrs. Pasquale.

"Hello, Mr. West," Mr. Mountmorris said.

Jec Banton stood behind him, but at a nod from Mr. Mountmorris, he wandered away, leaving us alone.

"I'm pleased that you all survived your adventure, none the worse for wear."

He sat down in the chair across from me.

I didn't say anything, keeping my eyes focused on the newspaper.

"Kit, I'm sure you realize that this war is going to change things for all of us. Your brother will be of use to BNDL, in a variety of capacities, once he's finished his Explorer training. As you saw, his bravery in battle has not gone unnoticed. Your sister will be pressed into service in the engineering sector. Miss Neville has already been inducted into an elite flying corps that will help to win this war."

The library was silent except for Mr. Mountmorris' low voice. Outside the high windows, I could see the snow falling slowly to the ground.

"What about me?"

Mr. Mountmorris smiled. "That's what I wanted to talk to you about. I think you are well suited for a *special* kind of job. From time to time, we need Explorers who can obtain information in . . . clandestine ways. With your knowledge of maps, you may be of great use to us in this war. After all, wars are mostly about lines on maps, aren't they?"

"You want me to be a spy? In Simeria?"

"Well, we don't call it spying. You would be a cartographer, of a sort. An information gatherer."

He gave me an evil little smile that made me shiver.

"What do you think, Mr. West?"

I didn't answer. I looked back down at the newspaper, at the map of Simer City. It was an oval of lines running this way and that, describing the roads of the ancient city, squares and rectangles representing buildings and parks. It could have been anywhere in the world, anywhere old cities were built before city planners decided to build roads along grids instead of following the ancient footpaths of humans and animals.

But there was something familiar about this particular arrangement of lines and squares and rectangles. I'd seen it somewhere before, only

made out of shells and stones rather than ink on paper.

The map to which Dad had led me, deep under the ocean, the map we had all risked our lives to find, the map that had led to the destruction of the underwater city—I was positive now—was a map of the ancient center of Simer City.

I looked up from the newspaper and met Mountmorris's gaze. "I'll do it," I said, thinking of Sukey's face, the way she'd beamed up at Zander, the way the snowflakes had melted on her lips. "Send me to Simeria. I don't care." I stood up, meeting Mr. Mountmorris's cold, green eyes.

"When do I leave?"

Acknowledgments

Writing a book is a little bit like going on an expedition. I am very grateful for my intrepid co-Expeditioners. Huge thanks to Esmond Harmsworth and everyone at Zachary Shuster Harmsworth, and to Andrew Leland, Brian McMullen, Sam Riley, Dan McKinley, Sarah Manguso, Bennet Wade Bergman, and everyone at McSweeney's McMullens. Thanks to Katherine Roy for her friendship and her beautiful illustrations. I am overwhelmingly grateful to my early readers, who made this book better in many ways: Lisa Christie, Sarah Piel, Griffin McAlinden, Zoe McAlinden, Remy Lambert, Sam Seelig, and Jon Secrest. I am so grateful to Amanda Ann Palmer for her friendship and for taking such good care of my kids. And big, Mammoth Elephant-sized thanks to my family, Matt, Judson, Abe, and Cora Dunne, and Sue and David Taylor, for going on this adventure with me.

About the author

S. S. TAYLOR has been fascinated by maps ever since age ten, when she discovered an error on a map of her neighborhood and wondered if it was *really* a mistake. She has a strong interest in books of all kinds, old libraries, expeditions, mysterious situations, long-hidden secrets, missing explorers, and traveling to known and unknown places. Visit her at www.SSTaylorBooks.com.

About the illustrator

KATHERINE ROY is an artist and author living in New York City. She loves adventure, history, and science, and is currently writing and illustrating a book about African elephants. Katherine is also the author and illustrator of *Neighborhood Sharks: Hunting with the Great Whites of California's Farallon Islands*. See more of her work at www.katherineroy.com.

THE
EXPEDITIONERS

BARBUDA

SAINT
BEATRICE

ANTIGUA

RUBY
ISLAND

GUADELOUPE

31901055748505